THE EXILE OF MUKUNDA

Born and brought up in Meerut (Uttar Pradesh), **Arpit Bakshi** pursued his engineering before moving to Mysore and then to Pune for his first job. Within three years, he shifted to upstate New York to pursue his master's degree. Having done his fair share of globe-trotting, Arpit now lives in Gurugram (Haryana).

His love for all things science and also his interest in mythic stories of yore inspire his writing. As a writer, he is known for his unique amalgamation of science fiction and mythology.

His idea of a perfect evening is sitting under a clear moonlit star-laden sky, appreciating the vastness of the cosmos.

Also by the same author

The Code of Manavas

THE EXILE OF MUKUNDA
MAHA VISHNU TRILOGY: PART 2

ARPIT BAKSHI

Published by
Rupa Publications India Pvt. Ltd 2021
7/16, Ansari Road, Daryaganj
New Delhi 110002

Sales centres:
Allahabad Bengaluru Chennai
Hyderabad Jaipur Kathmandu
Kolkata Mumbai

Copyright © Arpit Bakshi 2021

All rights reserved.
No part of this publication may be reproduced, transmitted,
or stored in a retrieval system, in any form or by any means,
electronic, mechanical, photocopying, recording or otherwise,
without the prior permission of the publisher.

This is a work of fiction. Names, characters, places and incidents are
either the product of the author's imagination or are used fictitiously
and any resemblance to any actual person, living or dead, events or
locales is entirely coincidental.

ISBN: 978-93-90918-80-5

First impression 2021

10 9 8 7 6 5 4 3 2 1

The moral right of the author has been asserted.

Printed at Rakmo Press Pvt. Ltd, Greater Noida (UP)

This book is sold subject to the condition that it shall not,
by way of trade or otherwise, be lent, resold, hired out, or otherwise circulated,
without the publisher's prior consent, in any form of binding or
cover other than that in which it is published.

To my cute little niece,
Shanaya Bakshi.
Hope you achieve all that you desire.
Always stay happy and inspired.

Contents

Cast of Characters ix

1. The Change of Guards 1
2. The Timid Past 12
3. The School of Thought 23
4. Blink of an Eye 31
5. The Good Captor 41
6. The Royal Welcome 52
7. The Desert Rose 62
8. The New Rules 72
9. Beyond Reach 83
10. Hope Is Good 94
11. A Pleasant Surprise 103
12. The Forgotten Friend 115
13. The Treacherous Track 126
14. The Useful Idiot 136
15. The Missing Links 152
16. An Outlandish Sojourn 166
17. A Home Away from Home 178

18. The Fabric of the Universe — 192
19. The Subverted Systems — 202
20. The Nandaki Arises — 213
21. A Good Thing Going — 226
22. For Vishnu — 237
23. Some Familiar Faces — 246
24. A Familiar Foe — 257
25. Beyond the Perceptible — 270

Additional Read: The Theory of Gravity — 289

Cast of Characters

CHINJHI: Xinjhua's wife
CHINJU: An engineer in Xarlok
GRUTVATOR: The collective consciousness of the Guru people
GURU PEOPLE: The residents of Gurupur
GURUK: The King of Gurupur
GURUVI: King Guruk's daughter
JHUCHING: The Emperor of Chinjing
KANHA: Mukunda's classmate
MADHAV: Mohan and Meera's son
MISS VAISHNAVI: School teacher
MUKUNDA: Krishna and Radhika's son
RAGHUNANDAN: Senior officer in Narayani Sena
RUKMINI: Raghav and Vallabha's daughter
SHRIPATHI: Senior officer in the Narayani Sena
XANDHRIN: The head priest of the Xarnakhts
XANUK: A high-ranking commander in the Xarnakht Army
XARDUKHT: The King of Xarnakht tribe
XARI: An automated flight control system
XARKI: Xandhrin's son
XARKSHA/BHAVYA: A huge flying bird revered by the Guru people
XARNAKHT: The ruling tribe of Xarlok
XARNIKA: King Xardukht's daughter
XHI: Commander in the Chinjing Army
XINJHUA: Mukunda's friend in Xarlok
XINNUN: Xarki's friend

1

The Change of Guards
Some Eight Prithvi Months Later

The mist had finally started to lift and the lakefront was now visible under the nascent sunlight. The tranquil blue water of the lake could be seen as far as sight could decipher, no matter in which direction one looked. It surrounded the city from all eight directions, acting as a natural boundary to it.

Those waters were not meant for charting and no one even ventured close to them. Give or take a few feet, the lake never encroached the shores. On most days of the year, the waters were placid and on many quiet days, even the sound of the waves could not be heard. More so after daylight, when, at dusk a thick layer of mist would, very systematically, make the lake invisible.

As soon as the last batch of Brahmportation landed on that lake island on Prithvi, Shyam gathered everyone and moved in quickly to constitute the city. It took him months to plan everything, from the bricks to the buildings, making sure that each facility was built exactly as it was in Madhavpur.

'You will have to do me a favour. Rather two,' said Shyam.

'Just spell them out,' said Shriram.

'Choose a name of your liking for the city and then rule over it with courage and wisdom.'

Shriram stood in silence, without even batting an eyelid.

'Having thoughts?' Shyam enquired.

'I remember the day when I made you wear that crown of thorns,' he said.

Now, Shyam was speechless. He realized how mechanized he had become, even more than those big construction machines that place one storey over another. As if he was running on some kind of fuel—a fuel that didn't power emotions.

'I gained my younger daughter back, while you had to leave behind your son,' said Shriram.

Shyam sighed. 'I am left with no further interest to oversee the daily management of our settlements. If you are not willing to head the state, I will probably have to reach out further. I do understand that you want to spend quality time with your daughters. And that's fine with me. But I, too, have an urge to retire.'

'I could have united us all on that very day, but I didn't. I owe you this one. I will take over all the affairs of Ksharanpur from here onwards,' Shriram replied.

Even while Shyam was making sure that construction of the city was going on in full swing, Shriram was visiting each family to make sure that everyone felt at home.

However, the person who mattered most to him was feeling completely out of place. Her eyes, still teary, were waiting for the heavens above to part and for miracles to happen. Soon her tears paved the way for cries; cries of loneliness and helplessness. She was already in pain of what she had to leave behind, when another pain subjugated the former one.

It was the eighth day of the waning moon when one cry peaked and tapered while another one rose. Both Shyam and Shriram were pacing up and down the hall, when Mohan and Raghav entered.

'I simply cannot believe that all of them had to go into labour, on the same night,' said Raghav.

'As if they get a vote,' said Shyam.

'Doctors are at it. They will be fine, relax you both,' said Shriram.

'I am more concerned about Radhika. I barely can look her in the eye. This pain is excruciating for her,' said Mohan.

'She is my daughter; I am sure she will come out strong,' Shriram muttered.

Just as Shyam extended his arm to reach out for his friend's shoulder, an elderly looking doctor came rushing out of the Operation Room. 'It's a baby boy for Meera and a baby girl for Vallabha,' he said.

'What about Radhika, doctor?' asked Shyam in a wobbling voice.

'It's a baby boy, but Radhika's parameters are weak,' the doctor replied, clouds of concern looming over his face.

Shriram dashed towards the O.R. and went straight to the bed by the window corner. Shyam followed.

As Shriram reached out his hand to grab that of his daughter, his eyes were arrested by the soft face of the baby. He clasped her hand with both his palms and said, 'Look at the child. He is the progeny of the one whom you miss so very much. He sacrificed everything for us, for you. You will have to pull yourself together to raise his son.'

'Let us see what we can do,' said the doctor.

Shyam nodded and convinced Shriram to leave along with him.

As soon as they left the room, the baby's cry emanating from the O.R. filled the hallway. Shriram turned midway, only to be stopped by Shyam.

'Please, Shri, a little patience. Let the doctors handle it.'

'That's my daughter and my grandson in there, they need me.'

'He is my grandson too, but right now they need medical assistance. You and I will only crowd the room.'

Shriram sighed.

'Have faith in Lord Rama, Shri,' Shyam said.

They both sat on the metal chairs placed alongside the hallway wall. As Shyam placed his back against the chair, he realized he was perspiring heavily. It was hard on him too, but he could not let his friend fall apart.

Barely a minute or so after they were both seated, the baby's cry subsided. Shriram got up from his seat, and this time even Shyam didn't stop him.

Rushing towards the O.R., he saw doctors emerging from the room. Shriram froze midway and sweat began to pour down Shyam's face.

'You both may come in,' one of the doctors said.

While Shriram rushed to Radhika's bedside, Shyam stood a few feet away. Unlike Shriram, he seemed more composed now.

'Her parameters look normal now, it seems,' Shyam said.

'We placed the baby alongside her, and placed her arm in an embracing position. The baby grabbed her finger and within moments it rejuvenated her heartbeat,' said the doctor.

Shriram couldn't hold himself back anymore and those long-held-back tears started rolling down his cheeks. He raised Radhika's arm and placed a kiss on her hand.

'He is no ordinary kid. He is a beacon of hope,' said the doctor.

'There is no doubt about that, he will liberate us all. He will be our *Mukunda*,' said Shyam.

As Shriram rose from the bedside, Mohan and Raghav arrived, each holding their babies in their arms.

'Do you see what I see?' said Shriram smilingly.

'Yes, indeed! Our boys aren't boys anymore. They have crossed over the threshold to being fathers. The batons are exchanging hands,' said Shyam.

A whole year went by. With Shriram bringing order to the city, Shyam was spending most of his time with his grandkids. He was now a Pita-Maha.

'Who is your favourite, of them all?' asked Vallabha as she walked down the pavement, the fresh evening breeze caressing her hair. She knew the answer and had heard the supporting arguments multiple times. Yet, she couldn't help but tease Shyam lovingly.

'Rukmini is the cutest of them all,' he said.

'Inferences are clear; Madhav isn't cute. He isn't a charming lad,' said Vallabha.

'I said—of them all. That doesn't make others less charming,' Shyam protested.

'Forget about pretty, cute and charming. Whom do you love the most?'

'See, all of them make us smile, but…' Shyam mumbled.

'Just pick a name,' she was barely able to conceal her smile any further.

'Mukunda,' he said.

To which she burst into laughter. 'He is all who matters to you. Isn't he?'

'You are being mean. I cannot think of spending my day without any of them. But, yes, by a fraction of a milligram, I care for him a tad bit more,' he protested again.

'We all do. And who wouldn't, he is the most mischievous of them all. His one touch brought Radhika back to life,' she replied.

Shyam nodded.

The sunset appeared just right. The thin lining of silver-greyish cloud, just above the horizon, adorned the setting sun like a silver ring would hold a ruby. It all felt right because these momentary visuals made every Manava forget that the circular placid lake made no sense. That was not how nature worked and its being there could not have been the work of nature.

The winds were building up and the sweet scent of the misty lake waters dominated the breeze.

'The evening is more pleasant than usual. Shyam, how about a stroll by the lakefront?' said Vallabha as they left the grass-covered pavement some hundred metres from the lakefront.

Shyam nodded. 'Let me hold Madhav and Rukmini.'

Vallabha took Mukunda from Shyam. Mukunda had no qualms expressing his displeasure about being away from his Pita-Maha. Looking at his heavy lidded eyes, Shyam couldn't help but laugh.

But again it was not Mukunda's fault. Madhav and Rukmini were equally fond of Shyam. Rukmini was giggling with sheer joy, lovingly embracing her Pita-Maha. Vallabha extended her arm and cupped Rukmini's right cheek. 'Love you, sweetheart,' she said.

'You asked her, right?' said Shyam.

'A number of times! But, she has a pile of administrative files to clear, she says.'

'She wasn't like this. But, probably, she needs more time by herself.'

'Radhika should come out more often. She cannot spend all her time in the palace,' said Vallabha.

As they stepped on to the golden grainy sand of the beach shore, they both noticed something. The wind grew wilder; the coconut trees (planted all along the shore line, by the lawn side) started swaying by the gusts.

'The weather here can be surprising at times.'

'The lake is responding to the winds, it usually remains calm,' replied Shyam.

'When will the lake be open for swimming in?' she asked.

'Not anytime soon, kid. We still aren't sure what it is.'

As they inched towards the lakefront, Mukunda started

growing restless and was constantly pointing towards the shores.

'You want to go there? Come let us sit by the lake,' Shyam said, smiling.

He pointed towards the yellow line drawn on the beach and said, 'Vallabha, let's sit by that line. Don't let any of these toddlers cross that, though.'

As soon as they sat by the line, the winds lulled. And even before they could face each other in amazement, a roaring sound grew in the background. The waves reared up and leapt for the line, as if they were ambushing them.

The cold lake water touched Mukunda's bare feet, and he started laughing and chuckling in joy and amazement.

Shyam and Vallabha, with kids still in their lap, crawled back.

'This never happens, the line is well studied and the lake never breaches it,' said Shyam as he got up and stepped back further.

The lake was growing even more restless now. They both quickly receded back to safety, and finally got off the beach.

'The first time we brought the kids to the lake, and this happens,' he said.

'It's just a lake, with cold clear water. Maybe we are being hyper-critical,' she replied.

Shyam nodded. But then he saw something and couldn't believe his eyes.

The mist had already started covering the lake, but this time the view around it was different.

The mist was light and some visuals started to appear on those mist screens. Shyam turned and looked around, lest somebody was playing tricks and projecting something onto the mist.

There was no one else in sight. The visuals were now gaining coherence and getting more pronounced. They were images of Madhavpur.

Shyam and Vallabha couldn't help but gasp in astonishment.

They were both busy taking brisk steps away from the lake when Vallabha noticed something. Rather, she heard something.

'Did he just say something?' she hollered.

Shyam while still pacing towards the city looked towards Mukunda. He, with his forefinger still pointing towards the lake, had his eyes fixed at the shore.

'Pa...Pe...Pa...' Mukunda mumbled.

'He did. He just spoke his first babble.' Shyam laughed.

Vallabha brought herself to a halt and cupped his soft little cheek. 'Speak again for your aunt.'

'Pa...Pa...' this time around he was more clearly audible. Shyam now slowed down too. 'Look! He is muttering papa,' he said.

'He is probably babbling Pita-Maha. He loves you a lot,' she countered.

'I myself find it a bit of a tongue-twister, why would he try that particular word as his first?' said Shyam.

Amidst all this celebratory chatter of uttering his first syllables, Mukunda was still staring at the lake; his index finger pointed towards the shore, with no sign of relenting. His eyes were steadfast, as if he could see something, which the others couldn't.

·◆·

A year or so passed. The city was taking shape and growing it's own identity. There was enough work for everyone in Ksharanpur. But, only two in the whole populace used to go through their day with inexplicable rigidity.

One was Radhika, who would look into the daily affairs of the palace and subconsciously leave no time for anything else in her daily schedule. And the other was Mukunda, who would sit by the window in his room and either play by himself or gaze at the lake at length.

After that incident, no one ever took Mukunda anywhere near the lake or for that matter anywhere outside the palace. Shyam would often visit him in the room and on certain occasions, seeing him playing all by himself, would stand by the door and just watch.

On one such occasion, Vallabha came unannounced and stood by Shyam's side. 'Where is Radhika?' she said.

'Must be somewhere in the palace.'

'She should be attending to Mukunda more often. He is growing a little reclusive for his age,' she said.

'I am not sure what is happening around here. This is not the world that Krishna envisioned,' he replied with dismay.

'It seems Radhika has receded into her own cocoon and doesn't want to form a bond with anyone. But one thing is for sure, I cannot see him suffer like this, lying in a corner, unloved,' she said.

'But what can we do?'

'Look at him. All he wants is to be by that lakeside. He cannot think of anything else. Just allow me to take him to the shore. Just once,' she pleaded.

'Don't you remember what happened the last time around?' Shyam said, inhaling deeply.

'I do. But can we let fear define our everyday life?'

'Of course not; alright, pick him up, I will accompany you.'

As they were moving out of the palatial gate, they saw Radhika standing by the lawns. Shyam pointed towards her, and drew Mukunda's attention to his mother. Mukunda waved and chuckled, as if his happiness knew no bounds.

Radhika acknowledged the greeting with a very measured smile and then waved back.

'Where would you like to go for a stroll?' asked Shyam.

To which Mukunda reciprocated, 'Papa where…'

Radhika burst out laughing and started moving towards them. As she inched towards them, Shyam handed Mukunda over to his mother. For a quarter of a minute or so he was happy and embraced Radhika with his small, soft arms. But then he started looking towards Shyam again. After all, he knew that his mother's love would not get him an evening's stroll outside the palace, in real Ksharanpur.

'He adores his Pita-Maha,' said Radhika, still smiling with ecstasy.

'He sure does. But he knows the fact that only Pita-Maha will cave into his demands. He is a true wanderer by nature,' replied Vallabha.

Mukunda was now growing impatient and wanted to be back with Shyam. He started moving his hands vigorously, mumbling again.

'Here! Enjoy your evening, you guys. I will finish my work and see you at dinner,' said Radhika, handing Mukunda back to Shyam.

As soon as he was with Shyam again, his babble turned into 'Papa where…'

'To the shores…' replied Shyam.

Radhika waved and then went back to the lawns.

As they stepped onto the pavement beside the shore, Shyam was more cautious than ever. But this time around, neither did the winds grow stronger nor was there any apparent lull.

Mukunda was trying to spring from his embrace, eager as ever to reach the lake. 'Papa where…' he repeated.

'To the shores…' Shyam repeated.

'When will he speak his first coherent sentence?' enquired Vallabha.

Even before Shyam could think of a reply, Mukunda raised

his finger and drew in a deep breath. 'Where Papa?' he said. And then in rapid succession uttered, 'Where is Papa?'

Shyam grew a little confused and then Mukunda spoke again. 'Where is my Papa?'

It was his first coherent sentence.

They both were now looking towards him in amazement. Shyam then turned his gaze towards Vallabha, to which she nodded.

They both knew what Mukunda was seeking an answer to.

'He is beyond that realm,' replied Shyam, pointing towards the lake.

2

The Timid Past
Some Four Prithvi Years Later

Mukunda was now five but as argumentative as a 50-year-old. He was cute, cheerful and confident. But humility was not his forte.

He wouldn't take no for an answer and let anyone get away till he was done explaining his point of view. To add to the woes of those stuck in the crossfire of his words, he was very athletic and would not mind chasing down the person in question, just to narrate his story. If you disagreed with him, he would take it upon himself to make you understand his views. Neither time nor energy was a constraint for him.

He was the star of Ksharanpur, nonetheless. Anybody who had some time to spare would sit down with him and listen to his stories.

'Shoes are more comfortable than slippers,' said Raghav. Vallabha chuckled; she knew he was now in deep trouble.

'No. Slippers are awesome, Uncle. Am I right, Aunt?' Mukunda demanded an affirmation from Vallabha.

'Don't know. I don't even know how to differentiate a slipper from a shoe,' she said, holding back her smile.

'Why, in heaven's name, am I always surrounded by people who know nothing?' he shot back, frustration apparent on his face.

'You mean to say we are idiots?' queried Raghav, with both his arms on his flanks.

'Not you, Uncle! You at least can tell a slipper from a shoe,' he said, poker-faced.

Vallabha's laughter and joy knew no bounds. It was like watching a vamana challenging King Bali.

Mukunda sat down on the floor holding his robe; he knew the establishment of the slippers' superiority would take some explaining.

'Aunt! A slipper is a shoe with little or no hassles. You can slip in and out of slippers in a jiffy.'

'Never thought of it that way,' she said.

'A shoe is like this palace, you need to cross so many doors and so many hallways just to reach your room. While wearing slippers is like camping outside, under the moon or by the lakeside. No dearth of fresh air.'

The smile on Raghav's face was replaced by amazement at the analogy. 'He is right, palaces are no fun.'

'Just like shoes are no fun,' Mukunda said.

'Not yet, dear! Not yet!' said Raghav.

Mukunda sighed and murmured something inaudibly. Probably ruing his efforts going to waste. 'What else do you need to agree with me?' he asked.

'How about this? Can you race me in your slippers? That too when I am wearing shoes?'

'Why would I race you? I would rather go to the beach and pour sand on my feet.'

'Let me guess! This entire discussion is centred around your dislike of shoes and your liking for beaches and camping. Don't you want to go to school?' said Vallabha.

'I never said that,' Mukunda said, a look of innocence on his face.

'You did and that too quite tacitly. What's the matter? School doesn't interest you anymore?' she queried.

'A school is a school, where you are schooled. I don't like getting schooled,' he replied, crossing his arms in anguish.

'Don't you enjoy the company of Madhav and Rukmini?'

'Madhav—yes, but Rukmini is an altogether different story.'

'What about her?'

'She behaves like my nanny. She thinks she cares for me, I think she pesters me.'

'Beware, young lad, you are talking about my daughter,' said Raghav.

'No, Uncle, she is good. But her goodness often wanders into the dark territories of nuisance,' he replied.

'Did she eat from your lunch?' enquired Vallabha.

'No. I don't mind sharing my lunch.'

'Then what on Prithvi did she do?' said Raghav.

'The other day I was too sleepy, because, you know, the previous night those imageries were all over the lake…'

'Mukunda, we don't look at the lake when that happens. You should sleep when it's time to,' interrupted Vallabha.

'And I watched that beautiful play of colours all night long. So, I was tired and dozed off in Miss Vaishnavi's class and she told the teacher about it,' he continued as if Vallabha's words hadn't made their way to his eardrums.

'She did it for your own good. You would have missed the lesson,' said Vallabha.

'She embarrassed me no end,' he added.

'You are five, you will get over it,' said Raghav.

'It's not only about her. I have finished reading all my books at the beginning of the session. There is nothing much to learn in school.'

'Then what on Prithvi do you want? No more beating around the bush, tell me straight,' she said.

'I want to play with Samganak.'

Vallabha raised her arm and made a call on her wrist-phone. 'Here, tell it to your Pita-Maha.'

The holographic image wobbled for a fraction of a second and then captured a full foot-by-foot of two-dimensional space in the hall.

'Hey! Mukunda. How is my buddy doing?' said Shyam.

'I am perturbed. Aunt Vallabha thinks I am not smart enough to be around Samganak.'

'Did I ever say that?' she screeched.

'The thing is, your grandson doesn't want to go to school. He thinks its below his dignity to sit among commoners,' Raghav said.

'Pita-Maha! Please ask Madhav how much I love going to school. Where else would I nap, if not there? And mind you, Uncle! Those commoners are my friends. Ridicule a man, but never his friends.'

Vallabha picked him up in her arms and started tickling him left, right and centre. 'Now tell me! Is this a man who is chuckling or a ticklish boy?' Vallabha said as Mukunda burst out into peals of laughter.

'Pita-Maha! You see, Aunt cannot tolerate me making headway in life,' said Mukunda, still chuckling.

'What headway? What do you want, Mukunda? Vallabha, will you stop that for a few seconds?'

'He wants access to Samganak,' Raghav answered.

Shyam raised his eyebrows and thought for a moment. The hologram wobbled as he moved his right arm swiftly to reach his wrist-phone.

'Mohan is now in Holo-Con with us. Mohan, the lad wants access to the Samganak. As our chief scientific advisor, it is for you to decide,' Shyam said.

'Samganak! Hmm!' Mohan murmured, his eyes widening in disbelief.

'I am fine with it, Mukunda. You can visit anytime and see what Samganak looks like,' he then said.

'I swear, Pita-Maha! I will not talk to anybody if these pranks do not stop right away,' Mukunda said.

'Why what happened?' said Mohan, trying not to burst into laughter.

'Am I visitor here? Why would I ask for a guided tour? I want to code Samganak.'

'Then you need to pass a test. How do we know that you deserve to be anywhere near that big machine?' said Mohan.

'Fair and square! Mohan, he is an ambitious lad and must I say smart too. Test him right now,' said Shyam.

A half-complaining and a half-sobbing grunt emanated from Mukunda's agape mouth.

'Your only key to Samganak is to answer this question. Spell Samganak,' Mohan said.

Mukunda regained his composure; he knew this was doable. He could already see the titanium frame of Samganak glistening in front of his eyes. 'Es-Aa-Em-Ge-Aa-En-Aa-Kh,' he replied.

'Can't help, Shyam! The boy is right. There is no stopping him,' said Mohan.

Shyam stood there in amazement. 'The boy's a genius!' he said, drawing a deep breath.

'Not only genius but brave too, unlike my father,' Mukunda said and embraced Vallabha.

'Wait! What?' said Shyam.

'I am brave, he was not!' he exclaimed, affirming what Shyam had just heard.

All the joyful pretentions and smiles vanished from everyone's faces, more so for Shyam, who froze.

'Your father is a brave man, Mukunda,' he said, still trying not to choke on his own breath.

'He might have been intelligent...but brave? I have no reasons to believe that.'

'He built this wonderful place for us to live in. He reunited Shriram and us.'

'That's what, Pita-Maha; no doubt he must have been smart. But not brave. I am brave. I never step back from what is required to be done. He couldn't join us here, when he was needed the most,' he replied.

'The choices a man makes, make him brave. He sacrificed his own spot to make sure we all reach here safely.'

'Now don't tell me a hundred thousand people could make it but he could not. Moreover, it was Uncle Mohan who defeated Kamsa. Uncle Mohan is brave, Krishna was not.'

'Go to the lawns and enjoy your day. You want access to Samganak, you will have it,' Shyam said, exhaling in despair.

Vallabha gently placed Mukunda down and he rushed out with both his hands up in victory.

'Who has been feeding him all that?' said Shyam.

'Even we are yet to figure that out. No one in Ksharanpur talks like that about Krishna. No clue who conjured these notions in his head,' she replied.

'It's tough on the boy. He needs his father by his side. Probably his way of coping,' said Raghav.

'Mohan! How many Bhoomi year's must have lapsed?' said Shyam.

'We simply don't know how to calculate time-factors for outward Universes. I have no clue. But, must have been eons.'

'Use the last available Bhoomi to Prithvi timescale.'

'Few thousands then, if not more,' he said, knowing well what Shyam was trying to back-calculate.

'How much Bhoomidium was left, back home?'

'All of it! It cannot just vanish or get used up.'

'Any chances…' the image wobbled.

Communication deterioration and disruption was the norm when tides turned. Whether it was the moon's gravity or some kind of interference from the lake's changing water levels, no one knew.

'Shyam, Bhoomidium or lack of it doesn't matter. Bhoomi collapsed unto itself, Madhavpur must have sunk by now.'

The bitter realization of the fact that he might never see his nephew again sent Shyam down the dark aisle of despair and helplessness. But he was not an uncle anymore, he was a Pita-Maha, with more responsibilities than ever before.

He didn't say anything, just nodded in nonchalant agreement and got off the call.

'Carry on, Mohan! Let me and Raghav go and see where the kids are,' Vallabha said.

Mohan nodded and disconnected his wrist-phone.

Standing on the porch of the entrance to the main hall, Vallabha could see Mukunda playing with Madhav and Rukmini. What Vallabha saw next took away at least an ounce or two from her already heavy heart.

Madhav, for some good reason, was pestering Rukmini. Mukunda stepped in and reprimanded him.

'He is bitter and hurtful in his words alone. Soft and kind in his actions,' said Vallabha.

'To what levels have we stooped? We are judging a toddler, that too for his talkativeness?' said Raghav.

'Wish that cloud would show up again and somehow Krishna would make it,' Vallabha muttered.

'I agree.' Raghav nodded as he made his way to the administrative office.

Sufficient arrangements were being made for Mukunda's Samganak classes. Miss Vaishnavi was instructed to let Mukunda off the hook by lunchtime. Mukunda was instructed to either finish his lunch in 20 minutes sharp or be prepared to forgo it. And napping was not allowed in the System Chamber; he was warned beforehand.

It was his first day and he could not help but stand and stare at the 'Café Evolution'. It was sweltering hot, but he refused to enter; rather, he simply wouldn't listen. He counted the number of floors almost six times. And then counted them again.

'There were four floors in Krishna's Café Evolution, why are there three here?' he finally said.

'There were just three in the original one too,' Mohan replied, tugging him by his hand in a bid to take him inside.

'No! Mother has narrated tales about Café Evolution to me. And it was four.'

'Your mother barely visited the lab. And I used to work there, you stubborn kid,' he said.

'Pita-Maha! Uncle Mohan always call me names,' he said, amply displaying his grudge.

'He was never my favourite too; let's drop this idea about Samganak. We want neither him nor his fancy toys,' Shyam replied, twisting his torso, as if preparing to retreat.

'This trick won't work on me, Pita-Maha. Uncle Mohan cannot wish me away so easily,' he said, resuming his counting.

Mohan grabbed him by his hand and picked him up. 'Come on in. Your relentless counting won't change the architecture of the building.'

A foot from the entrance, Mohan closed his eyes and issued a thought command. The door slid open, letting in a burst of light into the main hall. The floor to the walls to the ceiling were now shining in bright daylight. But none of that could match the glittering brilliance of the dark metal of the Samganak's chassis. Its contours dipped in the slanting rays of sunshine, and it seemed as if it was coming to life.

'That's pure titanium on it, isn't it?' Mukunda said, shaking his legs vigorously.

Mohan placed him down.

Awestruck, Mukunda started taking little steps towards the machine. Starting from the left side of the vast panel, he began sliding his palm over it.

'Pita-Maha! See, I can't even reach the Command-Panel. How will I work on it?'

'You will. But before that you need to learn the basics. What these big computing machines are all about and the kind of respect they deserve,' said Shyam.

'When can I get access to the main control panel?' Mukunda asked turning towards Mohan.

Mohan couldn't help but notice the similarities between then and now. Krishna withheld encryption codes from Mohan, for his own good. And Mohan craved for them as if he was being denied a fundamental right. Now he could see the flames of the same desperation and want engulfing Mukunda.

'Why do you want access to it? You can always ask Pita-Maha for a wrist-device to play games and prepare class reports,' he said.

'Pita-Maha! Uncle always does that…'

'Does what?' enquired Shyam.

'Looks down upon me! He doesn't love me. He loves Madhav,' he replied.

'I definitely love Madhav, because he is my son. And yes, you are right, I don't love you.'

Mukunda frowned, looking towards Shyam in despair and anguish.

It was then that Mohan picked him up and tickled him under his chin and on his neck. 'I don't love you. I adore you. Not only because you are my nephew, but also for your tantrums and foolhardiness, you little brat,' said Mohan.

'Are we sure he isn't lying this time?' Mukunda turned around to ask Shyam, still chuckling from the soft tickle.

'Of course! Why would you ask that?' said Shyam, troubled by Mukunda's endless skepticism.

'Nothing much! Just that he is known for switching sides way too often,' Mukunda said, laughing mercilessly.

Shyam took a fraction of a second to get the reference, but when he did he could not help but burst into fits of laughter.

Mohan smiled. 'You are no less evil than Kamsa, I won't mind siding with you.'

Mukunda grasped his uncle's face with both his palms and kissed him on the forehead.

Mohan then placed him down and said, 'You won't get access to the Samganak until next year. You will have to learn extensively about the machine, then prove your worth by presenting us with a detailed road map of what you would do differently with your access. How would you put it to good use for all Manavas.'

Mukunda nodded. This time he didn't find faults with his uncle's plan.

Meanwhile, Mohan turned towards Shyam to discuss the details of the training programme and the logistics required to bring Mukunda to Café Evolution. Mukunda placed his left ear on the cold surface-plate of the Samganak. He could feel the chill travelling up his skin towards his head. As he swept his face across the machine, he could hear some voices underneath.

He knew that the humming was actually noises emanating from the Samganak's circuitry, but his heart wanted him to believe otherwise. It was as if the Samganak was whispering something in his ear. Maybe, narrating the tale of what he had been through. How he had seen the rise and fall of Madhavpur. How he colluded with Mohan to defeat Kamsa. How his soul was Brahmported from his earlier home to his new abode, in a pen-like device. And, how when he gained consciousness again on Prithvi, his original Master was nowhere to be seen.

'I will pick him up from school tomorrow afternoon and bring him along,' said Shyam. Then he turned towards Mukunda and said, 'Let's go.'

As they were stepping outside the main door, Mohan ruffled Mukunda's hair and said, 'I will be teaching you skills that I have not even taught Madhav. So, never doubt my love for you. I will always be on your side.'

Mukunda smiled and then walked alongside his Pita-Maha down the Bhoomi Avenue, eastwards.

3

The School of Thought
Five Prithvi Years Later

Just a few hundred metres from the colossal Council building, stood another relatively small but exemplary marvel of architecture.

It was designed in such a way that the first rays of the sun never directly reached its façade at any time of the year but was reflected from the huge OM symbol embossed in shiny metal on the front of the Council building. Drenched in the reflected light of the first morning rays, the Central Knowledge Embodiment Council (CKEC, pronounced See-Kek) displayed colours and hues like none other in the whole island. The evenings were a bit different though. The wonder of Manava genius, the façade of CKEC would glow in the setting sun's direct light.

Set firmly above twenty-four columns of varied lengths, the arches met midway. Twenty metres off the ground on both extremities, they rose to thirty metres (about one-fifth the distance from the centre), and finally settled at twenty-five metres at the juncture.

The twenty-four columns (each about ten metres above the ground) were not placed equidistantly. Each variation of gap symbolized an exclusive pathway for students of different standards. There weren't many though, just four—Shishu, Baal, Tarun and Paripakv (in that order). Each spanned three years of student life. Shishu were the youngest of them all, mostly toddlers. They had exclusive rights over the exact midway section of the staircase, through the twelfth and thirteenth column. That was the shortest way to reach the central hall. The pathway was separated from the rest of the staircase by a parallel set of handrails.

The Paripakvs were supposed to use the outermost section of the staircase, the longest route to the central hall. But once you stood beneath the arch, it was a sure-shot way to catch breathtaking glimpses of the island-city. Not to mention, it offered a view of the ever-tranquil lake too.

Mukunda was now a Tarun(ite), and so were Madhav and Rukmini. Mukunda was still the smartest and the most boisterous of them all, but it was Madhav who aced the academics. One reason, proposed time and again, for this unexpected occurrence, was the effort and time that Mukunda had to devote to his Samganak classes. Although, the most surprising of them all was Rukmini. She was exceptionally good at athletics while being fairly good at academics as well. Her last summer paper on 'Ergonomics of moving around in a perfectly circular Island' had brought her some rapid recognition and appreciation across CKEC.

The three of them were good friends, just not on the school premises. There, they had their own social circles to oblige.

Madhav mingled with the folks who knew their life goals early in life (which was mostly getting into the administrative services). Rukmini used to hang out with easy-going and fun-loving folks (mostly girls).

But, it was Mukunda who had everyone worried. The guys he used to hang out with were rebels, in one sense or; people who knew they were carved out of a special clay and had no qualms admitting it and were always at war with anyone who tried imposing their authority on them.

One such prince of his own delusional world was Kanha. He was their classmate or rather a mate. He avoided classes, thanks to his extraordinary conflict-seeking skills. He would always find some issue with the school management. Or he would pester the management on the pretext of helping out a distressed student.

Funnily enough, the management was happy to lend an ear, as long as some (imaginary or not-so-imaginary) problem was solved.

Kanha and Mukunda never got along well, due to their constant upmanship. Mukunda thought that Kanha was wasting his intellect by wandering from pillar to post and Kanha was generally of the opinion that Mukunda was wasting his time by sitting around in Mohan's lab.

But then, the highlight of their rivalry was that they never confronted each other, ever. Wordplay was all that they deployed to crack open the hull of each other's colossal wisdom. And that witty wordplay between the two titans was the attraction of the school. Students (majorly Tarunites) used to help out the star of their liking with confidential information about the rival. They sure added fuel to the fire.

These days, it was Kanha who was ruling the roost. He seemed to have his network in place—precisely guessing each and every move of Mukunda.

This used to bother Rukmini more than it bothered Mukunda. She had her own friends who used to visit both sides of the fence and would provide her with the latest tidbits of news.

The current one doing the rounds was bothering her immensely. She had no choice but to rush to the person himself.

'Mukunda, you need to postpone your presentation,' she said.
'What for?'
'Kanha has got his hands on the content of your work. He will try his best to counter you on all levels.'
'Good for him, (am) happy to keep him busy.'
'You don't understand, do you? If he discredits your work, the

public consensus can turn against you and the lab.'

'The lab doesn't run on consensus. Moreover, he is just a kid, nobody takes him seriously.'

'We too are school kids. If he discredits your work, he discredits you and the chief family of Ksharanpur.'

'He won't. Just like all other residents of Ksharanpur, he too respects Krishna. He won't do anything that goes against the family.'

'He reveres Krishna, and that's the sole reason he doesn't like you. You oppose Krishna on so many levels,' she said.

'I will not postpone my presentation. It shall take place at 1:30 p.m. right here in the school library. Café Evolution is a high-security and limited-access area. There is no way Kanha can have access to my work.'

Rukmini turned around to walk away; she knew no amount of convincing would work. Besides, she had an assignment to complete before the lunch-hour event.

Within the atrium of the school building rose another discreet façade, behind which was a building that housed a big hall. It practically was a building inside a building. A smaller replica of the school façade, it was built of a much glossier pearl-ivory-finish marble. The glossy coating gave it a distinct glow even in dim daylight. They called it 'The House of Knowledge'.

The House was brimming with Taruns and Paripakvs. The Tarunites were there to cheer for their league-mate. And, the Paripakvs were there to gain ideas about new administrative projects, so they could align their choice of higher studies with them.

The lights were dimmed and the holographic projection being prepped. Mukunda nodded and Madhav started the projection of the presentation.

'The Samganak is older than most of us here. He is wise and

has seen the ebbs and flow of time. He was instrumental in the survival of civilization and deserves respect,' he said.

The house applauded in consonance. Amid that loud uproar of applause, Mukunda was trying to read the expressions on Kanha's face, who was sitting midway through the hall, on the extreme right. But there were none. He appeared focused, displaying no expressions, which was comforting to Mukunda.

'As we all know, he was transported here in virtual form and was built again around the data. Since then, he has been instrumental in building this great Ksharanpur,' he added.

'It was not Samganak who built Ksharanpur; it was your father who was instrumental in building Samganak, which in turn is helping us run the island. Your father faced great perils, but still handed all his know-how to Mohan. He upkept Bhoomi, and now his contributions help us survive on Prithvi too.'

Mukunda didn't have to turn around to see who was speaking. He knew it was Kanha, trying to unnerve him.

'The wheel must turn, no matter who pushes it. It's Mohan and Samganak who make this island inhabitable for us,' Mukunda said.

'He's got a point there; we all revere Krishna but let's not undermine Mohan. After all, he is the one whom Krishna passed on the baton to,' said Miss Vaishnavi.

As usual, no one countered her. And it was not because of fear or respect or the seniority she held at the school. The fact was that nobody wanted to argue with her.

She started out by teaching Shishu standards and then went on to become a Tarun teacher. Basically, as the batch progressed, she got promoted to teaching higher standards too.

She knew everybody inside and out, and would often make snide remarks, pinching where it hurt the most.

For Mukunda, it was 'You pampered kid' and for Kanha, it

was 'Everyone's unjust and you alone are right.'

The rest of the presentation was a boring mundane affair; the sparks of rivalry had been nipped in the bud (by Miss Vaishnavi).

Everybody knew something or the other about Samganak, and during the presentation they did get to know more about the new projects too. But the one thing that everyone in The House of Knowledge sought that day (of course, except Miss Vaishnavi) was Ksharanpur's renowned rivalry.

Those who cared knew who was to blame. Clearly, Rukmini, while making arrangements had forgotten to factor in Miss Vaishnavi.

Madhav and Mukunda were now busy collecting their stuff. Mukunda packed his hand-scribbled worksheet and reference notes and then packed the projector back in the box. They were then supposed to hand it back to the Library Master.

'Some pretty impressive stuff there,' Miss Vaishnavi said.

'Thanks for the kind words, Miss,' he replied and nodded.

As they turned to go back to their classes, Madhav heard a loud thudding sound. It was Kanha, who had just intentionally bumped into Mukunda, who flared up. But that didn't stop Kanha. He didn't pace away either. He kept on walking, with his head turned back towards Mukunda, still smiling.

Madhav held Mukunda by his wrist and whispered, 'This is the library. If scores need to be settled, then at the least not here.'

Mukunda nodded, his hand searching the contents of his right pocket, which seemed heavy.

Days went by, but Mukunda was nowhere to be seen in school. For the first couple of days it didn't bother anybody, but when Mukunda didn't turn up at school on the third consecutive day, Rukmini had no choice but to call up Radhika, who was equally amazed. After all, Mukunda had been leaving for school on time.

By midday, Rukmini grew restless and concerned. In the middle of an important lecture, she found herself staring at the skies outside, in a near stupor.

As her gaze shifted from the clear skies above to the horizon, she noticed something. It was unusually breezy for a clear summer day. Her gaze quickly shifted to the windowpane and then onto the third row from hers. She held her gaze, wishing Madhav would take notice.

She was twitching her right brow vigorously. It was a pre-agreed upon signal for sneaking out and thankfully Madhav caught her making the gesture.

They made it straight to the peripheries of the island.

'There is no way he can be sitting around on the beach without getting drenched by those bewilderingly odd waves,' said Madhav.

'But he is somewhere around here; it's not supposed to be so breezy around this time of the day.'

'He must be on the cliffs, to the western side of Ksharanpur, away from the palace,' said Madhav.

They had to run on the hot sand for at least a couple of kilometres or so before they could see the cliffs on the horizon.

'There he is!' she pointed out, running towards him, with Madhav following her.

On reaching the cliff-top, Rukmini was about to scold Mukunda, when Madhav signalled her to stop.

'What bothers you?' Madhav asked Mukunda.

Without even thinking for a moment, Mukunda pulled out a beautifully carved peacock blue-coloured wooden box from his pocket. Madhav took the box from him and gently opened it.

'Venu,' Madhav murmured.

'It's the flute my father used to posses,' said Mukunda.

Rukmini and Madhav smiled. It was the first time Mukunda

called Krishna 'his father'.

'There is a note along with it,' said Mukunda, pulling the note from beneath the flute.

'What does it say, which script is this?' she said.

'It's Brahmi. A script that pre-dated our own civilization.'

'What does it say?' said Madhav.

'Out of torment arises the pearl,' said Mukunda.

'He encrypted the message,' Rukmini said.

Mukunda nodded.

'You are not going to try that. You are absolutely not,' she exclaimed.

'What?' Madhav asked, holding Rukmini's arm.

'He is sitting here for The Eye. That compulsive hater has made him believe that The Eye opens the door to the realms.'

'Is this true, Mukunda?' Madhav asked.

'The eye does that, its true. But, I was not sitting around here to jump into it.'

'You do realize that Bhoomi might have aged a million or a billion years by now. We don't even know whether Bhoomi even exists or not, let alone Krishna,' he said.

'I just needed a quiet place to contemplate, but thanks to you both, I failed,' said Mukunda.

'You are coming with us. We are going to the palace,' said Madhav.

4
Blink of an Eye

The evening had gone quite well. Everyone from the family had gathered. There was interesting conversation, great food and plenty of fun and frolic. Tea was served in the garden, amid blossoming flowers and the chirping of birds. That was not all! Dinner too was served under a brilliantly shining full moon. Rukmini and Mukunda chose not to talk about the Eye that day.

The next day, as the Tarunites gathered in the Central Hall for the school assembly, Mukunda was again nowhere to be seen. Rukmini surreptitiously sneaked out of the hall and dashed to the reception area, from where she called Mohan.

'Yes! The Eye has formed. It was early this morning,' he confirmed.

'Meet me there, Uncle. And please don't bring anyone else along,' she requested.

Rukmini had no time to rush back to the hall to fetch Madhav, so she left for the cliffs alone.

'The Eye is closing now,' said Mohan as they both reached the cliff.

'Did he just…' she said.

'The monitoring drones should have been around. Let me see if I can pull up some earlier visuals,' he said.

Mohan started projecting the visuals from the drone feed. A minute or so of skimming through the feed and the fully developed Eye could be seen just a few feet from the cliff, right at the place they were standing.

'That's Mukunda standing by the cliff. He seems to be waiting for the Eye to grow bigger,' Rukmini said, pointing to the feed.

The Eye did grow larger, and what they saw next left them aghast. Mukunda jumped off the cliff, straight into the Eye.

'He is gone!' said Mohan, his mouth agape.

'What do we do now? Can your wrist-phone command a drone? Can you spare one and send it into the Eye.'

'Let me see,' Mohan murmured as he fumbled to operate his wrist-phone.

'It's about to close, Uncle. Hurry up!'

'Okay! I now have access to one of my drones.'

The drone appeared on the horizon from their right and dashed into the shrinking Eye. As soon as it crossed the threshold, the drone went off the radar and Mohan lost control of it.

'That drone is gone too, isn't it?' she murmured.

'How do I explain this to Radhika?' he murmured, cold sweat running down his face.

'I am not sure. Maybe wait for some sort of signal from that drone?'

'It's a wormhole, Rukmini; nothing will ever come out of that,' he replied, his voice trembling.

'What do we do, Uncle? How do we tell Pita-Maha about it? He will be devastated.'

'Everyone will be. Do you think it be easy on Shriram and Radhika?'

'Where is he now? Is Mukunda safe?' she asked, anxious.

'He must have wanted to reach Krishna by travelling through the Eye,' Mohan said.

'Will he?'

'I can't tell for sure. None of our calculations work beyond the realm. I simply don't know where that wormhole will land him,' he said, shaking his head.

'How do we break this news to the family? I should have raised an alarm when we found him lingering on the cliff yesterday. We feared embarrassing him in front of everybody. I never thought he would actually do something like this,' she said woefully.

'You guys had a chat with him? We need to get to Shyam immediately. He might be able to suggest something.'

The mood grew sombre in the palace when Rukmini and Mohan broke the news. Radhika was at a loss for words, Shriram had to be by her side each passing moment.

'This is all my fault,' Radhika said, sobbing inconsolably. 'Rukmini told me about him missing school, but I didn't do anything about it.' She stopped only to catch her breath among the sobs. 'I scolded him for cutting school but didn't bother to find out where he had been going,' she said as Vallabha and Meera tried to console her.

Meera cupped her head and hugged her. 'This is not your mistake. This is our collective failure.'

Shyam too was shocked beyond belief but had to hold his composure. He had been in the lab with Mohan for hours, frantically searching for some way to bring Mukunda back.

'I wish Krishna was here,' said Mohan, ruing his helplessness.

'How I wish both Krishna and Mukunda were here. We couldn't hold on to either of them. What have we done?' said Shyam in a choked voice.

'Things will get better. They will have to get better, believe me,' Mohan said, hugging Shyam.

•◆

As the news of Mukunda's disappearance spread, the whole island was engulfed in a cloud of grief. A part of a legacy had just vanished.

Days went by and the people of Ksharanpur gradually resumed their daily routines. However, the palace was yet to see any sign of normalcy, it was as if time had stood still. Shriram and Meera spent most their time with Radhika, who was counting on Shyam and Mohan to come up with some miraculous solution to find Mukunda.

On the seventh day, by when Mohan and Shyam had done everything in their power to arrive at a solution, Shyam called for an Empowered Council Meet, which was attended by Narayan, Gopal, Vitthal and Shriram.

'The situation is grim. Isn't it?' said Gopal.

'Beyond belief,' replied Shyam.

'This shouldn't have happened. None of us realized that something was troubling Mukunda,' said Vitthal.

'The next time our civilization is under threat, the people will have no one to fall back on,' said Narayan.

'We do understand, gentlemen. He was to be our beacon of hope. But he was too young to understand the shoes he had to fill,' replied Shriram.

'For God's sake, locate Mukunda. We need him more than ever,' said a perturbed Gopal.

'That is why we are here, gentlemen. Our current surveillance cannot track him down. We might have to set up the Omechta module again,' suggested Mohan.

'What are our chances?' asked Vitthal.

'Almost zero to none. But if he is safe in some alien world, we will get to know of it. Then we can plan an extraction,' Mohan replied.

'Sounds complicated. Any downsides?' asked Vitthal.

'We will have to shut down at least half of Ksharanpur to gather enough power for the project, and we have no idea what kind of realms and spheres we might open up,' Mohan replied.

'You mean our cover could be blown? We can be approached by beings of other realms?' said Gopal.

'There are inherent risks involved in such operations,' said Mohan, nodding.

'That's why we have gathered here, folks. We have done all we could. More search operations would mean pulling down the camouflage which Krishna had prepared for us,' said Shyam.

Pushing for an advanced search mission meant putting the entire Manava race at risk and vetoing a search mission meant letting Mukunda go. The council members were at a fix.

'He was my grandson, amongst other things. But even then, I cannot put everyone's security in jeopardy, just in the hope of finding him,' said Shriram.

'Let's not stop trying. We should hope for the best,' said Gopal.

'Seal all roads leading to the lake. Also keep a strict vigil on any activity in and around it,' Mohan spoke into his wrist-phone as the meeting concluded.

⋅◆

Meanwhile, it was first day of school for both Rukmini and Madhav after a long gap. They both waited eagerly for lunch break. As the clock struck one, they both started looking for Kanha. The annual sports meet was just a week away and Kanha was nowehere to be seen. After a frantic search they found him sitting beneath a tree in the playground.

'Are you happy now?' Rukmini yelled as she approached him.

'If it's about the sports meet, then yes. If it's about Mukunda, then no.'

'You gave him that flute. Where did you get it from?' demanded Madhav.

'It was a replica. I just wanted to inspire him to find a goal in life.'

'By asking him to chase torments?' she said.

'Look! That was an innocuous quote, nothing more.'

'If that is so, then why was it encrypted in Brahmi?' said Madhav.

'It was just to make him realize that he was among an elite few. That he knew things beyond the ordinary. I wanted the best for him. But if you feel that somehow I am responsible for his disappearance, that's okay. I understand.'

'We didn't mean that. How could you be responsible for anyone's action arising out of his own free will?' said Madhav, to which Rukmini glared at him in anger.

'You know more about Mukunda and the Eye than us,' she said.

'That might be true,' he said.

'Did he talk to you about it?' she asked.

'That day, a week before the incident, I went and sat next to him in the library.'

'We didn't know that. I thought you both couldn't stand each other,' said Madhav.

'We talked about the Eye. I had just come to know that it might appear again in a week.'

'You told him about the Eye, didn't you?' she said.

'He worked at Café Evolution, he already knew everything about the island. That's why I had approached him. I wanted access to the Eye's data. I wanted to study it up close,' he said.

'Why didn't you approach the Office of Weathers for it?' said Madhav.

'We are commoners, we do not have those privileges.'

'That's not true,' protested Rukmini.

'What did he tell you?' said Madhav.

'He referred a book, which he said had theories to explain such phenomena.'

'So you do have some understanding of the Eye?' she asked.

'I haven't read that book yet.'

'But you did want to study them, didn't you?' she said.

'I did, but Mukunda told me that this Eye was an insignificant one. That the major one would open up a couple of years from now. So, I dropped this Eye from my priority list for now.'

'He was concealing the facts from you,' said Madhav.

'He was lying, flat out lying. This one was major. He didn't want much attention around it,' she said.

'To execute his own plan, without drawing much attention,' said Madhav.

'Look, I didn't make him jump through that Eye,' said Kanha.

They both nodded.

'We are going to the Uncle Mohan's lab. Will you mind accompanying us?' she said.

'What for?'

'It would be much easier to get bionic access to the lab,' she replied.

'I am not sure if Pita-Maha and Dad would approve of that. Not everybody gets access to the lab, not even us,' said Madhav.

'Well, whether they approve of it or not, he is getting his accesses done. We need all hands on deck to safely crack open that wormhole again. I want Mukunda back in Ksharanpur,' she replied.

They reached the lab just when Mohan was stepping in. 'Good to see you all,' said Mohan, perplexed to see so many guests at his workplace.

'Dad! This is our friend Kanha, he would like to see your work and, of course, the lab,' Madhav said.

'Uncle, he is Kanha, the second-most brilliant kid in school, after Mukunda. Now that the most brilliant kid has left your lab and decided to jump into a wormhole, you might require a new recruit,' Rukmini said.

'Hmm! It's not as easy as it sounds, kids. There are security clearances required, then general consensus has to be built among the empowered elders. There is training involved too…a hell lot of it actually! Look, I would love to listen to you, but give the boy a breather. He looks overwhelmed,' said Mohan, pointing to Kanha.

'But we don't have much time,' she said.

'Its better we take our time and weigh our options, rather than taking wrong decisions in haste. Kanha, can you make it to the palace this evening? Do you want to be a part of this?' Mohan asked.

Kanha nodded.

'Be there then and don't tell anyone about it.'

⋅◆

An elaborate spread was laid out in the royal lawns. Almost everybody from the family was there.

'Come here, boy. Make yourself at home. I heard about what you said the other day about being a commoner. As a matter of fact, everybody sitting here, except me, are commoners. I am not a commoner because I head the state of Ksharanpur, therefore I get to live in the palace. These people live here because they are my family. Otherwise, they are all commoners too, just like you,' said Shriram.

'With all due respect, I don't see the purpose of such extravaganze,' Kanha said, referring to the lavish lawns and grand palace.

'Everything serves a purpose. Everything. We Manavas have a history. We were mortals once. We not only respect authority, we crave it. We need to know that someone is at the top, overseeing everything. That's what gives us a sense of security and that's what reinforces our conscience,' he said.

'So, ultimately, this grand palace is there to serve the people. It belongs to them?'

'It does. But till the time I am at the helm of affairs, I am its protector and guardian. Whosoever inherits the throne will be the protector of Ksharanpur and its treasures.'

'And that can be anybody?'

'Anybody. If you grow up to be a wise and just, it can be you,' he smiled.

Kanha smiled too. It was smile of relief and hope.

'Enough about the future, people! Our present is still wobbly. Kanha is our guest this evening and he want us to listen to him,' said Rukmini.

'I would like to join Café Evolution,' Kanha said.

'Tell them what you bring to the table,' she said to him.

'I, with my intellect, hard work and dedication…'

'He is our only hope to save Mukunda,' Rukmini interrupted him. 'He has been reading about those wormholes and can help us understand them better. Tell us what you know so far, Kanha.'

Kanha was not sure where and how to begin. He didn't want to come across as either dumb or overly ambitious.

'Kanha, if that is so, it's important that you help us in finding Mukunda,' said Radhika.

'This was a local wormhole. It appeared almost parallel to the horizon,' he said.

'How local?' said Mohan.

'Could be a next-door kingdom or a nearby planet. Perhaps a not-so-faraway galaxy.'

'Okay! Local as in a non-Omechta wormhole,' said Mohan.

'Mukunda is still in this universe, probably on some inhabitable land,' he replied.

'How do we know that?' asked Shyam.

'These kind of local wormholes crop up when there is an energy mismatch. The universe finds its own way to balance it out through such vents.'

'So, an uninhabited planet will have no major disequilibrium to trigger a wormhole?' said Mohan.

'This is what it is. Some intelligent race did something grand and insane to tweak the equilibrium,' he replied.

'Someone did it on purpose?' said Radhika.

'Doesn't seem like it. Not for now,' he said.

'Anyway, we can recreate one and pull him back?' said Shriram.

'We can do something to saturate our own realm with a tremendous amount of energy and wish for a wormhole to open up somewhere,' suggested Mohan.

'One more thing…the drone that you directed into the wormhole won't need charging for thousands of year to come,' added Kanha.

'Right! The wormhole must have super-charged the drone and super-vitalized Mukunda,' said Mohan.

'But you are missing something here,' Kanha said.

'In case of loss of signal, the drones are programmed to follow and protect the tagged residents; Mukunda being one the select few. Since he works at the Lab, I had synced his ID to the drone security and surveillance system,' said Mohan.

'That is exactly how he fooled everyone and jumped right through the wormhole. The drones didn't see him as a hostile entity leaping into the forbidden lake,' said Kanha.

'I like this guy!' said Mohan, pointing to Kanha.

'He is good to go. Welcome onboard, Kanha,' said Shyam.

'I appreciate everyone's generosity and willingness to help. I understand that we all want Mukunda to be back, but the safety and security of Ksharanpur and its people are paramount. Do not start something that spirals out of control,' warned Radhika.

5

The Good Captor

The sky was bright and clear, letting the bold and bright midday sunshine pass through it unhindered. But the horizon was not. That mix of sand ruffled by desert winds along with the wobbling mirages was anything but clear.

Dunes after dunes, crafted out of the golden sand, added to the monotony of the barren landscape. The hot desert winds were blowing uninterrupted, hugging the terrain below. And wherever they found an obstruction in their path, they circumvented it. But that didn't happen without some of the sand being deposited on the surface, forming small dunes. Then there were some obsolete-looking dry vegetation and shrubs that had too much sand all over them. In that dry and cruel landscape, someone lay half buried under the shifting sand. As the figure started tossing and turning in the sand, it was growing evident who he was. The drone hovered some ten feet above him, dusting the sand off his back with its exhausts.

'Master! Somebody is keeping an eye on us. We should leave this area immediately,' said the drone.

Mukunda raised his neck and looked around. He saw somebody standing to his right, about fifty feet away. The person was sitting on the hot sand, staring at him incessantly.

'Who are you?' he asked, turning to face the drone.

'I am Garuda of Airborne4 Division. I was assigned to find you, Master.'

'Good! Now that you have found me, take me home. This place doesn't look very welcoming.'

'All data links to the control command have been severed, there is no way back. But I will go with you, wherever this new world leads us to,' said Garuda.

'Then go ask that person why he is staring at us?'

The drone flew off and started circling over the stranger. He was unlike anybody Mukunda had seen back home. He had long hair, brused back. He had narrow and thin eyebrows. His nose bridge was flat and the cheekbones rose up to his eye sockets. He was short and stout. Seeing the drone hovering over him, he was both excited and perplexed.

'Who are you?' said Garuda.

'Am I talking to a metal Xarksha?' shouted the stranger.

'I am Garuda of Airborne4 Division. I am metal, but not Xarksha.'

'Of course, you are not. You do not have any wings to flap. You cannot outfly a Xarksha,' he said, giggling like a baby.

'Show us the way back home. We are lost,' shouted Mukunda.

'This is home.'

'What is this place?' he asked, perplexed.

'Xurabhur desert in the territories of the great Empire of Xarlok,' the man replied.

'Is there a more hospitable place around? Where we can stay for a few days?'

'No.'

'None?'

'You will have to accompany me to the nearest checkpost,' the stranger said.

'Why should we accompany you?' asked Garuda.

'All foreigners need to be deposited at the checkposts. That's mandotary.' 'Deposited? We will not accompany you or anybody. We can find our way back home,' said Mukunda, leaping to his feet.

'Narrating the procedures to you was my duty. If you choose not to, the soldiers will find you anyway.'

Mukunda stared at him with his eyes wide open.

'You cannot cross the border of the Kingdom. And the moment you make your cluelessness apparent around here, people will know,' the stranger said, grining ear to ear.

'If we get apprehended by the soldiers, what follows?' asked Garuda.

'If you are not accompanied by a local and are not on your way to be deposited, they will kill you. There and then.'

'Master! That's scary. I will follow him any day,' said Garuda.

'He is just trying to scare us. Don't worry!'

'I am not. This is a xenophobic society; being with me can give you immunity. If I deposit you, they will take you to the King. And, if the King is in a good mood, he might spare your life.'

'I will follow him, Master,' said Garuda, his voice trembling.

'On one condition, you will tell me more about this great kingdom of yours,' Mukunda said.

'Xinjhua will now be your guide,' the man said, smiling.

'How far is this checkpost?'

'An overnight journey, not much.'

'Master is tired, he cannot walk overnight.'

'I know, that's why we will be heading that way,' he said, pointing towards his right.

At first, Mukunda couldn't see anything, but as he strained his eyes, he caught glimpses of a tiny and wobbly speck on the horizon.

'That's my home,' Xinjhua said, poiting towards the horizon.

'Garuda, will you fly past that and see if it's clear?' Mukunda ordered.

As Garuda flew past Xinjhua, he let out a deep sigh. 'Oh! How I miss Xarksha.'

'Who is this Xarksha that you talk about?' Mukunda asked.

'Oh! You will see.'

'You promised to show us around,' said Mukunda.

'Some things cannot be put into words,' he said, grinning.

When they received a green signal from Garuda, they started making their way towards a hut-like structure in the distance. It was a cylindrical-shaped hut made out of sand and mud, and covered with a thatched roof. It did not look impressive, but served well as shelter against the dry desert winds.

As Xinjhua pushed open the door of his hut, Mukunda got a glimpse of his family. His wife was crouching on a makeshift bed, playing with her two young children.

They came across as a small and happy family, with just enough to make it by. 'Chinjhi, these are our guests,' Xinjhua said to his wife.

A vague smile grew on her face, which then faded and gave way to wrinkles of concern.

'Hey! We do not mean any harm. We are friends,' said Mukunda.

'She is very happy to see you,' he said.

'Then why did she go pale?' murmured Garuda.

'One, she doesn't come across talking flying creatures so very often. And two, she knows what being a guest here means,' Xinjhua replied.

'That we will soon be subjected to the King's mercy?' said Mukunda.

Xinjhua nodded.

'How old are they?' he asked, pointing towards the two young kids, who were in awe of the drone hovering above them.

'They both are two. Twins,' she replied.

'They are adorable and cheerful,' said Mukunda.

Hearing this, a smile reappeared on her face.

Garuda was now hovering quite low, seeing which Mukunda said, 'Enough! Don't hover so close to them. Lest you startle them or they pluck your rotors.'

'Why would they? I think they like me,' Garuda replied.

'Kids do that. Believe me. I myself have dismantled many of your brethren when I was a toddler,' he said, a nasty smile sparkling all over his face.

Garuda first gave Mukunda that blank 'How could you!' look and then flew up to hover at a secure height.

'What do we do now? Do we stay over? Or do we eat something and move to some checkpoint?' Mukunda said.

'We stay. We shall eat and rest. And then, in the morning, make a move,' Xinjhua replied.

'What if someone finds out that we are putting up at your place?'

'We are in the middle of a very vast desert. No one will bother us here,' he replied.

Mukunda found a chair and sat on it. Chinjhi, meanwhile, got up and started fixing an early dinner for all of them. Garuda too found a safe corner away from the kids and landed.

Xinjhua was sitting on the floor beside the bed. He was pensive and had a million thoughts racing across his mind. Mukunda noticed his sense of unease but chose not to ask anything. 'You are not from around here, are you?'

'No, we are not. We lost our way and then the desert heat knocked me out,' Mukunda replied.

'I have been to all kingdoms, surrounding and far away. And I have seen all kinds of people losing their way. But you are not like any of them. This flying friend of yours is made up of metal. You come from another world? Or the heavens above?'

'Not from the heavens above. You could say we belong to a different kind of world.'

'You need to be honest with me.'

'I am stuck here. I cannot afford to look or sound like a total stranger.'

Xinjhua nodded. Meanwhile, Chinjhi placed the food on the floor. Mukunda looked around. Xinjhua noticed the specks of sand on his hands and offered him a piece of cloth.

'The water we have is barely enough for drinking,' he said.

Accepting the piece of cloth, Mukunda wiped his face and hands. The food was not to Mukunda's liking. It had a pungent after-taste.

'What is it?' he asked, trying not to make his displeasure apparent.

'It is Xarrika leaf soup. Heavenly, isn't it?'

'Well, yes,' he said, looking at the copious amounts of soup left in his bowl.

'We cannot afford it as an everyday meal. I serve it only to the best of our guests.'

'You mean things could have gone more south?' Mukunda asked.

'Well, we are already south of Chinjing and the ancient kingdom. There is no farther south,' he replied, seemingly baffled.

'Master meant that the soup could not have been more bitter,' clarified Garuda.

'Never mind,' Mukunda said.

'We should be sleeping by now. We have to start early tomorrow,' Xinjhua said.

They all finished their meal and Xinjhua cleared the pots and utensils. He then proceeded to make a makeshift bed for Mukunda, but was clueless where to accommodate the flying one. Garuda, sensing the bafflement of his host, flew and settled on a high altar on the wall. Xinjhua smiled and muttered, 'Smart! Very smart, just like Xarksha.'

He then tucked his own kids into bed and turned off the lamp.

Mukunda lay there, unsure of the events that were to follow. Through the open vent on the wall he could see the clear desert sky outside. As he was listening to the little voices of doubts and assurances in his head, he realized something. He had jumped into the wormhole in search of Krishna, but it was his mother he was missing the most now. He wondered about how lost he had been in seeking his goals that he had almost forgotten all that he would have to leave behind.

When everybody was fast asleep, Garuda flew towards Mukunda. 'Master! You seem perturbed. I have tranquilizer shots with me. If you wish I can knock them out and we can run away,' he whispered.

'Please don't. I know you mean well, but don't. Look at their sweet and innocent faces. They have been good hosts to us, we should not betray or trick them.'

'But they will turn us in tomorrow.'

'We will be fine,' assured Mukunda.

Garuda blinked his illuminated eyes in agreement and flew back to his altar.

As the stars slowly slided across the sky and the thin clouds floated past the moon, Mukunda too slipped into deep slumber. He was woken up by the early morning sunshine streaming in through the window and Xinjhua calling out his name. Garuda was already up.

'We need to move. We have to reach the checkpost before midday,' Xinjhua said.

'Any urgency behind this proposition?' Mukunda asked.

'This way you can be presented before the king today itself. Else, they will lodge you in their custody. The king will be out on military campaigns from tomorrow.'

Though they started at sunrise, the ascent of the sun to the zenith didn't take very long. Within a couple of hours, the sunlight grew glaring and the heat was unbearable. Mukunda could already see wobbling mirages on the desert's horizons. He was perspiring profusely. Xinjhua, seeing this, subtly nodded to Garuda. He descended and pointed his rotors towards Mukunda. The breeze wafted from the rotors and ruffled his hair.

'What is this? This is annoying,' he said.

'You shouldn't be sweating so much, we have a long way to go,' said Xinjhua.

'You yourself are an outsider? Aren't you?'

Xinjhua was astonished upon hearing this, but he immediately curtailed his emotions. 'How do you infer that?' he asked.

'A couple living in a reclusive hut, surrounded by nothing but sand, no neighbourhood, no community. It is quite obvious that you aren't from this place.'

Xinjhua paused for a moment or two. 'No, we aren't,' he blurted.

'Apart from xenophobia, how is law and order in Xarlok?'

'It is brilliant beyond words. Xarnakhts are highly organized people.'

'Xarnakht?' Mukunda asked.

'The people who inhabit this desert kingdom, the owners of this place and beyond.'

'Tell me more about them.'

'They look a bit different. They are not someone to be messed with. They enjoy higher rights around here. They might look friendly sometimes, but…' Xinjhua paused.

'But what?'

'How do I explain this? They will never be your true friends, ever. They were made to rule everyone else.'

'How many of your people are being held here in Xarlok?'

'I do not have a count. But if we play our role in society, we are treated reasonably well.'

'Why are you people here? Droughts? Epidemics?'

'It was something far worse and far more obnoxious—the sound of Xar,' he said.

'A sound scared you away? Why fear the sound? Why not fight them?'

'They hit themselves on the left of their skull and become mindless war machines when they hear the sound. They become a swarm. They turn ruthless, and they fight in unprecedented formations, with unimaginable coordination.'

'Something like a swarm of locusts?'

'Indeed. But never talk about them this way when they are around,' Xinjhua murmured. 'Never!'

'What weapons do they have?'

'Just the basic stuff, the rudimentary ones—swords, axes, maces and a few trebuchets.'

Mukunda was a little baffled and kept looking at Xinjhua for answers.

'It is not about weapons; it is how they use them. They just overwhelm you and give you no time to respond.'

Mukunda was still staring at him, mindlessly.

'What?' Xinjhua said.

'So, you do know about advanced weaponry?' said Mukunda.

'This flying metallic bird of yours, that is smart. They do not have anything like this.'

'No, you meant something else,' Mukunda reiterated.

'Maybe, the Xarksha is their most potent weapon now. But they will never be as smart. Look, I cannot talk about this any further. Nothing good will ever come out of this.'

'Tell me more about this king of yours,' he said.

'Xardukht. He is a man of reason…well, somewhat. If you do not make him insecure, he will let you be. He wants to be unchallenged, the sole ruler of Prithvi.'

'Prithvi? What Prithvi?' Mukunda feigned ignorance.

'All countries, lands and sea combined…that's Prithvi.'

Mukunda now turned joyous. A spark of hope could be seen in his eyes. Any mention of the word 'Prithvi' meant that he was still on the same planet. Out of his fortified dreamland, but still on Prithvi.

'He isn't the sole leader?' Mukunda said.

'He conquered my part of Chinjing, but to the east of it, the Greater Chinjing area remains free.'

'So, you still have a country to live in. You can escape to Greater Chinjing, for a better future.'

'There isn't any better future. The whole of Prithvi is suffering due to the tyranny of the Xarnakhts. If all of us, captured slaves, start escaping, he would have us chased by his ruthless army and ransack the remaining Chinjing,' said Xinjhua.

'How is Greater Chinjing now?'

'They are doing all right.'

As Xinjhua was speaking, he saw some figures on the horizon. He raised his hand, shading his face from the sunlight and rechecked. 'There! That's the nearest garrison I have to deposit you at. Don't ask any questions and pretend to be an asylum seeker. And lose this flying toy of yours, at least for the time being.'

'How do I? He is programmed to follow me.'

'Shhh! Now start moving quickly. The quicker we reach, the

better,' Xinjhua said.

Mukunda followed him.

'I am warning you again, pull down that flying friends of yours, he will definitely startle them and drive them into a frenzy.'

Mukunda turned towards Garuda. 'Would you power down?' he said.

'I cannot, Master, I have to guard you,' he replied.

'Then hibernate and pack. I want you to hide in my pocket.'

'That I can, Master. But do not turn me off.'

'Sure, I won't. But do not wake up again until I ask you to.'

Garuda blinked in affirmation. It then flew down and landed itself on Mukunda's palm. The rotors slowed down and came to a halt. It then packed its wings and turned into a compact cube. Mukunda secured the drone in his pocket.

'Now let's move. And let me do the talking,' said Xinjhua.

The outpost was just outside a village wall. It was a thirty-feet-high tower, with a small mud hut beneath it. There were just three or four royal guards stationed there. They saw Xinjhua approaching from a distance.

'I am not making a run again to the king's palace. Execute whatever he is bringing along,' said a guard to another.

'It seems he is bringing a kid along. This hasn't happened before. King may need to see him,' the other guard replied.

6

The Royal Welcome

'Now tell me, what will my wife and kids do?' said Xinjhua.

'I said, I apologize. It was not intentional,' said Mukunda.

'Why did you let that metal head out of your pocket?'

'They were manhandling me. He came to my rescue. That is his job.'

'And pushing and apprehending an intruder is their job.'

'Excuse me! I am a crown prince back home. I have guards at my service.'

'Poor guy! Wait till the king sees you with your nasty little flying bird. Your kingdom will need a new prince,' he said, scoffing.

They were being carried in a horse-driven carriage. It was already evening now. Just then the carriage came to a halt.

'Now behave! Don't get me executed. Please, I beg you,' Xinjhua said, trembling.

'He is your king, ask him not to.'

Xinjhua grunted in frustration. With their hands still tied behind their backs, Xinjhua and Mukunda were taken to the royal court. As the guards waited for the king to arrive at the royal court, a minister walked up to them. 'Who are they?' he asked, pointing to the handcuffed strangers.

'This boy here is a foreign spy,' said one of the guards pointing to Mukunda.

'And how do you know that?' said the minister.

'He has a very strange metallic pet bird with him for spying.'

'Where is that bird?'

'In his pocket, it folds like a piece of cloth,' said the guard.

'It better be!' said the minister before storming out of the hall.

Within a few minutes, the minister re-emerged with the royal entourage, lead by King Xardukht. The king climbed the stairs leading to his throne and settled down upon it. 'Is it stranger than Xarksha?' the king asked the minister.

'That is what I have been made to believe, your majesty,' he replied.

'What's the name of this boy?' said the king.

To this, Xinjhua spoke, 'Majesty, per my limited interaction with him, his name seems to be Mukunda.'

'What kingdom is he from?'

'Your majesty! Per my limited understanding, he is not from anywhere around.'

'Some nomadic tribe?' The king enquered.

'Not any that we know of! None of the tribes, kingdoms or countries around have people with such names,' he replied.

'Where is that metal bird?' the king was now growing a little perturbed.

Mukunda took a few steps backward and so did the guards who had brought them to the palace.

'What is it?' said the king in a slightly raised voice.

The guards apologized with folded hands. 'That bird is dangerous. Last time we tried apprehending the boy, it attacked us with intangible arrows,' said one of the guards.

The king stood up and ordered his palace guards to be on alert. He then signalled his trusted commander Xanuk to point his sword at Mukunda. 'I need to see that creature now,' he yelled.

Mukunda shook his head and took a few steps back again. Seeing which Xanuk paced towards him and grabbed him by his arm. As his grip grew tighter and as Mukunda grunted, a noise began to grow which then grew into a distinct rumbling. Before Xanuk could even locate the source of the sound, Garuda leaped out of Mukunda's pocket. Its magnificent rotors then unfolded and after a yard of fumbling, it got into a steady flight. Garuda fired its particle gun and broke Xanuk's sword. And then made a single low-pass fly over Xanuk's head. Xanuk ducked and then ran towards safety beyond the hall's pillars. By now all the palace guards had drawn their bows and were taking aim.

'Bring that thing down,' shouted the king.

Garuda was flying close to the ceiling, trying to dodge the shower of arrows. Mukunda and Xinjhua both knew what was to follow and had taken cover by now.

'Stop this madness,' shouted the king.

The guards stopped there and then, while Garuda got into position to go on an all-out offensive.

Seeing this Mukunda yelled, 'Stop, now! And hibernate. It's an order.'

Garuda retracted his particle gun and flew close to Mukunda. He then powered down and landed on Mukunda's palm and he stowed him away in his pocket.

'Who are you? And what was that?' said the king. The undertone of authority was now missing from his voice.

'I am from another place and time. We never knew that kingdoms beyond ours existed. A storm pulled me in and left me in this desert.'

'You are a non-resident and an intruder. You will have to serve your punishment for that,' said the king.

'I happily would. But as soon as this flying friend of mine finds me in trouble, he springs into action. And who knows, he might summon a bigger army of flying warriors from my land,' he replied, trying to hide a grin.

'He can?'

'I am a prince. He surely can and would.'

'You are of royal blood?' the king asked, turning to look at his ministers, who looked clueless. 'We can waive any sort of punishment then. But you have to be of some use to us.'

'None that I can think of,' he said.

"Well then, how about this, let me have you killed in one stroke. I don't care about the collateral damage. These men will lay their life for me, if need be,' the king said as he signalled to his soldiers.

As the king's men sprang into action, Mukunda raised his hands and yelled, 'Stop. I can help you with something.'

'Make those flying warriors for me,' the king demanded.

'They are too complex,' he replied.

'Then get me those beams, the ones he was setting forth on my soldiers,' he suggested.

'Majesty! These are energy-based guns. If I do succeed in making those, they will create imbalances and destroy the fine ecology of your system,' said Mukunda.

'And how is that?' the king said.

'They borrow primordial energy from the air to create particle burst. Just like those arrows are made from wood. But if you go on an overdrive to make arrows, you will run out of trees and forests.'

'I can get more trees and forests planted. Or annex a kingdom that has more. I never run out of resources,' Xardukht replied.

'Sure you can, Majesty! But we are talking about weapons that leave air dry and crumbling. We cannot manage that,' Mukunda protested,

'I will forbid their use in our territory. Now help us make those,' the king reiterated.

'I am afraid I cannot,' Mukunda said curtly.

The Xarnakhts standing there, seeing their King being

reprimanded, started growing impatient. A few disgruntled courtiers could now be heard mumbling.

Sensing the soaring tension around, Xinjhua stepped in. 'My majesty! Give us time, maybe he can do something else for the empire…'

To this Xardukht rose up in anger and yelled. 'I do not negotiate. I do not talk.

Apprehend the accomplice of this boy and kill him first thing tomorrow morning, Xanuk.'

The palace guard rushed towards him and caught Xinjhua by his arms. Mukunda saw the gleam of helplessness in his eyes. 'Wait… I will make those for you,' he said, feeling helpless.

'But you need to understand something. I am not an arrow-maker or a workman. I am a prince. I will have to figure it out. I will also have to figure out the required raw material. It might take a while and the process could be very slow.'

'What all do you require?' asked Xardukht.

'I will require all kinds of tools, workmen, peace of mind, time and sand.'

'Sand for what?' the baffled king queried.

'That's what we use to extract the material required for making the internal working of such gadgets.'

The court men were now murmuring in amazement.

'We have ample of that,' said Xanuk.

'Now please let us go back to his place. I will start work as soon as I receive all the required material,' Mukunda pleaded.

To which the king laughed. 'You are brave, intelligent and witty. But you still think that this is a court full of children? That we will give in to your whims and fancies. You will stay *here* and work.'

'Okay, then make sure Xinjhua reaches home safely,' Mukunda pleaded.

'He is your trusted friend isn't he?' The king said.

Mukunda nodded in affirmation.

'He too shall stay here. He will be your collateral.'

'Fine, but I deliver you the know-how and we both shall leave,' Mukunda said as a last resort.

The king nodded. 'Xanuk, these two shall not be treated as infiltrators or guests. They are palace people. Have them taken to their new place and take utmost care of them.'

Xanuk nodded and escorted them from the court.

Seeing all of this, the royal priest stood up from his seat. 'My majesty! Having these people as our guest could be perilous.'

'Mukunda is a kid. He wouldn't harm us. If he wished to, he could have ordered his flying companion to do so. He probably has ventured outside his kingdom and is now unable to find his way back home. Clearly he doesn't belong to this realm,' assured the king.

Meanwhile, Mukunda was familiarizing himself with the palace. He was yet to see his room, but he was counting each and every step and turn from the court to wherever he was being led.

'Is the king bluffing?' whispered Xinjhua.

'He is not. You will be safe here,' said Mukunda.

'Will I meet my family?' he again asked in a muffled voice.

'Definitely! Let me weigh all the options, then maybe I can request the king to have them over here.'

Xinjhua smiled and an inexplicable joy was now apparent in his gait.

Even though it was dark, Mukunda couldn't help but notice that in the heart of the palace was a garden. The administrative halls and residences were built on the periphery of the palace. But in the middle of it, a substantial part of it was a stretch of a garden. No matter which part of the palace you were in, you could always see the garden.

'Here! This is where you two will stay,' said Xanuk.

'This place looks comfortable,' said Mukunda.

'Splendid, I would say,' said Xinjhua.

'I will make sure you have a comfortable stay. But remember what you are here for,' saying this he left.

Their personal chamber was a big hall with intricate engravings on the walls.

'What are those depictions?' said Mukunda, curious.

'I haven't had the privilege of ever being in a palace, but from what I have heard, these are depictions of all the battles that the Xarnakhts have fought and also some portraits of their glorious ancestors.'

They both were now settling in and finding their own corners in the room.

'You are bluffing about making them these new weapons, aren't you?'

'I am not,' Mukunda said.

'But they might use those weapons to propagate their rule of tyranny and subjugate more kingdoms.'

'Did we have a choice? They would have killed you and your family.'

'But now they will have you build those fancy weapons and then kill everyone in Chinjing.'

'I am a ten-year-old; I did what I deemed best. Don't worry, things will work out.'

Xinjhua nodded in agreement. Suddenly there was a knock on the door. They both looked up. It was the head priest of the Xarnakhts, Xandhrin.

Even though Xinjhua had never seen him up close before, he knew from the sacred Xarksha feather on his robe. He leaped up from his seat in awe and respect.

'This is a temporary arrangement. Both of you will get your own places,' he said.

'I like this room,' said Mukunda.

Xandhrin smiled. 'So you will stay here and Xinjhua will get a bigger room where he can stay with his family.'

Xinjhua first smiled and then started clapping and giggling with joy.

'But make no mistake. You both are on a mission. The king wants what he wants. His eastern campaigns have been a stalemate for a while now. He needs new and more powerful weapons,' he said. 'Xinjhua, you are from Chinjing, I suppose.'

Xinjhua nodded.

'You don't want the Rule of Righteousness to govern the fate of Greater Chinjing, right?'

There was an uncanny silence in the room. Mukunda spoke up, trying to ease the tension. 'Who wouldn't want that? We all want the Righteousness to prevail.'

Xinjhua was still silent and Xandhrin was waiting for him to speak. After a moment or two of reckoning, he spoke up. 'The Rule of Righteousness demands war. And war demands men. It's a huge price to pay for Righteousness, my lord.'

'I see. Your heart aches for your own people. Which makes sense. Which is what good people do…care for their brethren.'

'If I may take the liberty of speaking, the constant wars and extension of the Righteousness has reduced Prithvi's population by half in the last thirty years. It has left kingdoms after kingdoms in a rubble. You are the upholder of Xarnakht Wisdom, my lord. You should speak up and help getting a moratorium on further annexations.'

Xandhrin nodded. This was not a nod of agreement but rather acknowledgment of the fact that Xinjhua was concerned and was willing to speak up.

'Did you know, we here, in the palace have always respected you. You have always stuck to the duty that you were assigned to, so religiously,' he said.

This was enough to bring some joy and light back to Xinjhua's face.

'There have been cases of people venturing in, spying and then leaving our other borders. But not in Xurabhur desert frontiers. Not on your watch,' he said.

'I have accepted the Rule of Righteousness here. I know it's my fate. It is everyone's fate. But for some reason, I cannot bring my heart to accept the cost of it. The constant war, the suffering that the rule demands, don't make sense.'

Xandhrin drew a deep breath and walked up to the big window of the hall. He stared blankly outside the room. Mukunda looked at Xinjhua, concern written all over his face.

Xandhrin laughed and turned towards them. 'We have been so self-absorbed with our issues and differences that we forgot there is a young visitor among us.'

Mukunda smiled. 'Thankfully, someone in the room is thinking about me.'

'What do you feel about our kingdom, son?' he asked with a smile.

'To be Honest, Sir, nothing! I am not very judgmental and take my own sweet time to form opinions.'

'True! It's us who are coming to terms with your superpowers. How did you say the guards apprehended you? They themselves seemed so scared.'

'He pleaded to me,' said Mukunda, pointing to Xinjhua.

'And on your command that tiny bird ceased the attack on our guards?'

'Not at all! But Xinjhua then pleaded to Garuda and then he ceased.'

Xandhrin looked at Xinjhua in amazement.

'My Lord! I might not look like a Xarnakht, but when I say that I have accepted the Rule of Righteousness in my heart, I mean it.'

'If you are so appreciative of the Rule, why didn't you stop the bird in king's court?' Xandhrin said.

'I was dumbfounded, My Lord! It all happened so fast that I was awestruck, couldn't utter a word in the presence of His Majesty!'

'Why is it that I am having a hard time believing you?'

'I say nothing but the truth, My Lord.'

'Nothing but the truth?'

Xinjhua nodded.

'Or were you scared that if the Border Guards were hurt, the whole Xarnakht Army would be in search of the one person and his family, who brought the trouble along?'

'If further truth be told, that was not on my mind. I was trying to avert misunderstandings. If Mukunda had hurt our people and escaped, there would have been a blame game between Chinjing and Xarlok. Partly because I too was involved.'

Xandhrin nodded. 'You do have a heart of gold.'

Xinjhua nodded and smiled.

'But this world doesn't deserve a heart of gold. It only understands a battle-ready iron fist. If we do not rise to the moment, these tribes on Prithvi will fight against each other and crumble,' he said.

'And I shall do everything in my capacity to help in the Lord's cause,' said Mukunda.

'You will start receiving everything you need in a day or two. Meanwhile, rest and maybe take a tour around the palace.'

7

The Desert Rose

It was just a little past dawn when Mukunda woke up, the immense burst of light from the big window hitting his face. Xinjhua was fast asleep. Mukunda rose from his bed and walked up to the window. The view outside was in complete contrast with the palace's indoors. It was nothing but a huge sea of sand. An ever extending and a never-ending desert outside the palace walls. It was beautiful.

As the golden sand crested and troughed over the landscape, the winds were doing their part by ruffling the dunes ever so lightly. Between the azure-blue skies and the radiant golden sand, there were hoards of gazelles and deer, leaping and hopping from one dune to another in search of foliage.

In the distant corner, two gazelles were locking horns. Seeing the two gazelles fight playfully, Mukunda smiled.

'Why are you smiling?' Xinjhua asked, rubbing his eyes.

'The desert outside is full of life. There! That's a Fennec Fox, I guess. He is so tiny and almost elusive.'

'I haven't seen one earlier.'

'Are these real? Or did the Xarnakhts bring them here, you know, as a part of landscaping?'

'Wouldn't know. I haven't been here before,' said Xinjhua.

'But you have heard stories about them, right? Tell me something or anything about them and this palace of theirs.'

'I haven't heard about the outdoors much. But I have heard much about this palace,' he said.

'Tell me all.'

'They say that the gods planted the eternal curse, right in the midst of this palace. No building, wall or room ever stays there. The Xarnakhts tried but in vain. So they turned the area into a garden.'

'Was the palace already there when the eternal curse was planted here?'

'It wasn't,' he said, walking closer to the windowpane. 'The palace wasn't always here. Xarlok was not always the capital of the empire. They had to move it to Xarmatik out of fear.'

'Fear? Is there someone who can instill fear in them too?' he said.

Xinjhua smiled. 'For once, you did too.'

Mukunda smiled. 'But who were they?'

'This is the least appropriate place to talk about them. We are standing in the imperial palace and you are asking me about them.'

Mukunda was getting irritated. He stared at Xinjhua in annoyance.

'Okay! But first move quietly and peek outside the room to make sure no one is eavesdropping on us,' Xinjhua muttered.

Mukunda nimbly walked towards the door and peaked outside. There was nobody. He could hear some kids playing in the distance, but apart from that there was nobody. Closing the door, he crept back.

'Those kids you heard playing outside, they are from the royal family and other high ministers,' said Xinjhua.

'I don't want their story, I want the story of the palace.'

'They are the palace. Nonetheless, back to the story. They, among all beings, were the tallest in wisdom, heftiest in courage and relentless when it came to principles. They were the Evil Wise people.'

'What is an Evil Wise?'

'They were wise because that is how everyone saw them and evil because that is what Xarnakhts considered them to be. They were the people of Gurupur,' he said.

'But they were wise, right?'

Xinjhua nodded. 'Even Xarnakhts couldn't deny the fact that they were wise.'

'Where are they now?' said Mukunda.

'They are long gone. Not a trace of them now remains.'

'But you said that no one ever had the courage or capability to take them on. Who killed them?'

'Their own sincerity killed them. The reverence and respect in their heart for their loved one, proved to be fatal for them.'

'How so?'

'Some twenty years back, Xandhrin went to the king with a plan. A plan that was their only hope to expand their kingdom eastwards. Xandhrin wanted Xanuk, the valorous commander, to defect to Chinjing and ask for asylum there.'

'For what?' said Mukunda.

Xinjhua started to narrate the story.

Xanuk ordered his own men to beat him up. Bearing those deep wounds and lacerations, he travelled through the Xurabhur. Then he circumvented Gurupur, the kingdom of Evil Wise. For twenty days, he ingested no food and drank very little water. When he finally reached the gates of Chinjing, he almost fainted in front of the guards. They, being benevolent, took him in and cared for him till he recovered. After ten days of illness, when he felt fit enough to speak, he narrated his story to the wise ministers from the High Council. How he was suspected of being an agent of Gurupur and was about to be murdered when he fled the evil kingdom of Xarlok. The ministers were baffled as to why he sought asylum with them and not Gurupur. It was even closer to Xarlok.

Xanuk then told them that in such proximity, they would have sent undercover agents to find and kill him. The wise ministers were confused and they left the decision to Emperor Jhuching. The emperor soon visited him and found his condition to be pretty miserable. He chose to believe in his story and gave him asylum. They were still sceptical and kept him in out-houses of the fort in army garrison, under close watch. He started making friends in the garrison and working his way up, he befriended the whole garrison in a matter of a month. He would teach them the Xarnakht styles of fighting. Reveal his own army's secrets. His presence came to be cherished in the fort.

One day, the emperor visited him. 'You are a Xarnakht?' he asked.

Xanuk nodded. 'They will come looking for you. For us, you are trouble.'

Xanuk looked up, fear clouding his eyes. 'I have nowhere else to go.'

'But are you ready to assimilate here for life?' the emperor said, taking pity on his condition.

Xanuk nodded.

'What work are you apt at?' he said.

'I started as a caretaker of the Royal Stables and made my way up to being an army commander. I can be a good stable caretaker at the least.' Xanuk said.

The emperor agreed to give him that job and he put his heart and soul into it. As word of his dedication and hard work spread, Xanuk got promoted to the mentor of the garrison.

·•

It was the Annual Military Day of Chinjing and Xanuk was asked to help the forces prepare for the same. A day before the parade, Xanuk finally got to see what he was in the enemy's camp for—Bhavya. There were at least five squadrons of Bhavya, which were loaned to them by the wise people of Gurupur. The majestic being with wings was as huge as a house. Its huge, beautiful, violet-coloured wings could cover the midday sun like a rain-laden cloud. Its beautiful beak could pierce through fortified walls. Its neck was long, flexible and yet strong.

Xanuk, like any other Xarnakht, had seen a Bhavya only in battlefields. It was for the first time that he had seen a Bhavya, or Xarksha, as they used to call them, from such close proximity. Xanuk ventured close to one of the Bhavyas and tried to pet her. She turned red and wailed at the top her voice. A swing of her neck, a flap of her wing, and Xanuk was flying in air. He landed several feet away. Seeing this commotion, her trainer rushed to help Xanuk.

'They are easily startled, let me reintroduce you to her,' said the Airman in charge of the Bhavya. Xanuk walked along with him and stood at a distance from Bhavya. The airman patted her gently. The tinges of red faded and her skin was a now light shade of violet again. She turned her neck and took a good look at Xanuk, lowering her head to the ground.

'Now you can reach up to her and talk to her gently,' said the airman.

Xanuk mustered the courage and walked up to her, and this time, he managed to tame her.

The very next morning, the commander of the garrison knocked on Xanuk's gate. 'You have been introduced to Bhavya 1144, haven't you? Her airman took a fall while practising and is injured, you will have to fly her for the parade.'

Thus, Xanuk finally got an opportunity to fly a Bhavya. On the day of the parade, he flew in a formation and did a vertical climb, disappearing into the clouds. As the other climbers descended and reappeared from between the clouds, Xanuk and 1144 were nowhere to be seen. There was an outcry. People feared that Bhavya might have hurt her new airman. But very soon, they both reappeared on the distant horizon, with Xanuk headed for Xarlok. The rest of the squadron gave them a good chase, but they were helpless as they were not allowed to shoot arrows in Bhavya's direction. Xanuk escaped, circumventing Gurupur, and reached Xarmatik, where he was received like a hero. The Xarksha was tied and kept in confinement. He told his king that neither the army of Chinjing nor that of Gurupur could ever defeat an army commanding the bird, for fear for its life.

'But we need more of these creatures to completely overrun them,' said the greedy Xardukht.

It is then that Xanuk revealed the secret about the Xarkshas. There were no male Xarkshas. A female Xarksha lays eggs only when they feel threatened, to increased their numbers. The king couldn't believe his ears. The Wise Evil had borrowed this quality from some naturally occurring reptiles and introduced the same into the bird. And it is true that some reptilian lifeforms do procreate in this manner. On hearing this, the king hatched an evil plan. He would take the bird to Xurabhur desert and let it starve there till it laid eggs. The ruthless king's plan was successful. After days of pain and hunger, the bird finally laid half a dozen eggs on the tenth day which were taken back to Xarmatik, where they hatched after a month. The infant Xarkshas were raised and trained by a dedicated team, under Xanuk's strict supervision. The little ones grew up thinking Xanuk and his men as their family. Their mother too had accepted her fate, obediently training under Xanuk. The Xarnakht army now had a full-fledged Xarksha squadron.

No one in the kingdom was as happy as Xardukht; he could now fulfill the dream of his forefathers. The deployment of Xarkshas would leave Gurupur defenseless. And even if they did retaliate, they didn't stand a chance against the Xarkshas.

Columns after columns of military units were moved closer to the borders of Gurupur. Sereval sub-commanders were apprehensive and scared of the idea. They knew full well that Gurupur possessed state-of-the-art weaponary, but once Xandhrin and Xanuk introduced them to the specialized Xarksha squadron, their confidence was somewhat restored.

Meanwhile, the formations on the western borders had alarmed Gurupur and they too moved their combat troops to the far west. However, as soon as the news of the stolen Bhavya and that of its progeny being deployed by the Xarnakhts reached King Guruk of Gurupur, he made his troops fall back. The western front was now echoing with the sound of 'Xar', the war cry of the Xarnakhts. A yajna ritual was performed in Gurupur to atone for the sins of humans, who had carried out untold atrocities on the magificient bird. The soldiers of Gurupur were ordered to hold fire till the council came up with a solution.

His council of ministers approached him and told him that this probably was an elaborate bluff that Xardukht was playing on them. They were very sure that they had some demands and would not risk engaging Gurupur in a direct combat. But then the Xarnakht troops breached the western fronts of Gurupur and started fast approaching towards the Capital. The council was now highly alarmed and was scrambling for solutions.

Gurupur, among all their potent weapons, had the Sound-Chasing weapons.

The blood-lusting Xarnakhts used to raise their Xar slogans in unison before mounting an attack. They also kept humming the sound during any combat.

The Gurupur councilmen thus ordered the Sound-Chasers to

be set to this particular humming sound.

When the Xarnakht army reached Gurupur, Xanuk went flying over the town on his Xarksha. Suddenly, a flurry of Sound-Chasers came chasing him. Then something strange happened; not only did Xarksha deflect most of them, she also imitated the sound of Xar. When the Sound-Chasers deflected towards her, she smashed them with her wings. Xanuk was unharmed. The Xarnakht army captured the entire kingdom of Gurupur.

Mukunda stared in disbelief as Xinjhua finished narrating the story. 'I am sure there was some foul play involved in the battle.'

'No one knows.'

'If Gurupur was such an easy victory, how come they are averse to capturing Chinjing?'

'With Gurupur conquered, Chinjing is no longer under the Gurupur Accord. Chinjing is now free to use all the weapons they acquired from Gurupur on anyone, including Xarksha. When Xarnakht forces were busy plundering Gurupur, Chinjing already had a few of its men moving the arsenals of Gurupur.'

'So both were like vultures?'

'Gurupur was established to protect the whole of Prithvi and to upkeep the righteousness. The arsenal was to be removed at any cost. Chinjing did the right thing, and thus became the last bastion of the righteous.'

'But why did they not intervene and save the Evil Wise?'

'What can I say? This is how things used to work back then. The Gurupur Accord didn't let any of that happen. They never thought that the Xarnakhts would raise an army of Bhavya. They were left blindsided,' said Xinjhua.

'Too much of righteousness killed them all. Maybe they were more Wise-Fools than Evil-Wise,' said Mukunda.

'Have some respect for the wronged, Mukunda. Some respect.'

'Why don't your people just take the Xarnakhts to task and liberate everyone now?'

'They will still have to fight these maniacs. And believe me, these Xarkshas are not Bhavyas. They are neither revered nor pampered. They are trained day in, day out. Moreover, off late, several small kingdoms have been mushrooming in the south of Chinjing. If the kingdom of Chinjing stretches itself by fighting the Xarnakhts here, those southern tribes will swoop down on their unguarded kingdom.'

'I wish someone would tame these Xarnakhts and I can then focus on finding a way back home,' he said.

Just then something thumped against the door of the chamber. Xinjhua signalled Mukunda to stop talking, A well-adorned girl, almost of Mukunda's age, appeared. She was wearing the most sophisticated silk, her hair was done up and her skin glistened in the morning sun. 'Can we have our ball back?' she said, pointing towards a yellow ball in the corner of the room.

'Certainly, Princess Xarnika!' said Xinjhua as he stepped forward to pick up the ball for her.

Another young lad, younger than Xarnika, came rushing in. He picked up the ball and gave it to Xarnika. She then turned towards Mukunda. 'You must be new here. What is you name?'

'I am Mukunda and he is Xinjhua. We are His Majesty's guests.'

'Will you come play with us?' she said.

'They are Xarmik, Princess. And we don't know him well yet,' said the young lad.

'Don't call him a Xarmik. I think Mukunda can be our friend too,' she said.

Mukunda turned to Xinjhua. 'What is a Xarmik, for Prithvi's sake?'

'Well it could mean many things; an outsider, for once.'

'And?' he queried.

'It also means someone who doesn't enjoy full rights of the palace. A slave.'

'That little Xarnakht just called me a slave,' said Mukunda.

'Who told you he is a Xarnakht?'

'Is he a Xarmik then?' said Mukunda.

Xinjhua smiled. 'That's the beauty of this system, a Xarmik displaying bigotry towards another Xarmik.'

'They have accepted their fate, haven't they?' said Mukunda.

8

The New Rules

Mukunda was pacing up and down his room while Xinjhua was sitting on the corner settee, watching him.

'Is this what I am now? A Xarmik? The grandson of Shriram, the Chief of Manava clan, is now a Xarmik?' Mukunda said.

'Time changes, hold tight and your glory shall return,' said Xinjhua.

'If only holding tight would do. I am a second-class citizen here,'

Xinjhua shook his head. 'No, you are not. Forget what that kid said. You and your flying friend can bring the whole palace to its knees. They respect you. They need your expertise.'

Meanwhile, those chuckling voices of children playing outside grew louder. Xinjhua rose and smiled. 'Do you want to be absolutely indispensable to this palace and be treated well?'

Mukunda nodded.

'Go and befriend the princess. No one will then dare call you a Xarmik again.'

'Are you certain?' he said.

'Trust me. You wouldn't.'

Mukunda stepped out of his chamber. Slowly traversing the hallway, he stood beside a pillar, near where the kids were playing. Mukunda could now view the central garden in its full glory. Covered with exotic fruit- and flower-bearing trees on the periphery and rows of berry-bearing bushes on the interior, the garden was the focal point of the palace. At every twenty steps or so, at the junction of those bush rows, there were small musical fountains from which gushed out ever-changing colours of the rainbow.

The surrounding high chambers meant that only during midday would the full burst of desert sun cover the garden. Due to the vegetation and the shadows of the adjacent walls, it remained cool for most of the day.

Everyone, except for one person, was always hiding behind a bush, and that one person would run seeking the others, with the yellow ball in hand. Whosoever was spotted would become the next seeker. This time it was Xarnika's turn to hide. She was giggling and laughing, trying to evade the seeker. Finally she reached the periphery closest to where Mukunda was standing. She was hiding behind a tree, the same tree under which Mukunda too was standing, leaning against the pillar.

She was busy concealing herself from the lurking seeker, totally oblivious to the fact that he was standing right behind her. She was also oblivious to the fact that the current seeker had already crossed the shrubs in front of that tree.

The seeking kid was very close to the tree, a little ahead but nearby. If he had just turned to look back once, he would have spotted Xarnika. And then, as Xarnika moved to peep again, the leaves beneath her feet rustled, alerting the seeking kid. He was about to turn around when Mukunda leaped forward, held Xarnika by her wrist and pulled her behind the pillar.

'That is not how you evade somebody,' he said.

She was still puffing and wheezing from the rush of that sudden pull.

'It isn't? I wasn't doing it right?' she said, with her eyes wide in amazement.

Mukunda maintained his calm. 'No!'

'No wonder, every day, just before lunch they spot me and toss the ball at me.'

'Why just before lunch?' he asked, curious.

'Because of the rule of the game! As the sun ascends to the zenith and it gets hot outside, we have to stop the day's play and move indoors for lunch.'

'But why target you only towards the end?'

'The one who gets spotted the last has to help with the kitchen's lunch services. So, they sit merrily and I am always the one to serve them food and water along with the palace team.'

'And, His majesty, your father, does not frown upon this?' he queried.

'He doesn't. He wants us all Xarnakhts and Xarmik children to be placed equally.'

'Today you won't,' he said, stepping forward.

Mukunda kicked the dried leaves on the ground and then shook the tree with his hand, making ample sound to attract attention. As soon as the guy doing the spotting heard, he turned around and hurled the ball. Mukunda caught the ball with his right hand, before it could hit him.

'Come here! Will you?' Mukunda said.

'Is this how you toss things at your princess?' he then yelled.

The boy took a few steps forward. 'Rules are rules.'

'Xarki is right, I guess! I will head towards the kitchen arena,' said Xarnika.

'Stop! He did not spot you. If rules are already set, it's either him or I who should run the kitchen service,' said Mukunda.

'It's a noble cause, feeding everyone at the same table. I have no qualms taking up this duty,' she said, looking a little scared because of the commotion.

'But you were not spotted. And as Xarki himself said, rules

are rules. So, I will leave it up to him to decide, either him or me,' he said.

'I will not serve the kitchen. I played my part and won, the ball was off me by the last game,' Xarki hurriedly said.

'But you clearly missed your intended target. That is called losing,' Mukunda said.

As Xarki was fumbling for words, his friend Xinnun stepped in. 'Xarki won. Because rules also mandate that whosoever interrupts the game will have to bear the title of the vanquished and will have to serve the kitchen.'

'So, me it is,' Mukunda said, looking towards Xarnika.

She was smiling in relief. They then headed towards the kitchen arena. It was on the opposite side of the palace, quite a distance from Mukunda's chamber.

For the first time in a while, the special chair at the children's dining area, meant only for Xarnika, was not going to be vacant. The little, yet beautifully, adorned chair was one of its kind. Placed at the head of the oval table, it was plated in shimmering gold and was adorned with the finest of silk. The gold was carved with everything beautiful: flying horses, laughing clouds, humming stars, talking suns and smiling fairies.

As she approached her chair, Xarnika couldn't help but look at all those special engravings on the chair. She ran her fingers over them. They filled her heart with joy. Then her eyes wandered towards the Royal Emblem embossed on the top of the chair. It was the Xarnakht War Helmet with two spiked horns on each side and a full-bodied moon engraved in the the front. The emblem could be seen on everything royal in the palace. It stood for valour and battle-readiness.

As she ran her fingers over it, she could feel the gush of the Xarnakht valour coursing through her veins and she stood erect.

The feeling was so strong that it gave her goosebumps all over her arms. Her eyes widened and her shoulder blades pulled back. One of her hands was now grabbing the top of her royal dining chair and the other was tightly clenched. She looked up. All the other kids were settling down.

'Get up!' she said in a loud but firm voice, her eyes raging with anger.

Startled, everyone sprang to their feet.

'This is Xarlok, land of Xarnakhts. Here, the rule of Xarnakhts prevails. Nobody takes a seat before a royal Xarnakht does. First and foremost, the Royal Chair on this table shall be occupied and only then will any other chair will be filled,' she said.

Everybody on the table nodded, be it other Xarnakht kids or Xarmik kids. By now, even the kitchen staff had come running hearing the raised voice of the princess. Mukunda was also standing along with the staff. He heard everything and smiled. On seeing him, she relaxed a bit.

'This is why we keep her away from that commanding chair. She gets to handle those high positions with royal insignias and the sleeping royalty in her rears its head,' whispered Xarki.

'That new boy altered all our settings. He is a new nuisance that we will have to deal with,' said Xinnun.

Xarki nodded. 'After lunch.'

Meanwhile, Mukunda was now done helping with catering for the day. He moved into the adjacent chamber, where other support staff was having their lunch. Xinjhua was seated at one of the tables, chatting to someone.

As he saw Mukunda, he got up from his seat and walked towards him. 'Have you had your lunch?' he asked.

'I am skipping lunch,' Mukunda said.

'Let's head back to the chambers. You need to know a few

things about the power dynamics here,' Xinjhua said.

'You saw what happened over at that table?' he said.

Xinjhua nodded. 'We heard.'

'Did you have anything to do with that outburst?' Xinjhua asked as they stepped out.

'Yes! Remotely, but yes.'

'Xarnika is otherwise known as a people's princess. Very soft spoken, complacent and ever accommodating. All thanks to her father. What brought that out today?'

'It turns out they play a little game of fancy hide-and-seek every day. And a rogue few gang up against her. The rule says whosoever gets sought in the last game of the midday will assist the kitchen staff. So these rogue kids systematically make Xarnika the sought one every day,' he said.

'What changed today?' said Xinjhua.

'I made her realize that she was being tricked into it. I pulled her aside from where she was hiding and made them seek me instead. So I ended up serving food and doing dishes and she was free to be a royal again.'

'And you being uninvited to the play, no one protested?' he said.

'Oh! Few loud mouths did. But I managed to take the kitchen service and saved Xarnika somehow.'

'I just wish and hope Xarki was not one of them,' said Xinjhua.

'He could be, I do not remember their names. What about Xarki?'

'He is the son of Xandhrin. He is very easy to offend and on some occasions, he does overrule the authority and hierarchy of Xarnika,' said Xinjhua.

They were headed for their chamber when Xinjhua suddenly noticed some strange shadows lurking behind the next pillar. Before he could make sense of them, the shadows pounced and grabbed

Mukunda by the neck. It was Xarki and behind him was his friend Xinnun. Xinjhua froze, not knowing how to react. He was neither a Xarnakht, like Xarki nor a prince of any tribe, like Mukunda. He was a mere Xarmik, the inferior ones. He didn't dare touch Xarki.

'What is the matter?' said Mukunda in a muffled choking voice.

'You know very well. You interfere with our matters and we interfere with your life,' said Xarki.

'Fair enough. If protecting the heir to the throne of Xarlok is interfering, I was interfering. You are free to act in your best interest,' he said, with his eyes blood red and nearly popping out. As the grip of Xarki tightened across his neck, he couldn't help but let out a deep grunt in pain. And that sound triggered a chain of events—few beeps and then a sound of mechanical whooshing. The sound brought a little relief to the terrified Xinjhua. Xinnun was looking towards Mukunda and what he saw next left him pale. Garuda had sprung into action and jumped from Mukunda's pocket. After its ritualistic fumbling, it regained balance.

As Xarki raised his head to see the flying bird, his grip around Mukunda's neck loosened.

'Stop him, before he kills these boys,' Xinjhua yelled.

Xarki and Xinnun stepped back in fear.

What kind of a flying devil is this?' Xarki shouted.

'This is your end,' said Mukunda.

'Mukunda! Stop him. If anything happens to these boys, the whole palace will turn against us,' Xinjhua pleaded.

'I won't. Garuda! Shoot these two vermins,' he shouted.

Garuda adjusted his guns. Xinnun was already on the ground, Garuda aimed at him and fired. Xinnun promptly slid and rolled behind a nearby pillar.

'Wait, Garuda! Now I want you to introduce His Highness to fear, choking fear. Let him know what it looks like,' said Mukunda.

Garuda trained his guns in Xarki's direction and took a shot. Xarki ducked and barely dodged being hit.

By now, Xinnun and Xarki were crying and Xinjhua was trembling in fear. Xinjhua folded his hands. 'Let them go, Mukunda. In greater interest, please.'

Mukunda looked at Xarki and Xinnun, and they too were looking at him with their hands folded, pleading.

'Step back, Garuda,' Mukunda said. 'How do we play this, going forward? What if any of you get tempted to ambush and choke me again?'

'We will never try harming you, ever again,' said Xinnun, while Xarki nodded in agreement.

'Stand down, Garuda,' he said.

Garuda quietly landed on Mukunda's palm and hibernated. Xarki and Xinnun both got up and fled.

'You need to have a little more patience,' said Xinjhua.

'Patience! Some crazy zealot was trying to choke me and I am the one who needs to be patient?'

'I am happy that Garuda came to your rescue, but you shouldn't have let him attack them both,' said Xinjhua.

'I wanted to see fear in their eyes. I am pretty sure they will not be plotting against me any further,' he replied.

'I wish and hope they don't,' said Xinjhua.

But before they could speak any further, they heard approaching footsteps. It was a small group of soldiers, lead by Xandhrin. As they were rushing towards them, Xinjhua sighed. 'Stay calm,' instructed Mukunda.

As Xandhrin approached them, he yelled, 'Are you two fine? 'I heard what my knuckle-headed son did to you. I really apologize.'

'We are fine, please don't reprimand them. They are just kids,' said Xinjhua.

Xandhrin nodded. 'Xarki has grown without his mother; he is a difficult kid to handle. Pardon him for his follies.'

Mukunda nodded. 'I, of all, can understand. I am away from my family and homeland too.'

'I was heading to your chambers when the palace guard told me what happened.

Anyway, we have earmarked a place nearby for your workshop and we want you to visit it. I will accompany you there. It's in the middle of the desert, but we can landscape it with a beautiful herb garden.'

Mukunda nodded. 'I am eager to visit and see the place.'

'All right then, please carry on. I will pick you up from your room a little prior to sunset,' said Xandhrin.

Everybody dispersed and Mukunda along with Xinjhua reached their chamber.

The garden outside the chambers was now totally isolated. 'Where are all the other kids now?' said Mukunda.

'As far as I know, after midday, they are taught various subjects. The classes are held indoors though,' he said.

Mukunda nodded and they both went in. Mukunda sat beside the window, remembering his homeland, while Xinjhua took a nap. Mukunda was contrasting the landscape outside with that of his homeland. He and many other kids of Ksharanpur had grown up listening to the tales of Madhavpur. They were told that Madhavpur was their original home and that they had to move to Ksharanpur due to adverse circumstances. But right now, Ksharanpur was all that mattered to him. He kept thinking of the saying, 'Out of torment arises the pearl.' Suddenly, he was not interested in that pearl. He was feeling overwhelmed by the torment that he had chosen. In the mist of this dismay which clouded his mind, only one question echoed. Why did he give up on things that mattered?

Did he really care? Was the torment a result of his long-suppressed emotions: his love for his father? His mood grew somber as he saw the sun going down.

He then heard a loud knock on the door. 'Get up! Xinjhua,' he said.

Xinjhua woke up and walked towards the door to open it. He as well as Mukunda expected it to be some palace guards or Xandhrin himself. But what Xinjhua saw next, left him astonished and in tears. Xandhrin stood there with Xinjhua's wife and two kids.

Xandhrin then spoke up, 'They have just arrived, but we all agree that you have a very sweet family, particularly the kids. I hope they enjoy the palace education and the company of the other palace kids.'

'I cannot thank you enough,' Xinjhua said.

'We have noted a new chamber for you and your family. It's a few chambers down the same gallery. Mukunda can now have his own place. But before that, while your family rests here, we have to go and see the workshop,' said Xandhrin.

They both nodded and picked up the essentials they would require for the tour.

•◆

They were seated comfortably in a horse wagon as they rode on makeshift paths through the desert. On the way, Mukunda spotted more deer, bucks, large rodents and small foxes. They ploughed through some smooth and rough patches through the desert, finally reaching a spot where some construction work was being carried out. The workers were divided into two groups, one emptying the place of sand and the other raising some sort of a structure.

'We will have huge walls here to evade sandstorms. We are building a workshop here, almost as high as the place. We have kept the floor layout quite flexible. We will try to provide you with everything that you may need,' said Xandhrin.

'How much time will it take to have the workshop built?' asked Mukunda.

'Perhaps a few months. We chose this site because storms here are not that massive. It is close enough from the palace to commute and, at the same time, far enough to protect the palace from future harm, if any, arising from this workshop and that work that will be carried out here. Also, if any of our eastern enemies try to reach this place, they will have to cross two of our heavily armed garrisons,' Xandhrin replied.

Mukunda nodded. 'A few months is good. I too will require some time to recall what I had studied and figure out the way forward. We will have to start everything from scratch.'

Xandhrin nodded. 'I understand. Our intelligence says that our eastern enemies already have those magical weapons. We want everything to be better than them.'

Mukunda nodded in agreement.

Xandhrin smiled. 'Why don't you two go ahead and inspect the place? I will have a word with the foreman here.'

As they took a few steps, out of anybody's earshot, Mukunda said, 'They are serious, aren't they? They want huge weapons of mass destruction. They can then turn against anybody, even us.'

Xinjhua nodded.

'Can we escape? Before I am made a part of this madness?' asked Mukunda.

'They will have us hunted down before we can even make it to the borders,' Xinjhua replied.

Mukunda stared at him with dejection.

9

Beyond Reach
A Year or so After Mukunda Left

The midday sun had just ascended to the pinnacle of the sky and was now shining brilliantly. The day was lightly breezy and the remnants of the morning cold made it pleasant. The bell had just rung, and Rukmini and Madhav were headed home. They were both tired beyond belief and had excused themselves from the post-recess classes. It was, anyway, just a Social Responsibility class for which Kanha had volunteered to speak.

As they were about to begin their descent down the staircases leading to the main gateway of the school, someone came rushing towards them from behind. They both were too tired to even to turn back and look. But as the footsteps grew louder, they both knew who it was. Kanha, puffing from all the running, said in a wheezing voice, 'You both won't be in the class, I was told.'

'We are as sleepy and droopy as we can get. We can barely bat an eyelid without napping. So, no, we will not be there for your big day,' said Madhav.

'Why what happened?' Kanha enquired, pacing alongside the two.

'There was no power supply the whole of last evening and last night,' said Madhav.

'None of us at the palace got any sleep. I particularly was bumping into things, candlelight didn't suffice,' said Rukmini.

'And you have no idea why?' Kanha said.

They both gave him blank looks and said nothing.

'Has this been happening a lot lately?' Kanha said.

They both nodded in unison.

'And Mohan is always away at work?' Kanha then enquired.

They nodded again, in unison.

'And you didn't think it was a coincidence?' he said.

They both gestured in negation.

'Okay! Here is the deal. Sit through my session and you will have an idea about the frequent power outages.'

They both again wiggled their head in negation. They picked up their pace and started climbing down the stairs with extra vigour. Kanha couldn't catch up with them. He couldn't help but find this odd. They said they were too exhausted to sit through the classes but the swiftness in their gait was narrating an altogether different story. He gave up and climbed the staircase and stood waiting under the Arch. Rukmini and Madhav took the first right, straight to the palace, but for Kanha, it was still not adding up enough. He stood there waiting.

As soon as they both traversed the first street, they surreptitiously took the first left. Kanha first smiled and then burst into laughter. He now knew what the duo was up to. He raised his wrist-device and made a call.

'What kind of an erratic breeze is this? Very windy one second and a complete lull another,' said Rukmini, a little concerned.

Madhav nodded. 'These are the very precedents and signs we are in search of.'

'Let us head out to the far left. We may find something near the cliff overlooking the lake,' she said.

'That area has been cordoned off since the past year. There is no way we can breach the secure cordon,' he said.

'I secretly downloaded the module required to breach such

safety measures,' she said.

'Where from? Won't it leave trails?'

'I copied it from your father's wrist-device. And then did a little tweaking to add a log cleaner. No one would know,' she said.

'Brilliant! But won't we have to hide from surveillance drones?' he asked.

She nodded. 'We will manage.'

They picked up their pace again and started walking up to the cliff. As they reached the vicinity of the cliff, the cordon fencing was visible. 'Hurry! We need to find the entrance access to the cordon,' she said.

Madhav spotted the access point and pointed it out to her. She rushed through the beach sand and flashed her wrist-device to the point. She was expecting a chime and then a grant of access, but it did not work. She tried a couple of times, when she heard a voice from behind. 'You can keep trying the whole day, it won't work,' said Kanha.

'You disabled it! This is blatant misuse of your lab accesses,' she yelled.

'I don't see it that way. I am not the one hacking through someone else's accesses,' he replied.

'Enable it right away!' she said in a commanding voice.

'I thought you were headed home, but when I saw you turning left, I knew you were in search of the Eye,' he said.

'We are! And we want this access very desperately. Now give me back my access or I will find one way or another to get you out of the lab,' she replied.

'You won't.'

'This is our last chance to save Mukunda. I will not let anybody stop me from that,' she said.

'That is exactly the reason you won't. Do you know why there have been outages in the palace? We, at Café Evolution, are trying hard to harness the upcoming Eye to trace and save Mukunda. Samganak needs huge amounts of power to run simulations for the same. We are this close to locating him,' said Kanha.

'We don't care. We don't understand what goes on in that lab. And what we don't understand, we don't trust,' she replied.

'Actually, I do understand some functioning of the lab and the Samganak. I think we should give him a chance,' said Madhav softly.

As Rukmini turned towards Madhav, Kanha said, 'Moreover, Mohan is spearheading all the rescue efforts. Don't tell me that you don't trust your uncle and his father.'

Hearing this Madhav turned to look at Rukmini for a response. 'Okay! But when does the Eye open up next?' she said.

'Tomorrow, but only with a probability of 95 per cent,' said Kanha.

'What about the remaining five per cent?' she said.

'Those are things beyond our control,' Madhav said.

'Look! Ninety-five or five, these are just numbers. I can do something for you. Let me take you people to the Lab. Mohan can explain everything to you,' said Kanha.

Rukmini nodded. 'But not a word about this cliff incident.'

Kanha nodded and led the way. They had both visited the lab only on certain occasions, Madhav probably more than Rukmini. Madhav was also offered an internship at the lab, but he had turned it down. He had consulted his mother, Meera, and she also preferred him growing up without that extra responsibility. She understood that when you have access to such powerful systems, you have to use every waking hour of yours for the good of Manavas.

'Back in our days, one missed class and there was a price to be paid. I see your school is growing lenient in that department,' said Mohan, seeing the trio there.

'Drop the act, Uncle! You know why we are here,' said Rukmini.

'No, I don't. This is my office and the right to entry is reserved, now make yourself scarce,' he said assertively.

'We won't leave until you tell us about tomorrow,' she said, standing her ground. Mohan turned to look at Kanha.

'I didn't tell them. They found out, nonetheless,' said Kanha, shrugging his shoulders.

'Rukmini and Madhav, just go home or go to school, wherever you belong. Let us handle this,' said Mohan.

'This is a matter of concern for us too. I will not leave until we know what is being done to rescue Mukunda,' she said.

'Mohan is right. This is a sensitive issue. The more people get involved, the more difficult it will be for us to keep it rational. The chances are already bleak, no one is more worried about Mukunda than Mohan,' said Kanha.

As soon as Rukmini and Madhav heard the word bleak, their faces turned pale. And seeing them overcome with despair, Mohan said, 'Kanha is wrong. The chances are good.' But looking at the despair in Rukimini's and Madhav's eyes, Mohan gave in. 'Fine! Have a seat. I will explain it all to you.'

They both sat on the couch, adjacent to Mohan's desk. 'Bleak too is good, Uncle! We haven't seen him for a year, even if there is the slightest chance to bring him back, let's try our best,' she said.

'This is not how it works. If we get even a trace of information about his location and/or his well-being, it will be a big leap forward,' said Mohan.

'Father! Can we be of some help? I hope our zeal is not hindering your work?' said Madhav.

'As a matter of fact, we require Rukmini's work on Ksharanpur's topology,' said Mohan.

'The Eye is due to appear tomorrow, when were you going to ask for it?' she said.

'We weren't. We have already picked it up from your school server,' said Kanha.

'So, you don't need me. You wanted my work and now you have it,' she said.

'None of us understand your work; it's not our field of interest. We have assigned it to Samganak and it may take some time to process. But now that you are here, you can help us pick relevant data from the report and punch it into Samganak,' said Mohan.

Rukmini nodded. 'Can you share some more details on what our plans are for tomorrow?'

'Tomorrow early morning, the Eye or the wormhole should appear around the same cliff area. This will be a minor one. Something exceptional, but not great, must have happened in a realm nearby. Let us wish and hope that we can transmit and receive some data from the Eye,' said Mohan.

'If we find some trace or whereabouts of Mukunda, what do we do next?' said Madhav.

'We don't know yet. Once we do get a trace, we will have to calculate the risks associated with breaching the realm. Then, with the collected data, it is up to the administration to decide the best course of action,' said Mohan.

''How do we breach the realm?' she said.

'We have no clue yet. We are advancing one step at a time,' Mohan confessed.

'Even if you get to know, please do not share the information with any of us. We are too young to be trusted with such sensitive data,' said Kanha.

Mohan nodded and one could see that Rukmini was getting a little angry. She knew what Kanha meant.

'Now go and help Kanha punch in all the relevant topographical data into Samganak,' said Mohan.

Kanha handed her a printed copy of the report and lead her to the Samganak.

'Now, if you will allow me, I must go home,' said Mohan.

'But we need to arrange everything by tomorrow,' said Rukmini.

'Kanha knows whatever needs to be done. I will be back this evening anyway.'

Mohan picked up some stuff from his desk and left the lab. As he exited the lab, he called out to Shyam. 'Meet me in the lawns, and please bring Radhika along.'

·◆·

As Mohan entered the palace, he instructed the guards not to let anybody in or out of the palace. Shyam was already there, sitting around the tea table. Tea, coffee and other snacks were now being arranged.

'Where is Radhika?' said Mohan.

'She will be here,' said Shyam.

As Mohan pulled out a chair for himself, Radhika appeared from the other end of the lawn. He got up and pulled a chair for her too. 'I have some update regarding Mukunda,' said Mohan.

Radhika looked at him. 'Something hopeful or something hopeless?'

'Hopeful,' he replied.

Radhika thought for a moment. 'Even then don't tell me about it.'

'Why wouldn't you be interested if there is still any hope?' said Shyam.

'Perhaps no one is more interested than me. But I don't have the courage to be disappointed again,' she replied.

'Let's be a little practical and pragmatic here. We do not have a magic wand that can bring Mukunda back here in moments. But we do have an opportunity. All I want to do is to discuss my strategy with you both,' said Mohan.

'This is a matter of larger concern. Shouldn't we have everybody else here?' said Shyam.

'You are the only two people I can trust right now, because you two are the most rational and practical of the whole lot. This is sensitive information. And things are so fragile right now that I do not want our strategies to get muddled with emotions. Whatever we need to do, we will have to do it with a cool head,' said Mohan.

'What is this opportunity and what's your strategy?' said Radhika.

'There is this Eye opening tomorrow… similar in nature but smaller in size than what took Mukunda away. We can use it to peek through to the other side of it. But we have to be very cautious. We cannot let our existence be known to another realm,' he said.

'But why was there no such info publicized? I mean, the day and date of any wormhole appearing on the horizon is made public for safety reasons,' said Shyam.

'To begin with, this one is smaller and may appear for a very short duration, so it's less of a safety concern. And do you know that today someone was trying to gain access of the cordoned-off area, probably in a bid to gain access to the Eye?' said Mohan.

'Who was it?' said Shyam.

'I don't know yet, but I will find out. The bigger issue is: people and especially those who cared about Mukunda might want to toy with the idea of rushing across the Eye. We can't allow or handle that. One person across it is a menace, many more will be a disaster,' said Mohan.

'Rukmini?' said Radhika.

Mohan nodded. 'In most likeliness.'

'Among all the young ones, she is the one struggling the most with the absence of Mukunda. She is a natural leader and caregiver and always thought that the onus of every young person's well-being was on her,' said Radhika.

'She is a well-meaning kid and I am pretty sure that now that Mohan knows, he will ensure that she remains safe,' said Shyam, looking at Mohan for an affirmation.

Mohan nodded. 'I have already taken measures to keep the Eye away from her reach. She can try anything but won't be able to get within its working range.'

'Now back to the topic, what are our plans for tomorrow?' said Shyam.

'I have aptly equipped drones for this purpose and have kept them up and ready. As soon as the Eye begins forming, they will start attacking it with energy beam pulses. Then they will try capturing any energy outbursts emanating from it. The data will then be transmitted to the lab, where it will be Samganak's task to make sense out of it,' said Mohan.

'What are we looking for?' he said.

'Energy signatures! The Eye forms when something extraordinary happens, which disturbs the energy balance between spheres. We now know that these sorts of wormholes are not linear. They transmit energy and data, which are bewilderingly non-linear. So, an incident happens, say a year ago, they build up and then show up maybe a year later. They radiate the balance out and if the balancing was not perfect, they soak some energy back in too. The energy, which is also data for us, stays trapped in such wormholes for days or weeks and then reaches the other side. Now here is the most bewildering and fun part, energy or a person trapped inside the Eye can remain there for days. And the time spent inside the Eye would seem like a fleeting moment,' said Mohan.

'It sounds way too complex. So is there a chance that Mukunda might have survived inside this wormhole or the Eye?' said Radhika.

'Absolutely! Because in the end, that time spent inside the wormhole didn't even exist for the traveller,' he replied.

Shyam and Radhika smiled in relief.

'There is more to it, but promise me no word shall travel out of here. There will be more Eyes opening in succession within a period of a few months. Something remarkable is happening! And the more they show up, the better we will get at understanding them,' he said, tyring to contain the excitement in his voice.

'What do we do if we find a clue to his well-being and whereabouts?' asked Radhika.

'Then I prefer that these words not travel outside of our close group,' said Mohan.

As Radhika grew perplexed, Shyam said, 'He means the Empowered Council. If we are to breach those wormholes and bring Mukunda back, we must let the Empowered Council know the risks associated with it.'

Radhika nodded. 'He is right. The safety of the Manava society is paramount. And no matter who is in question, interest of one person should not and will not dictate the interests of a larger group.'

'But we will get there when we do. Before that, we need to tread cautiously and understand those wormholes and in the process perhaps find out about Mukunda's whereabouts,' said Mohan.

Shyam nodded. 'Well then, do whatever you deem necessary. We will talk once we have some inputs.'

Mohan nodded and smiled in agreement.

'Hey! We should do this more often. Sit together, have some coffee. Just like, good-old Madhavpur days,' said Shyam.

'Good-old Madhavpur days! I was not even there in Madhavpur,' said Radhika.

'I meant more or less. Moreover, there wasn't a day when Meera or the rest of us did not miss you. We are all so very happy that you are here now,' Shyam replied hesitatingly.

'I am pretty sure you were reminiscing about the time with your buddies, your boys—Mohan and Krishna,' she replied.

Shyam smiled, but his smile had signs of embarrassment and cover-ups all over it. Seeing which, both Mohan and Radhika had a good hearty laugh and then Shyam joined in too.

'This is fun. Let me have the rest of the guys called in,' said Mohan as he signalled an usher nearby.

10
Hope Is Good

It was five in the morning. Mohan, Kanha, Rukmini and Madhav were standing near the main panel of Samganak while Shyam was racing up and down the lab hall.

'Who sent out the invitations?' said Mohan.

'No one did, Mohan! We all are worried about the matter. Please stop looking at us, and keep figuring out the essential,' said Shyam.

'Well everything is in there, in Samganak. As soon as the Eye appears, it will start all procedures and modules. Again, who told you all that this will be a public broadcast?' said Mohan.

'Uncle! We didn't get a minute's sleep last night. You cannot even begin to understand what Mukunda meant to all of us. Agreed, he was a bit different, or for a lack of better word, esoteric. But nonetheless, we adored him no end,' said Rukmini.

Mohan nodded. 'Any minute now, the Eye should appear and Samganak will begin procedures. The power of half of Ksharanpur will be rerouted to Samganak. With the lab's cooling unit down and Samganak running at full throttle, this place will be one hot furnace. Let me see how many of you stay then.'

'No one is moving out, Uncle!' replied Rukmini.

'Well then, be my guest,' replied Mohan and smiled.

Mohan then turned towards Samganak, where, in an inset on the screen the actual visuals from the site were being streamed. A red dot at the bottom right of the inset screen started blinking.

But still nothing was visible on the screen.

'Is Samganak fumbling?' said Shyam.

'All this is new and complicated for Samganak too,' said Mohan.

But then Rukmini stepped forward and leaned in closer to the screen.

'Samganak is not fumbling. We are missing visuals,' she said, pointing at the topmost right-hand corner of the inset.

There it was—a very small turbulence on the horizon. The Eye was barely formed and flickering.

Mohan stepped forward too, narrowing his eyes. 'Even the drones on duty are picking up the visuals.'

Kanha then leaped forward. 'They need some help. I am going for a manual override,' he said, grabbing the control panel.

He then started guessing the Eye's coordinate vis-à-vis the drone's and started uploading those numbers manually.

'Start the beams! We cannot miss this chance,' said Mohan.

Kanha then started the irradiation beams on all the three drones there. But the Eye was rapidly flickering and the drones kept missing their target.

'This isn't working!' sighed Shyam, when something strange happened.

The Eye multiplied. The flickering Eye did a rapid swirl and then spawned a new one of the same size. Before anyone could react, the newly spawned Eye started swirling in turn. It then spawned another one. There were now five Eyes on the horizon, rotating at a outrageous speed.

'Cut the beam! Cut the beam!' yelled Shyam.

Kanha, without even waiting for Mohan's confirmation, disabled the beam guns on the drones.

Mohan grew perplexed at this but then it struck him as to what concerned Shyam. 'They are soaking energy from those irradiation beams and are multiplying,' said Mohan.

Shyam nodded. 'Let's wait and see how they behave in the absence of those beams.'

The Eyes slowed in rotation and were not multiplying.

After a minute of silence, Mohan spoke up. 'It was the beam. We might have to rethink our approach.'

But then, the Eyes started spinning and swirling again at great speeds and after a fraction of a minute spawned five more Eyes.

'It wasn't the beam; it's their nature. And to know their nature we have to peep into them,' said Rukmini.

Mohan and Kanha looked at Shyam for his affirmation. He nodded. Kanha then signalled re-initiation of the beams.

The drones were now irradiating all ten Eyes with precision. They all started swelling up in size and started slowing down in spin speed. Then something even more marvelous happened. The Eyes started merging and the spin speed decelerated further. After a dozen or so complex spins, they merged to form a single Eye, big enough to pull anything, even a house. Owing to the suction pressure from the pull of the Eye, the drones were operating both on rotors and propulsion.

'Hope this doesn't grow further,' said Mohan.

Meanwhile, Samganak started receiving data from the drones. The Eye remained on the horizon for a good ten minutes, during which time the drones were extracting whatever they could from it. Then the Eye started shrinking and the spin speed started increasing. And in a matter of a minute, it had closed.

'Let those drones be there on the look out for a while. Do not recall them just yet,' said Shyam.

Mohan nodded.

'Let me command Samganak to start the analysis of data,' said Kanha.

'First, send a copy of it on my wrist-phone. I will go through it myself,' said Mohan.

'You can do that? Analyse that encrypted data?' said Shyam.

'That painful procedure that Vasu had made me go through to bump up my cortical categorization, to match that of Krishna's, is paying off,' he replied.

Shyam smiled. 'Talk about a silver lining.'

Mohan nodded. 'I will require some time to go through all this. Let us meet in the evening, I will let you know what all we have.'

As everybody was exiting through the main door of the lab (including Kanha), Rukmini paused and came rushing back to Mohan. 'Uncle! Just a preliminary guess! Do you see Mukunda beyond those tumultuous Eye formations?' she said.

'I wish I had an answer for you, but I just do not know yet. Trust me, I am as scared and concerned as you. The only difference is that I am willing to put my fears aside and work towards even the slightest of hope,' replied Mohan.

·◆·

Rukmini and Madhav looked around for a shaded spot in the school playground. The Indoor Cafeteria got overcrowded at lunch break and was way too noisy to have any meaningful conversations in. As they finally found a cozy bench to sit on, Kanha came rushing towards them. He was in so much haste that the lunch tray in his hands was shaking wildly.

'Slow down! Where is your group? Why are you here with us?' asked Rukmini.

It's about me and Mukunda!' he said, taking a deep breath.

'What about him?' replied Madhav, curious.

'I will tell you all but promise me that it shall remain between us.'

They both nodded.

'First, about me! I too can read the raw encrypted data, in bits and pieces though,' he said.

'You mean like Uncle Mohan?' replied Rukmini.

He nodded. 'But only a few portions of it. It has just started making sense to me a few days back. But I don't want to tell this to anyone of the elders. I am not sure how they will react.'

'True! They can behave strangley at times. And your work in the lab is important. But at the same time, you cannot confirm with anyone whether your interpretation is right or not,' replied Rukmini.

Kanha nodded.

'When was the last time you got your Cortical Categorization tested?' asked Madhav.

'When I was a kid and had just begun school. I was a CD2++, like everyone else,' he replied.

'Then don't go rushing for a test just now. Enjoy your new acumen. Maybe working on Samganak has given you a boost,' replied Rukmini.

'And what about Mukunda?' asked Madhav.

'From what I saw, there were multiple signatures of high-energy beams from a drone in there,' Kanha replied.

'An Airborne that followed Mukunda through that eye?' said Madhav.

'Hopefully, yes!' replied Kanha.

'What else could you see in there?' said Rukmini.

'Those signatures were all that I could see and they could mean anything,' he replied.

'Could those be mere bounce-back reflections of beams from our drones that were irradiating the Eyes?' said Madhav.

'I narrated what I saw,' said Kanha.

'But if they were the original signal, then perhaps we can find the realm that Mukunda is stuck in,' said Rukmini.

•◆•

As the sun made its descent over the horizon, the mysterious lake shimmered in the soft glow of the evening sky. But then something magical happened. As the periphery of the sun touched the horizon, its rays, instead of forming a streak, spread radially over the lake. The sight was unparalleled in its beauty.

Meanwhile, Mohan reached the palace. Shyam was already present in the lawns, waiting for him. His eyes were fixated upon the teapot shimmering in the golden glow of the sunlight.

'Is this sunset for real? Or is it as illusive as the lake that surrounds us,' said Shyam, transfixed.

Mohan shook his head as he pulled a chair back. He sat down and stared at the setting sun for a while. 'Never given it a thought! But now that you have pointed it out, you have ruined a perfect moment.'

Shyam laughed. 'So all this is as fake as that lake, isn't it?'

'I can't say. We can try walking up to the shore and find out about the existence of the lake for certain. But we simply do not have the resources to know what else is conjured around here,' he said.

'He treated us like kid. He didn't take any chances, did he? He placed us in a safe cradle. A beautiful safe cradle,' said Shyam.

'Well I betrayed his trust. So, he never told me about our landing site on Prithvi. He was protecting the Manavas from a person he could no longer trust,' replied Mohan.

'He had enough faith in you. He was protecting us from someone else,' replied Shyam.

'He indeed was,' said Radhika as she walked up the lawn towards the tea table.

She now had their attention.

'Who was it then?' said Shyam.

'I don't know who or what, but it was there in his eyes. I could tell that he feared something. As a matter of fact, in the last couple of days before the Great Migration, he had started keeping to himself,' she replied.

'Indeed, there was something. He stopped sharing project details with me. He said that he was too busy for that, but I knew it was something else,' said Mohan.

'Tell me one thing; you rebuilt Samganak from that device that he shared with you. Have you tried searching within Samganak for answers?' said Shyam.

'Answers to what?' he said.

'Why it happened? What went wrong?' said Shyam.

'But he backed up Samganak way before the Brahmportation operation, there might not be anything in it after all,' he said.

'There must be something, some clue in there,' said Shyam.

'I too have a strong feeling that there is something there. That we are overlooking it,' said Radhika.

Mohan's brow arched and his face grew a little stiff. 'How desperate are you to know what happened?' he asked.

'Quite!' said Radhika.

'Come along then!' Mohan said, rising up.

As the three of them reached the lab, Shyam had a vague idea of what was to follow. Mohan entered the lab and commanded each of the screens to be turned on. He then rushed to the main panel and kept on working the panel till the Omechta Key appeared on the screen.

'Are we opening the gate of the realms?' Radhika enquired.

'I hope not,' said Shyam.

'I am ready to pay the price. Just one command from you and

I will migrate back to Bhoomi and look for him,' said a worked-up Mohan.

'Don't! Even if you reach Bhoomi, a moment there would mean thousands of years here. We will all be gone by then,' said Shyam.

Radhika too nodded in agreement.

'Then at least let's open the channels and look what's left there?' Mohan said. Shyam nodded. 'But be sure that nothing harmful crosses over.'

Mohan opened the data channels between the two worlds. As the process started, the lab lights started flickering and Samganak too, started fumbling. Samganak's display too was struggling to keep up. But when it could, it intermittently started displaying in bold red letters the word 'HAZARD'.

Mohan, in a matter of seconds, leaped into action and closed the Omechta module. The lab lights, Samganak and its display stabilized again.

'What just happened?' said Shyam, flummoxed.

Mohan was busy watching the logs on the screen. It took him a minute or so before he could get a grasp of the situation. 'It's in an awful state!' he finally said.

'What is in an awful state? Samganak?' enquired Shyam.

'Samganak is fine. Bhoomi and its Universe, 0018, they are in a depleted state. They are old and are running out of energy.'

'So, when we connected to them, they started sucking energy from here?' asked Shyam, to which Mohan nodded.

'We, after all, might not have a viable way to find out what happened there,' said Mohan.

'There will be a way. I am sure you will be able to figure out something,' Shyam said.

'Let's call it fate and move on. Mohan, we met to discuss the results from this morning, didn't we? We digressed. Let's get back to the point,' Radhika said.

Mohan nodded and smiled.

'Enough suspense, tell us already!' Radhika said.

'The findings are a bit of a relief. We found energy signatures very similar to the drone that followed Mukunda,' he said.

'A big relief indeed!' said Shyam.

'Yet, nothing is conclusive. This is just a small speck of hope, that if an Airborne is still up and active, Mukunda might be safe too. But then, that's just wishful thinking. We need more concrete proof,' said Mohan.

'Yet, it's somewhat comforting,' said Shyam.

'Thanks, Mohan! Even this much of hope means a lot to me. But again, always keep Manava interest above everything else. Do not try anything which can endanger our last bastion, just to save one person,' she asserted.

11

A Pleasant Surprise

Xarnika was gazing into the vast and dark horizons on the west. The lower half of the horizon was inundated with silhouettes of sand dunes of varying sizes. For brief, intermittent moments even the sand being ruffled by the cool evening breeze could be seen in the starlit night. The rest of the horizon was covered with stars, planets and galaxies. Few of those stars were only to be seen in a tranquil cloudless desert sky.

'You said we came here for the moon. It's there, in the east! Why are you looking the other way?' asked Mukunda.

Xarnika placed her slender finger on his mouth and shushed him. 'That one is real, I am waiting for the surreal.'

Mukunda was baffled but he kept quiet, gently removing the finger from his lips. He then looked into her eyes and nodded. They were both now mindlessly gazing into the horizon when the unbelievable happened. A gleam, a light so ever-pure broke out on the western horizon. Mukunda gasped in disbelief and Xarnika gasped in amazement. Then that luminous piece of magic gently surfaced and it's radiance started illuminating the dunes on the horizon.

'What is that?' asked Mukunda.

'This is the surreal moon. It's very rare and precious, it appears only once in two years,' she said.

'That's impossible! A moon so big and bright cannot have such a big orbit!' he said.

'Let's not waste these special moments in search of reasons and explanations. Let's make the most of them,' she said, leaning in towards Mukunda with her eyes closed.

'What?' he exclaimed, still baffled from the sequence of events.

Xarnika paused. 'It is said that people who kiss under the surreal moon never separate. Their love becomes eternal.'

He nodded, gazing at her radiant face, which shone in the moon's light. Her glistening lips looked like rose petals covered in morning mist. She again closed her eyes and inched forward. Mukunda was still soaking in her beauty when the right side of her face grew dim and dark. Her face lost its sheen and her lips grew pale. Mukunda looked to his right towards the mysterious moon. It had turned dark.

Xarnika too sensed something odd and turned towards the moon. Something big was hovering across the horizon. 'They are looking for us!' she said. As Mukunda turned towards her, she continued, 'That's a Xarksha flying over the deserts in search of us.'

'I have never seen such a big bird. Its wings alone are concealing that mysterious moon,' he said.

She nodded. 'She is not any Xarksha; she is the mother of them all. If she is here, it means the palace is desperately searching for us.'

As she finished speaking, the moon cleared again and light started pouring onto the desert. But that big dark figure was now fast approaching them.

'We should be heading back,' Mukunda said, getting up.

But Xarnika held him by his arm and pulled him back in. 'The surreal moon is still young,' she said and leaned in with her eyes closed.

Mukunda looked at her trembling lips and shimmering face. He again inched forward. But before the two could meet under the sparkling moonlight, the Xarksha's loud shriek filled the desert.

Xarnika opened her eyes. She was now visibly perturbed. As Mukunda turned to his right, the Xarksha was only a few hundred feet away from them.

Xarnika finally got up and moved close to the Xarksha, which had landed close to them. She patted her on her neck. 'Take us home!' she said.

'It's probably Xarki, from the palace! He must have brought our absence to everybody's notice.' she hollered as the Xarksha cruised at full pace towards her destination.

'And then everybody else must have panicked,' he hollered back, to which Xarnika nodded.

As the Xarksha started its descent, they both grew a little curious. 'Isn't the palace a little eastward?' asked Mukunda.

'I know what's happening. I almost forgot. Today, to honour the surreal moon, they are conducting a prayer session for our ancestral god.'

'Ancestral god?' he asked.

'Our god, the God!' she replied.

'Does he have a name?' he enquired.

'He does, but we are not supposed to utter his name, only the high priest can and that too in prayers of high importance.'

'Tell me more about him,' he said.

'I respect our god and his ways. I don't know much about him, though I do know that he was the primordial ancestor of our ancestors,' she replied.

'Sounds complex and intriguing,' Mukunda hollered back.

'It is, isn't it? It is so hard to grasp that I couldn't learn more.'

As the Xarksha slowed down, the wind caressing their faces too mellowed down. A few lights were becoming visible on the horizon amid that barren desert. She dived a little further and reduced her altitude. Within a matter of seconds, the lights grew brighter and the people holding them became visible.

'There they are!' Xarnika said, pointing to the congregation.

'One more thing! I now recall that this year the high priest may ask me to lead the prayers,' she said.

The Xarksha was now flapping its wings slowly, with its head raised high, to breaks its own speed. She then landed a good fifty steps away from the congregation. As soon as Mukunda and Xarnika disembarked, Xardukht as well as Xandhrin came rushing to them.

'Where have you been, Xarnika? We were all so worried!' said Xardukht.

'I thought we would venture out a little to see the second moon.'

'You were not a little out! You had to be flown in!' said Xandhrin.

Xardukht now turned towards Xandhrin, but before he could say anything, Xandhrin murmured, 'He is not even a Xarnakht. It's a little embarrassing, seeing you venturing out that much with him.'

To which Xardukht finally raised his hand and said, 'Enough! Tonight, he will be initiated as a Xarnakht.'

'He can at best be an honorary Xarnakht! He is not one of us!' Xandhrin protested.

'It doesn't matter, he shall become one of us!' Xardukht said.

Mukunda smiled and nodded in gratitude, knowing well enough that having the king by his side would definitely make his life easier in Xarlok. Meanwhile, Xarnika rushed and hugged Xardukht, 'Thank you for trusting me, Father!'

'I have always trusted you and have supported you in every manner possible. But today is not entirely your day. This boy has helped us enormously and has won our trust with his sheer ingenuity and diligence. This is his day too. He, along with you, will lead the prayer, after which we will request him to inaugurate the weapon's workshop and make it functional,' he said.

These words of the king worried Mukunda no end, but he kept his calm. He had always wished that the work on the weapons workshop would never complete. But his options were limited. The Xarnakhts had a few captive engineers from the rival kingdoms. The captives didn't fully understand Mukunda's work, but they were brought in at regular intervals to make sure that someone could make some sense of Mukunda's work. So, he couldn't bluff. His only option had been to keep delaying the project citing one reason or another. But today was different. He had been caught romancing the heir to the throne of Xarlok and if Xandhrin had his way, his days would be numbered. *What will I tell Xinjhua?* he thought.

Mukunda nodded with a half-hearted smile.

Xarnika almost instantly read his face. 'What's the matter, Mukunda? Isn't it a good day to begin our new venture.'

'It indeed is! The day on which even the skies adorn two moons, how can it not be good?' he replied sheepishly. He then turned his gaze upward and saw the mystery moon again. *Even the heavens above are crazy today!* he thought.

'Time for the ceremony!' Xardukht announced, leading everyone to the altar.

On the ten-feet-high altar was a statue, which didn't look all that impressive.

Xardukht could sense that Mukunda had doubts about the divinity of the statute. 'We do not need a statue or any reminder to commemorate our guardian god. This one is special though. It was made by our founding father, the first modern Xarnakht. He made it with an alloy so special and rare that a grand statue was not possible. He wanted a simple symbol for himself.'

'It's beautiful! There is that mysterious energy around it. I can already sense a nurturing and caring divine presence around me,' Mukunda replied.

Xardukht smiled and signalled Xandhrin to begin the prayers.

Mukunda slightly leaned towards Xarnika and murmured, 'What am I supposed to do?'

'Just stand still with your hands raised.'

As she completed the sentence, everyone around raised their hands and Xandhrin started chanting the prayers aloud in Xarnaiki, the liturgical language of the Xarnakhts.

Xarnu xarnu, xarta xarnu
Xar ahane, xarta xarnu
Xar mimase, xarta xarnu
Maft hahini, xarta xarnu

(Victor of all victor of all, glory to you victor of all
Hail your kingdom, glory to you victor of all
Hail your support for us, glory to you victor of all
Uproot our enemies, glory to you victor of all)

As the prayer reverberated through the desert, several Xarnakhts joined in and chanted along with Xandhrin. With each sentence, the prayer grew intricate and Mukunda's ability to keep track of those alien words was withering out. But then something happened. As Xandhrin and the crowd chanted the last line of the prayer, an uncanny silence ensued. Everyone stood stiff with their lips sealed. Xarnika leaned in towards Mukunda. 'Don't try repeating what Xandhrin will say next, it's only for him to chant.'

Mukunda nodded with a feigned smile.

Xandhrin meanwhile rose and extended his hands further up in the air and regained his voice. Then, with all his might, he chanted:

Xarnu xarnu, xarta xarnu
Xar ahane, xarta xarnu
Xar mimase, xarta xarnu

Maft hahini, xarta xarnu

Xarnu xarnu, Kamsa xarnu

Suddenly, Mukunda couldn't believe his ears and his eyes widened in disbelief. 'Did he just say that?' he mumbled. 'Xarnika, did he just hail Kamsa?'

'Never ever repeat that name. Only the High Priest can say it out loud, not even the king can utter his name.' she said and muffled his mouth.

'Fine!' he said, removing her palm from his mouth and drawing a long labored breath. 'But did I get his name right?'

She nodded. 'You got it right. Don't utter his name again, no one takes his name in vain!'

'I won't! I have bigger problems to deal with!' he replied.

'What problems?' she asked.

'Nothing! Forget I said so!'

With too many things already on her mind, Xarnika nodded and feigned a mild smile. 'The prayer ceremony is over. They will take you to the workshop, I guess. Can I come along?' she asked.

'I would love that, but ask your father,' he replied.

Xarnika nodded and rushed towards her father. Meanwhile, Mukunda was trying to find Xinjhua. He rushed from one end of the congregation to another but to no avail. He was about to give up on his search when he noticed a dark silhouette sitting atop a dune, a little distance away. It was Xinjhua, who was sitting there unaware of the developments, sporting his trademark smile.

'Get up! You need to come with me *now*,' Mukunda said.

'I am a Xarmik, they will not allow me near the congregation.'

'The prayers are over, we are now going to the workshop,' he said.

'At this hour, why?'

'They want to inaugurate it and make it functional,' he replied.

'This should not happen, they will misuse the weapons and ruin every other kingdom around,' Xinjhua said, the smile from his face now gone.

'I tried! I tried for as long as I could. Those Xarmik engineers, they are beginning to understand the stuff. They are catching on pretty fast. I cannot think of another reason to delay the production,' he said.

'What will we do now?' Xinjhua said.

'That is why I am here. I want you to come along, we will try figuring out something on our way,' he replied.

Xinjhua nodded. Mukunda grabbed him by his hand and made him hurry back to the congregation.

The king, meanwhile, was perturbed by the absence of Mukunda. As he saw Mukunda rushing back with Xinjhua, he sighed a heave of relief. 'Hurry now! We have to reach there before the mystery moon sets,' Xardukht said.

Mukunda raised his head and looked at the moon in question. It was at the zenith. 'It seems we have ample time,' he said.

'It seems so, but once this moon nears the horizon, it moves with a greater speed and sets within no time,' Xardukht replied.

'How is that even possible?' he murmured.

Xardukht overheard, so he said, 'It is how it is! That is why it's a mystery moon.'

Mukunda nodded. 'Then we must be on the move now.'

Xardukht signalled Xandhrin and he then asked his men to get the special carriage.

'What is with the moon? Why do we need to boot the workshop today itself?' said Mukunda in a hushed tone.

Xardukht gave him a baffled look with a hint of doubt. Sensing this, Mukunda added, 'Never mind!'

'Because it is rare and does not show up every now and then. And the one whose legacy we are carrying forward was rare too,' Xardukht replied.

Meanwhile, Xarnika walked up to Xardukht. 'Father, I need to talk to you,' she said.

Xardukht walked away from the group he was standing with and signalled her to speak.

'Can I come along with you?' she pleaded.

'You don't need an invitation or permission! This whole kingdom is yours!'

She smiled and hugged her father. She went rushing back to Mukunda. 'I am coming along. Also, I was not required to ask.'

Mukunda smiled. 'I am happy for you.'

'You don't understand how important this is for me. I mean, once that workshop is up and running, we won't be able to meet much,' she said.

'Much of it will be automated; I won't be required much over there. So, we will catch up,' he said.

'But once you are a commander in the Xarnakht army, you will rarely be home,' she replied.

'I will be what? Who said so? I am not joining the army,' he said.

'You had better check on that with father, because this has been the plan all along. Hope you get to stay back,' she replied.

Things were now moving too fast for Mukunda. Just then, the background noises grew louder. A big horse-driven carriage arrived. Everyone standing there moved backward and made way for the royal entourage. Xardukht, Xandhrin, Mukunda, Xarnika, Xinjhua and a few other royal officials boarded the carriage. The horses were turned around and without any further delay, they started for their destination. Xardukht, knowing that Mukunda had many things on his mind, sat beside him.

After the carriage made its way into the desert and the lights grew distant and feeble, Mukunda finally said, 'Do I have to enlist in the army?'

'Yes, I see you as a man of substance. Someone I can rely on and someone who can hold this kingdom together once I grow incapable with time. I want you to be ready for any challenge,' he replied.

'But I am not a warrior. The place from where I have arrived, no one fights each other. This is not who I am,' Mukunda replied.

'I envision you and Xarnika together. I want you to be a warrior. So I know that Xarnika is in apt and safe company,' he replied.

Xardukht had made up his mind and Mukunda had no choice but to play along.

Mukunda now felt guilty of not being a worthy Manava. He was enjoying the lavishness of the palace and his proximity with Xarnika but he had failed to read the future. Now, he was just a pawn at the hands of these high-powered Xarnakhts.

Meanwhile, Xinjhua, who was sitting diagonally opposite to Mukunda, was growing impatient. Mukunda, who was worried about his own future, was staring blankly out of the window. Xinjhua kept on staring at him in the hope that he would sense his gaze and notice him. The carriage then hit some kind of bump and tossed everyone around a little. Mukunda finally looked at Xinjhua and noticed his sulking face. On top of it, he was frowning too. Mukunda could only reply with a shrug.

Xinjhua, to divert his own mind from the impending danger, turned his glare towards the window closest to him. For the rest of the route, the carriage was filled with an uncanny lull.

As the carriages gradually came to a complete halt, the doors opened and Mukunda climbed down in a hurry, walking up to Xinjhua, who by now had walked halfway towards the workshop.

'Look, Xinjhua! I was not prepared for this. I didn't even know about this moon thing. I thought we could keep buying time.'

'We have run out of time now!' Xinjhua replied.

'Tell me what to do and I will do it! I, myself, cannot think of anything,' he replied.

'Command Garuda to blow this place up!' Xinjhua replied.

'And then what?'

'Then you escape! Let them capture and kill me!' Xinjhua replied.

'Are you mad? And what will they do to your wife and kids? Have you thought about that?' he said.

'But if this happens, thousands of innocent men along with their wives and children will be slaughtered. There will be no stopping these Xarnakhts from ruling over Prithvi. Your one flying warrior can terrorize a whole regiment, a whole army of those can run over any kingdom.'

Mukunda nodded. 'I know! I am aware of what I have been made to do. But there has to be a better way. Owing to the Xarkshas that they are breeding here, they already have the capability to run over any empire.'

'They always feared that Gurupur transferred their weapon's knowhow to the eastern empires. And these weapons of yours will give these Xarnakhts an upper hand,' he replied.

'See, I cannot put Chinjhi and those two lovely kids in the way of harm by being rash. Moreover, there is something else too! Even if we refuse to play along, they will still figure out how to operationalize this workshop,' he said.

Xinjhua shook his head in disbelief and gasped.

'I am a kid myself; I can be immature at times. They cajoled me into not only building this workshop but also make it automated. It was not my suggestion. The Xarmik engineers suggested and I…

I don't know why... I complied,' he said.

'So now even if you don't cooperate, they can get the weapons?' Xinjhua said, shaking his head in disbelief.

'No! Not exactly! If I disappear right now, they will take years to make sense of all this,' he said.

'But they eventually will?'

'That's what I am regretting,' he replied.

'Are we actually left with any options? Or is this where it ends?' Xinjhua said as gloom and despair took over his voice.

'Let's hope... ' even before Mukunda could complete his words, he heard someone approaching. He turned and saw Xarnika coming towards him.

'Where have you two been? Come on now!' she said.

Mukunda nodded and then signalled Xinjhua to come along too. Mukunda's face bore a sense of guilt, but his eyes still showed a glimmer of hope.

12

The Forgotten Friend

Mukunda was working on the automation unit, but something was amiss and the system was not responding in the manner that it should have. Xardukht, meanwhile, was pacing up and down the workshop. Each time he passed by the automation unit, he would look towards Xandhrin and sigh.

Sensing his restlessness, Xandhrin said, 'Your Highness! There is still an hour or so to moonset. Mukunda will figure it out.'

But the words had the exact opposite effect on Xardukht and he was now more perturbed. Xandhrin seeing this, turned around and yelled, 'Who is in charge of the floor here?'

A Xarmik engineer stepped forward.

'You! Did it occur to you that the boy might require some help?' Xandhrin yelled again.

Xardukht stepped in and signalled Xandhrin to calm down. He then turned towards that Xarmik and asked, 'What is your name?'

'Chinju!' he replied.

'The boy there needs your help. Go see if you can do something about it.'

Chinju nodded and rushed towards the automation unit, which was a big box made out of dull metal and had a large screen, large enough to be seen from the production line some 20 feet from there. Beside that box was another small box connected by a few wires to the bigger one. It was after a year or so that a section of the workshop was functional. All the basic tools and gadgets needed for the main weapons workshop were manufactured there. The Xarmik engineers knew basic as well as advanced tool-manufacturing and once taught they were even able to put together the structure of the assembly line by themselves. But electricity and the electronic circuits were hard for them to grasp.

Mukunda, on the other hand, having worked at Café Evolution, knew the basics of circuitry and its manufacturing. And whenever he was stuck, he sought Garuda's help. All such drones had a whole online library stored in them along with several other survival know-hows. The information in that library was curated in such a way that it could have helped the Manavas create a whole new colony in a matter of months.

So, Mukunda having referenced the library, manufactured that automation unit for flawless operations in the workshop. Or so he thought. Because, it was not working, the way it was supposed to.

'Sir! Pardon me but I have tried reading those papers that you referenced for making this unit,' Chinju spoke.

'And?' said Mukunda.

'Just like that small box that you call repeater, it needs one more of that in the series. Otherwise there won't be enough power for the unit to operate on the required scale,' Chinju said.

Mukunda nodded. 'I am glad that you noticed that, but how much time will we require to manufacture the repeater?'

'I got it done! Not as a mean to correct you, but more as a hobby. To learn!' he replied.

Xardukht, upon hearing this, walked right up to Chinju and patted him on his shoulder. It was a rare gesture on his part, that too for a Xarmik. 'I like the passion and dedication that you have, young man,' he said.

Chinju nodded and folded his hand in gratitude and reverence. He then signalled other engineers of his team to bring in the repeater. As soon as it was placed near the unit, Mukunda started connecting it. The whole system was then re-energized and the booting sequence started. The automation units' display panel turned blue and all essential modules started loading. Thousands of lines of yellow text displaying system messages started being displayed on the screen. And with each display of cryptic codes and messages, it beeped and chimed.

'What next?' Xardukht said.

'We can only hope that it works as expected,' Mukunda replied.

'Is this the first time this machine has been switched on?' Xardukht then queried.

Mukunda nodded. 'It took an enormous amount of time and effort to just understand the architecture and build it in first place. Hope it works fine.'

'It will work fine, for it looks so beautiful with all those colours playing with each other,' Xardukht said, pointing towards the display.

Mukunda smiled. 'Did you know that while the upper body is made of metal, the inner working is made of the sand from this very section of the desert?'

Xardukht's eyes widened. 'This section of the desert is very holy to us. This is where our forefathers lived and died for the empire.'

Mukunda nodded and smiled. Meanwhile, the system kept on loading files after files and kept on displaying codes and commands on the screen.

'How long does it take? The moon is about to set,' said Xandhrin, growing impatient.

Mukunda turned to him. 'Any minute now…'

Before Mukunda could complete his sentence and turn back, the beeps and chimes paused. Still facing Xandhrin, he said, 'See, it's done.'

Mukunda then turned around, but he was in for a bigger surprise. The vigour, enthusiasm and speed at which he had turned back, dissipated at the first sight of the screen. 'Paramganak V2.0' the screen read.

Mukunda froze with his eyes wide open; he could sense a wave of cold pain running down his spine. After a lapse of several seconds, he gasped for air.

He finally found his voice. 'Is this some kind of a joke?'

Seeing a frenzied Mukunda, everybody else was now baffled too. Xinjhua stepped forward. 'Is everything okay?'

Mukunda turned towards him and yelled, 'Stay away!'

Xinjhua pulled his feet back and stood baffled. Mukunda then turned towards Chinju. 'Did you do this? Did you tamper with the codes of this unit?' he asked.

Chinju shook his head as a cold sweat of fear rolled down his temple.

'Relax, Mukunda! And tell us what is wrong?' said Xardukht.

Mukunda still overwhelmed from what he had seen turned around to face Xardukht. He was about to say what was bothering him, but then his saner side reclaimed him from his state of frenzy. He realized the fragility of his situation. Telling Xardukht about what the word 'Paramganak' meant to a Manava would have worked against him.

'The module! A wrong module has been implanted in this automation unit,' he said, controlling his nerves.

'What are the implications? Will it take time to get this unit repaired?' asked Xardukht.

'This is a far more superior and a highly dangerous version of what I wanted on this unit. It was not supposed to be here. This is a power-hungry automated programme which will overheat the whole workshop and destroy our work,' he replied.

'So it needs to be removed?' said Xardukht.

Mukunda nodded in affirmation. But before Xardukht could say anything, Xandhrin stepped in. 'But you said it is much superior!'

Mukunda was regretting using that word.

'Xandhrin! He says it's dangerous!' Xardukht interjected.

'Highness! What I am saying is that repair will lead to delays. How about all engineers remain here on standby and we let this unit run as it is for a day or so?' Xandhrin suggested.

'Not advisable, Highness! This needs to be shut down before it grows in intensity!' Mukunda pleaded.

'Just a day, Highness! If anything happens, I will be the one responsible.' Xandhrin said.

'Just one day then!' Xardukht said.

Mukunda somehow suppressed his urge to react. Instead, he nodded his head in agreement. 'I will stay here to monitor the situation.'

'You don't have to! You already look too perturbed, I think you need rest. Chinju and his team can handle this from here,' Xardukht said.

Mukunda nodded but refrained from speaking any further.

'Just a few moments to go before the moon sets,' announced Xandhrin.

Mukunda stepped forward and with a few basic commands, started the production line of the workshop. As the machines on the long production line started coming alive, the Xarnakhts burst into a collective chant. The whole of the workshop, and the deserts outside were now abuzz with the sound and echoes of the chant: 'Xar Xar Xar! Xar Xar Xar! Xar Xar Xar!'

Amid the chants, the Xarmiks stood with their hands folded and heads bowed; while, Mukunda and Xinjhua looked at each other in utter dismay.

The chanting lasted for half a minute or so and then Xardukht raised his arms in the air. Everybody stopped chanting and shifted their attention to the king.

'The moon has set and we now have what we wanted. This has all been possible due to the blessing of our forefathers and our protector above,' Xardukht said.

He turned and walked up to Mukunda. 'Let us go home. You catch up with Xarnika in the lobby outside and I too shall join you all in a while.'

It was on hearing this that Mukunda realized the absence of Xarnika. He was so caught up in all this that he didn't realize that she was not with them.

Mukunda nodded and started making his way home. Xinjhua too joined him. 'Why were you so angry and upset back there?' Xinjhua whispered.

'You know how I came from a faraway land?' he said.

Xinjhua nodded.

'My people are now without an enemy, but it was not always like that. There was this one traitor, who was an absolute villain. Now, somehow, it turns out that these Xarnakhts pray to the same traitor, Kamsa.'

'Two people can always share a name!' Xinjhua replied.

'I so want to believe that, but then that unit turned out to be a Paramganak!'

Xinjhua was now baffled and gave him a blank look.

'Paramganak was the biggest weapon in possession of that evil traitor. He used it to hatch a plot to enslave us all. Now out of nowhere all the modules I loaded on this computer have been overridden by that Paramganak module.'

'It sounds serious, Mukunda! If this person is the same Kamsa, he has control over the workshop now,' said Xinjhua.

'That is why I wanted it shut, but that high priest got his way. And now I seriously do not know what will happen,' he replied.

'How much time before the first batch rolls out of here?' Xinjhua asked.

'A fortnight or maybe a month; but they will need me for final testing. No computer can test the final weapon for these Xarnakhts,' he replied.

'We still have some time…' as Xinjhua said these words, they both heard footsteps approaching. Mukunda slightly gazed towards his left; it was a group of royal entourage. They discontinued their conversation.

'Xarnika! There she is!' Mukunda exclaimed as they approached the lobby area.

'Do not get entangled in something that you cannot free yourself from,' Xinjhua whispered to Mukunda.

Mukunda rushed up to Xarnika, and as they walked up to Xinjhua, he said, 'There are now plenty of carriages to take us home, I will have to find the one I am supposed to be in.'

'You will come with us,' Mukunda replied and Xarnika too nodded in agreement.

Chinju, meanwhile, came running towards the lobby and rushed towards Mukunda. 'Majesty and his officers say that they will start a little later. You along with Princess Xarnika can leave for the palace,' Chinju said.

As Chinju spoke, Xarki and Xinnun came rushing into the lobby too. 'We have been asked to do a little catching up. We will all ride back home together,' Xarki said with a smirk on his face.

Seeing this, Xarnika rolled her eyes and made her displeasure apparent.

'It seems Princess is unhappy seeing us! We can board the next coach home?' Xinnun suggested.

'She isn't and can we defy the Majesty's command by not accompanying them?' Xarki said.

'I guess you won't! Allegiance and obedience to the kingdom!' Mukunda's words were laced with sarcasm.

Xarki smiled and started walking towards the exit. As he stepped across the exit gate, he said, 'This place of yours looks mindboggling. Why don't you redesign the palace with some of those shining lights and roofs?'

'This place has been made keeping in mind the requirements of the people. Still, if you want all this glow and glitter in the palace, ask your father. He can sanction the same. But be aware, all resources here will have to be diverted towards the palace.'

'He won't allow the diversions, and you know that,' Xarki said with a big devious smile.

Mukunda smiled in return. As they approached the carriage, two royal guards joined them. They opened the carriage doors and made sure everyone was seated comfortably. The guards then signalled the carriage driver and they started towards the palace.

'You shouldn't have been out there!' Xarki said.

'Are you talking to me?' Xarnika retorted.

'No Majesty! I am talking to him. It was not your mistake, he should not have lead you to those dunes,' he said.

'Yes! From sunrise to moonsets, it's I who gets to dictate terms around here!' Mukunda said sneeringly.

'You cannot speak this way to him!' Xinnun said, albeit in a raised tone.

Xarki grabbed Xinnun's wrist and asked him to calm down.

'Xinnun! First, no one will his raise his voice or temper in my presence! Second, I sneaked away to see the mystery moon amid the desert, he was just accompanying me for my safety, at my request,' Xarnika said.

"You are right, Majesty! What I meant was, he should have taken the guards along for your safety,' Xarki replied.

Mukunda snorted out a derisive chuckle. Xinnun, hearing this, was about to blurt something, when Xarki held his arm again and signalled him not to.

Meanwhile, at the workshop, Xardukht was waiting impatiently for Xandhrin.

As Xandhrin appeared, Xardukht exclaimed, 'Where have you been? Why are we still here?'

'There is something that I wanted to confirm, Majesty!'

'You know I do not like sending the kids alone through the desert at this odd hour!' Xardukht replied.

'I have dispatched the royal guards with them, Xarki is there too.'

'What is it that you needed to confirm?' Xardukht asked.

'I had a little chat with our Xarmik engineers here. I made them check the health of the automation unit in question. Agreed, that they do not know everything about it, but with whatever they do, they say it will work just fine,' Xandhrin said.

'Mukunda seemed worried about that shadow called Paramganak,' Xardukht replied.

'Majesty! You have overlooked a very minute detail though!'

'What?'

'Whatever this uninvited shadow is, it terrified Mukunda. I still remember the royal court scene when he was brought to us. We were intimidating him with dire consequences and he was not afraid. He was standing amongst the most ruthless and powerful warlords and he showed no sign of fear. But this, this shadow terrifies him,' Xandhrin said.

Xardukht was even more baffled.

'Majesty, I have collected some information about this boy. He obviously does not belong here and it seems he does not belong to any other tribe on Prithvi either. He comes from worlds beyond and is here because he has no way back home. His folks would have rescued him but it seems they have not found him yet.'

'Do you already know who he is?' Xardukht said.

'He belongs to a tribe called Manava and they are supposedly wiser than the wise. Imagine, My majesty, if ever his folks come searching for him… They can run us over in a matter of hours,' Xandhrin said.

Hearing this Xardukht's eyes widened and a stream of sweat rolled down his temple and cheek.

'But this is what scares them, this very shadow. And, what scares a Manava can very well be a friend of ours,' Xandhrin said.

'Do whatever you wish to, but only build defenses. This Manava has been a good friend of us up till now. Do not harm him for any frivolous reason,' Xardukht said.

'Of course, Majesty!'

··•

The carriage with Xarnika aboard was now gaining pace and headed straight for a forest amid the desert.

'Why are we taking this route?' Xarki asked as he glanced outside.

Xinnun shifted to the seat just beneath the front window facing the carriage driver. 'Why are we driving through the forest?' he asked, sliding open the window.

One of the guards sitting alongside the carriage driver turned and said, 'Majesty, there was a sandstorm on the way back through the desert. For safety purposes, we have chosen this route. I will have the driver speed up the carriage. We will be through this forest soon.'

'This forest is infested with animals, be careful,' Xarki exclaimed.

The guards nodded and instructed the driver likewise. A silence ensued as everybody sat looking outside. The carriage then entered the thickest patch of the forest. Xarnika, seeing the trees outside, turned towards Mukunda. "These tall, slender trees with tapered outline are called Xarkoki. They are very beautiful. They remain green and thick throughout the year. But just before the winters, their leaves acquire many colours. For instance, leaves at the top may turn red, the leaves beneath may turn orange and yellow, and the leaves on the lowermost branches may turn purple. And in very rare instances, maybe one out of a whole forest, leaves of a special Xarkoki may start glowing like a herd of firefly,' she said.

As she spoke those words, a distant light started glimmering on the horizon. Mukunda was the first to notice this, and then everybody got fixated on the light ahead. As the carriage drove through the mud trail, that distant light grew brighter. It was now more apparent. A whole tree was glowing, as if a million glowing fireflies were residing on it. As they approached the tree, bright light from it started illuminating the inside of the coach. Xarnika looked towards Xarki, who was amazed at the sight.

'They never let us come to this portion of the desert,' she replied.

Xarki nodded and smiled.

'Now I wish we could see the forest in daytime, too,' she said.

As Xarnika chatted with Xarki, Mukunda was busy looking at the glowing tree, whose brightness was almost blinding. But with his half-open eyes, Mukunda thought he saw some shadows on the tree.

13

The Treacherous Track

Finding it difficult to see the way forward in the bright, blinding light, the drivers of the carriage struggled to keep the wagon on the road. Just as the carriage reached beneath the tree, it hit a bump, throwing everybody around a little.

The guard on the left side of the driver's seat fell too. Mukunda was the first to notice that one of the guards was missing. Before he could raise an alarm, the second guard fell too. And the carriage, still wobbling, sped up.

'Where are the royal guards?' Mukunda yelled.

'They were shot with arrows,' said the carriage driver, frightened. 'We are under attack. I cannot stop now. I have to drive you to the palace safely.'

Xarki panicked. 'Are there any swords, bows or any other weapons in the back of the carriage?'

'I fear not, my majesty,' driver said. But this time as the driver turned a little, Xarnika noticed something. He too had arrows protruding from his arms. He too had been wounded. And suddenly, in the blink of an eye, another arrow came hurtling through the air and pierced through his heart and he fell overboard.

The carriage horses were now running amok. Two horses were hit too. The carriage toppled beside the trees off the mud trail. Everybody was lying unconscious when the whirring sound started to grow. Garuda leaped out of Mukunda's pocket and unfolded. He took a while before stabilizing. 'Are you okay, Master?'

But Mukunda did not respond, seeing this Garuda panicked and repeated again 'Are you okay, Master?' He then flew very close to Mukunda inside the carriage and played loud sounds. Mukunda raised his head and with his blurry vision saw Garuda hovering over him. The loud noise was causing him acute pain in his head. Mukunda raised himself a little but now found his eyelashes getting drenched with something. He shook his head and then noticed a stream of blood trickling down from his head. He quickly got up and shook Xarnika. With her not responding, he shook Xarki and Xinnun. They both got up and before anything else, they started poking Xarnika, trying to bring her back to consciousness, but in vain.

'We need to get her out of here,' Xarki yelled.

Mukunda raised his arm and started tapping her cheek with his palms. She was still lying inert. He started tapping her face harder, with greater force. But she lay still. 'She is losing it!' he said, checking her pulse. He pinched her nose and opened her mouth. Placing his mouth firmly over hers, he started pumping her with air. He then again checked her pulse and there was almost nothing. He then gave rapid compression to her chest and again pumped in some air. The pulse was still growing feeble. Just then Mukunda heard a slight hissing sound.

'There is a barrage of arrows inbound, duck everyone,' he shouted.

It was a barrage of arrows along with some explosives. The arrows couldn't pierce through the hard shell of the carriage, but the explosives, which landed quite close to the carriage, exploded and ripped the roof of the carriage apart.

The shock wave from the explosion threw everyone off balance. But to Xarnika it did something remarkable. Her fingers moved and she suddenly gasped for air, much to everyone's relief. But fell back again. Mukunda, while cupping his own wounds, got up and started shaking Xarnika vigorously. She briefly opened her eyes, but then blanked out again.

'We cannot stay here! I will pick her up. We need to get out of this place,' Mukunda said.

'No! We are safe here. This carriage's body is armored! We just need to keep the doors locked till help arrives,' Xarki said.

But before Mukunda could counter his arguments, another bomb came hurling in their direction and shook the wagon wildly. The jolt brought Xarnika back to a semi-conscious state. Mukunda raised his gaze towards Garuda, who was hovering near the top of the toppled wagon. 'Peep through that gap on the roof and see how many people are out there, Garuda.'

Garuda flew towards the torn roof of the wagon and rose slightly above it.

'They are aplenty! They have some kind of stealth on and I am not getting the exact count,' Garuda reported.

'You have their approximate position? How far are they from us?' he asked.

'They are almost a hundred feet away from us; they are holding their positions,' Garuda replied.

'Which means they will shower more arrows, bombs and what not on us! Garuda! Calculate an escape route,' Mukunda said.

He then turned towards Xarki. 'Who are they? Any known enemy of the sate?'

'We have plenty of enemies but only few are bold enough to strike deep inside our state,' Xarki said.

'We aren't very far from the border. This forest lies quite close to our eastern border, we can make a dash for it,' Xinnun said.

'They are preparing their weapons again, brace for another attack in sixty seconds,' Garuda warned them.

'Get us a way out!' Mukunda yelled.

Garuda flew close to Mukunda. 'Unlock the doors on both sides, Master. I will blast the one on the left with full force and the one on the right very gently. Escape from the right door and I will manage the rest.'

'Hurry!' Mukunda shouted to the others.

Xarki unlocked both the doors and Garuda took position. Garuda then melted much of the right door with an energy beam and then turned towards the left side of the carriage. Meanwhile, Mukunda started hitting Xarnika on her face in a bid to wake her up. Xarnika opened her eyes and raised herself a bit. He grabbed her and pulled her away from the left door.

'Thirty seconds to the next attack!' Garuda said.

'Blow up that door!' Mukunda yelled.

Garuda then hurled a burst of very high-energy beams and continued to do so until the door popped and exploded outward, forming a huge ball of fire on the left side of the carriage.

'Exit from the opposite side...now,' Garuda ordered.

Xarki and Xinnun got down from the carriage and looked around for a safe place. Mukunda held Xarnika and helped her step down the carriage. Garuda then started holographic projections of the four of them on the leftward side of the carriage, trying to deceive the attackers.

The armed men who were still very close to the glowing tree, seeing the fireballs emitting from the left side of the carriage shifted their focus towards it. They then noticed the holographic projections exiting the carriage and walking towards the forest cover.

'They are out! Don't shoot now!' one of them said.

The men started pacing towards the projections.

'They have stopped shooting arrows it seems!' Mukunda whispered as he guided everybody into the thick vegetation.

'They are here on some kind of extraction mission. They are looking for someone,' Xinnun said.

'Are they your folks? Here to get you back? Ask them to stop attacking us then!' Xarki turned towards Mukunda and said.

'They are not here for me! There was only one high-value target in this carriage,' Mukunda replied.

Xarki's eye widened in horror and he said in a slightly raised voice, 'Shit! We need to grab Xarnika and rush her to someplace secure.'

With Mukunda already holding Xarnika by her right hand, Xarki swiftly grabbed her left arm and then they both started walking into the forest.

'Hurry! Before they realize that they are chasing our shadows and not us,' Mukunda said.

As the armed men reached close to the shadows, they noticed Garuda hovering just above the carriage. Perplexed, they halted and saw the shadows slipping into the thick cover of the forest. Four of those masked men went ahead and chased the shadows, while the remaining four prepared arrows to shoot down Garuda. But just then, a thumping sound emanated from the other side of the mud trail.

Xarnika while limping her way along with others had stumbled upon a rock. She, along with both Xarki and Mukunda, fell to the ground.

The four heavily armed men turned towards the sound. They now knew something was off and instead of targeting Garuda, started chasing the sound.

They were heavily built and yet were very quick and nimble on foot. The four kids stood no chance against them.

As soon as Mukunda saw them approaching, he got back on his feet and lifted Xarnika too. He turned and looked at Garuda, who was still busy projecting the holographs.

'Garuda, our cover is blown! Stop projecting the shadows and neutralize these masked men,' he yelled.

Garuda turned and locked on the masked men. He then fired beam after beam at them. But something unexpected happened. Their armor absorbed the high-energy beams, making them stronger.

Seeing the enemy approaching, Xarki and Xinnun both stood up and readied themselves to put up a fight. 'Take Xarnika along and run away southward towards the palace, Mukunda.'

As soon as the masked man got in their range, they kicked, punched and tried everything possible to stop them there. But, they were no match for those masked men. One of the men grabbed both and another punched them hard enough to lay them unconscious.

Mukunda meanwhile was tyring to flee into the forest, carrying Xarnika along.

But the masked men soon caught up with him, they grabbed hold of Xarnika and punched Mukunda till he lost consciousness.

Garuda could see the masked men fleeing but other than increasing his elevation and recording their route of escape he could not do anything else.

His core mandate was to never leave Mukunda alone. And now when Mukunda was hurt, his hardwired programming would not allow him to leave Mukunda behind.

•◆

The night went by and Garuda was still hovering above them helplessly.

As soon as the sun rose and the glowing tree finally dimmed, the royal guards and commanders reached there in search of Xarnika and the others.

Hearing the approaching foot taps of the horses, Mukunda was the first to come to his senses. He got up and looked around for Xarnika. Not finding her, he shouted out her name at the top of his voice.

Garuda lowered his elevation. 'She is gone, Master. They took her towards the eastern borders.'

Mukunda grabbed hold of his own head and shouted in anger again. He then looked around and saw Xarki and Xinnun getting up. It's then that he realized that Xinjhua was missing too.

'Where is Xinjhua?' he shouted.

'He is still in the carriage. In a bid to save Xarnika, you people forgot him there,' Garuda replied.

'How did this even happen? Is he safe?' he replied.

'I have been checking on him through the night. He seems safe, unconscious but safe,' Garuda replied.

Mukunda walked up to the carriage and found him lying in a corner. He had several cuts and wounds on his arms and legs.

Xanuk was the one heading the search party and as soon as they reached the spot, his first question was, 'Where is Xarnika?'

Mukunda was fumbling for words, when Xarki came forward. 'She was abducted after we came under attack. Both the carriage guards were killed and we tried defending her in whatever way we possibly could.'

'This is a disaster!' Xanuk muttered. 'Who told you to go through this forest?'

'The carriage driver did, he said the weather was inclement on our usual route,' Xarki replied.

'What do we now tell his majesty?' Xanuk yelled. He then looked up towards Garuda. 'He was there! Did he not put up a fight?'

'He did! But they had some sort of armour on, which his

weapon could not harm. They knew about his presence and were well prepared,' Mukunda clarified. 'One more thing! They have fled towards the eastern borders.'

Xanuk nodded and said 'For sure, they have.'

•◆•

'How did this happen? Anybody can now just walk into Xarlok and abduct the throne princess? How did this bloody happen?' Xardukht yelled.

Xandhrin then stood up. 'It's a lapse! And we do not know how they even managed to carry out such an operation.'

'Then who is supposed to know? What will be next? My head on a spike?' he shouted back.

'It was our collective duty and the royal court failed you, Majesty,' Xandhrin said.

Xanuk then intervened. 'Majesty! The biggest lapse was from my units. We were totally unprepared for attackers with such capabilities.'

'What do you mean?' Xardukht said.

'My men are now working on the reason for the lapses. And the first reports that have come in are quite baffling. The intruders had no problem crossing our borders and they sneaked away too very easily,' he said.

'How is this all even happening?' Xardukht said.

'They were wearing some kind of an armour that could not only deflect the attack mounted by us but also gave them enough stealth to execute the whole mission,' he replied.

'Have them located and then hunt them down,' Xardukht said.

'We already have that information. They are hiding in the abandoned cities of Gurupur,' he said.

'But that place is too toxic for anyone to inhabit. Isn't it?' Xardukht said.

'These men have capabilities beyond our reckoning. They have somehow camped there,' he replied.

'How many of them are there?' Xardukht asked.

'Apart from those men, there are around 200 civilians there,' he replied.

'What do they think; are they on a pilgrimage to Gurupur? Prepare and march an army of 2,000 of our most lethal men and slaughter everyone down,' Xardukht said.

Xanuk nodded.

'Anything about Xarnika?' Xardukht asked.

'From what my men have confirmed, she is in captivity but safe,' he replied.

'Prepare the assault force and rescue her. Decimate each and every living being in those camps,' Xardukht replied.

Xanuk nodded. Xardukht now turned towards Mukunda. 'When do we expect the workshop to produce those first few weapons?'

'In a matter of two weeks or so, majesty,' he replied.

Xardukht then got up. 'Everyone related to this matter, leave now and get down to work. Only Xandhrin shall stay.'

The royal court emptied in a matter of minutes and only Xardukht, Xandhrin and a few other royal guards remained. Mukunda walked towards his room. As he reached there, he saw Xinjhua standing. 'Whatever happened should not have happened!' Xinjhua said.

Mukunda knew what it meant. He walked towards the door and opened it.

As they both went inside, Xinjhua firmly closed the door.

'So those masked men were from Chinjing?' Mukunda asked.

'It seems so.'

'Now suddenly I am the good guy making lethal weapons for

the wronged party,' Mukunda said.

'You still cannot give them those weapons,' Xinjhua said.

'Your people are abducting kids and you are telling me what I can do and what I cannot do?' Mukunda yelled.

'They are not my people now! I belong to Xarlok, just like you do too. But those weapons will mean that neither Xarlok nor Chinjing survives,' Xinjhua said.

'What do you mean?' he said.

'Those people's capabilities have evolved. They could easily walk into the heart of Xarlok and kidnap Xarnika. They even rendered Garuda's weapons useless. Think about it,' Xinjhua said.

'So now they have tactical advantage over Xarlok and the first thing they do is abduct a defenseless girl? I think they need to be taught a lesson,' Mukunda replied.

'Come on! They know something that we don't! They definitely have a motive behind their actions,' Xinjhua replied.

'Yes! They know more than us and they are misusing the knowledge. And the only way this situation can be rectified is that Xarlok should get what it deserves,' Mukunda said.

'Can't you see, his majesty demanded 200 heads just for abducting a girl?' Xinjhua said.

'Just a girl? She is the throne princess to Xarlok! And those are the perils of harming a royalty,' he replied.

'You are saying so because you love her. You even left me dying in the carriage for her,' Xinjhua said.

'I am a teenager, and yes, I am infatuated with her. But that does not mean that I left you there to die. I panicked. It was a horrible mistake, but it was an unintentional one,' he replied.

'Any midway then?' Xinjhua said.

'Midway is I give enough weapons to his majesty so that he can keep these neighbouring empires in check,' he replied.

14

The Useful Idiot

Xardukht was pacing up and down his office. There was a big window, just beside his work desk, facing the corridor adjacent to the garden. Every now and then, he would peep through it.

Suddenly, he heard the sound of footsteps. He rushed towards the window and peeped outside again. He saw Mukunda approaching.

Meanwhile, Xandhrin, who was standing at the other corner of the office and had been watching Xardukht getting impatient, said, 'Pardon me! But this is very unbecoming of you, my majesty!'

Xardukht gave him a skewed look.

'Calm down, is what I meant,' Xandhrin said.

'My haste is unexpected of a king, but not of a father,' he replied.

'You have all the right to worry about Xarnika, but what I meant was you have to put up a nonchalant, brave and authoritative front to convince Mukunda,' Xandhrin replied.

'He will understand the helplessness of a father,' as Xardukht spoke, Mukunda knocked on the door.

'Please do come in!' Xardukht said.

As soon as Mukunda entered, Xardukht stopped pacing up and down the room. He offered him a seat and politely asked Xandhrin to leave.

Xardukht stood in silence for a few minutes, his face sombre and eyes dull with hopelessness. He wanted to speak but was too overwhelmed to do so.

'That evening when you arrived at my court for the first time, I wanted to get rid of you. You were an undesired interruption in my life and kingdom. But seeing your bravery and willingness to fight, I have grown fond of you. I took you for a son I never had. Even though you are quite young, I started looking up to you in times of trouble,' Xardukht said.

Mukunda nodded. 'Thank you for having faith in me. Please tell me what happened with that attacking party that you had sent.'

Xardukht could now see his fear reflected in Mukunda's eyes too. 'None of them barring Xanuk ever returned.'

Mukunda shook his head in disbelief.

'They are camping in the abandoned parts of Gurupur. Our team never had a chance against them,' Xardukht replied, shaking his head in despair.

'What about our new specially cast weapon? Were our troops carrying any?'

'They are immune to these new weapons and to Garuda's weapons too.'

'Did they use them as was instructed? On high-boost power?' Mukunda asked.

'They tried everything, but nothing worked,' he said.

'What message does the spared one bring?' Mukunda asked, visibly perturbed.

'They have asked Xanuk to let us know that Xarnika is safe for now.'

'And now what do they demand for her safe release?'

'You!' Xardukht said, drawing a long and heavy breath.

'That makes no sense! I was there with Xarnika, they could have taken me instead!'

'I am not sure why they are doing what they are doing, But they cold-bloodedly killed two thousand of my brave men, just to send back this one message,' Xardukht replied.

'If this secures Xarnika's release, I will be happy to turn myself in.'

'I was supposed to deliver this message to you. But I am in no position to tell you what to do. I do not have the heart to put you in peril,' he said.

'This is my decision. I want to go and get Xarnika released.'

Xardukht nodded. 'Well then! They have also sent the details of the meeting. They have allowed you to fly into Gurupur. They have allowed twenty guards to accompany you. They will see you alone, the guards will have to wait outside the city.'

'When do I leave?'

'Tomorrow morning,' Xardukht asked.

'As a representative of the great empire of Xarlok, what is it that I can promise them and what is it that I cannot?'

'I am a king, and for me, my subjects are most important, even more so than my family. Do not promise them anything that compromises the safety and security of my subjects. We may not have much bargaining power, so listen to them and then we can decide,' he said.

Mukunda nodded. 'Majesty, I shall take your leave now. I will be here tomorrow at sunrise.'

Xardukht nodded. 'Take care, son.'

It was few minutes to sunrise and Mukunda was still in his bed thinking. He had run all the details with Xinjhua the previous night. Xinjhua was worried. Earlier, when he heard about the weapons getting delivered he was upset, but now he was worried.

He thought Mukunda was playing right into the hands of the Xarnakhts.

'They can overwhelm every empire on Prithvi, but they have chosen to feign helplessness. They are using you to do their bidding,' he said.

'They see you as a useful idiot, they will get the most out of you and then abandon you,' was his opinion.

But Mukunda knew he had little to no options. And he knew he was an idiot to begin with, too. He left his beautiful homeland and loving people and jumped into a desert full of conniving aliens. So, in conclusion, there was no debating that he was, indeed, an idiot. And with no way back home, he would have died an idiot too. But now, at least to the Xarnakhts, he will be useful.

Every nook he went by, every aisle he crossed, every sunset he saw, he always wished a magic door would open to take him home. His mother, his brother, his uncles and his grandparents would often frequent his dreams. As he was lost deep in thoughts, the burst of sunlight piercing through the window grew stronger. It was now inundating the whole room. He got up and quickly went through the morning routines.

As Mukunda approached Xardukht's office, a young Xarksha was standing there in the central garden of the palace prepared for flight. Mukunda walked right up to her and patted her on her neck. She lifted her face and emanated a low-pitched sound.

Xardukht and Xandhrin walked up to him.

'Hope you slept well!' Xardukht said.

Mukunda nodded.

'If there is even a speck of doubt or fear in your mind or heart, just tell us. We will try finding some other way out,' Xardukht said.

'The only thing that is occupying my mind and heart right now is the safety of Xarnika,' he replied.

'Very well then! You and Xanuk will lead the way and the

guards will follow you. Xanuk and the royal guards will have to stay outside the camps though.'

Mukunda occupied the first slot on the saddle on the Xarksha. Xanuk sat behind him.

Xardukht, seeing this, said, 'He does know his ways. Be victorious!'

Mukunda nodded slightly, acknowledging his compliments and wishes and commanded the Xarksha to take off.

As the lead Xarksha took off and attained the desired height, the rest of the formation took off too. A lot was going through Mukunda's mind and among them was his eagerness to see Xarnika again. He should have been worried about her safety but a voice in his head told him that she was all right.

Every time he thought about her, he could almost get a whiff of her aromatic fragrance through the gust of winds caressing his face.

He was on one of the most perilous missions of his life and he should have been worried. But he couldn't care any less. Everything seemed perfect to him. The whizzing winds, the clouds drifting past, the distant land below, everything was beautiful. He was happy and confused at the same time. *Is it the eagerness to meet Xarnika again? Or is it something deeper?* he wondered.

As he was noticing the sun rising above the horizon and into the morning clouds, his attention shifted downward. He could literally see the desert ending.

A kilometre or so ahead, the dunes were paving the way to the flatlands. And those flatlands had vegetation. It was as if a massive golden-coloured pond converged into a huge beige-coloured pond with green moss floating over it.

'What magic is that?' Mukunda hollered.

'That's where Gurupur begins,' Xanuk hollered back.

As they passed over the desert's edge, Mukunda could now see an abandoned city in the distance. 'Is that the capital of Gurupur? What's its name?'

'Gurupur! They call it Gurupur! The kingdom was named after this town,' Xanuk hollered.

Mukunda nodded and then his focus shifted to another emerging feature on the terrain ahead: a criss-crossing network of something. It couldn't have been a river; it was too dull and lacklustre for that. The meandering network merged in the middle of the city and at that juncture stood a tall structure.

'What is that?' Mukunda hollered, pointing towards the structure.

As Xanuk looked, he seemed a little taken aback. 'We do not talk about it. We need to descend!'

Mukunda nodded and commanded the Xarksha to descend. Soon, they landed just outside the city limits. And all the other guards assembled there too.

'We expect someone from their side to show up and escort Mukunda for further talks. He shall go, but we will not move from our positions,' Xanuk then said.

'What if they play foul, sir?' one of the guards asked.

'We do not retaliate. We will try extracting Mukunda out of this place. Or else we will try getting back to the palace to report it all,' Xanuk said.

As they were discussing the further nuances of their plans, a group of five masked men showed up.

'Are we ready?' one of them said in his heavily accented voice.

'I will be coming along with you!' Mukunda said.

Mukunda started to walk and soon found himself out of sight of the other accompanying men. There was a very small hillock surrounding the inner part of the abandoned city. One that could be easily crossed on foot, without even struggling for breath and they were nearing that now.

As they were about to begin their ascent on those hillocks, Mukunda saw those vein-like features again. They were the dried beds of a network of rivers. Now that he could see them clearly, they seemed to be everywhere. They merged into one big riverbed, in the centre of the town. They started to descend. Mukunda now shifted his focus towards the other structures in the abandoned city.

The houses, though abandoned, were still beautiful. They were symmetrically arranged along the length and breadth of the city. They were of even height and had almost the same beige colour, with sporadic dark-brown textures.

The whole city had been thoughtfully designed.

As they approached closer, he noticed that vines were growing on the walls of many houses. And around many, there was a thick undergrowth of vegetation.

Mukunda now shifted his focus towards the tall tower in the middle of the city, just next to the confluence of the small riverbeds. The structure was broad and tapered as it gained height. It was made of shiny metal and must have been difficult to look directly at in the midday sun. As they walked closer to the city centre, he realized that the tower had a big room-like structure at its base.

But then something happened. As they started getting closer to the first row of houses, Mukunda's focus shifted to them again and he noticed something.

The coloured texturing was not any planned texturing after all. Those were marks from arson. And from a closer range, he could see that many of them had either collapsed or were in a dilaptated state.

He ran his fingers over the wall of a house he passed by. His fingers collected soot from those walls. It was black as charcoal. As he was inspecting the soot, he heard two of the guards letting out a curt chuckle. There was an undertone of sarcasm in it.

They now neared the riverbed channels. As he approached one, Mukunda turned back and looked at the masked men.

'These river marks were indeed revered around here, but you can walk over them,' said one of them.

As he approached the first riverbed, he saw a small broken bridge over it to his right.

He took a few quick steps and crossed the riverbed and kept moving ahead. Soon, there were many small riverbeds criss-crossing their way and Mukunda noticed many small as well as big bridges around them.

While crossing the one very near to the tower, Mukunda turned and finally asked, 'When the original inhabitants of this city built these bridges, was there water in these channels?'

'There was never any water in those as far as we can remember,' one of the guards replied.

'Yet, they used those bridges and never crossed these on foot?' Mukunda asked.

The guard shook his head 'They used to revere these channels and riverbeds.'

They kept walking and finally reached the riverbed where all the channels, small and big, merged. As Mukunda was about to near this particular riverbed, a guard said, 'Not this one! We shouldn't step over it! There is a bridge over there, we will use that.'

Mukunda nodded and corrected his course.

The bridge, which they mentioned, was on their right and it too was a little less maintained. But it was charming nonetheless. It was almost sixty feet high and was next to that magnificent tower.

As Mukunda started walking towards the bridge, he got nearer to the tower itself. He could now clearly see the base of the tower. There were some door-like structures on it. And the beige-coloured walls, which matched the colour of the soil below, had something scribbled over them.

As he approached the base, he could now see what the scribbling was.

They were sketches of an odd-looking demon chasing a group of three warriors. As he moved closer, he noticed more such sketches. In another depiction, which particularly caught his attention, one of the warriors was slaying the demon all by himself.

He walked past the base of the tower and looked up to see the magnificence of the tower from upclose. But it was hard to see anything in the glaring daylight.

He lowered his gaze and approached the bridge. It was still useable but not in the best of shape. At places, it even wobbled and was creaky.

Mukunda, while holding the siderail, started moving across the bridge. The bridge, which was steep at ends, quickly gained height. And from here, Mukunda could now see the tower in more detail.

He used his cupped palm as a visor and looked up. The metal or alloy, whatever it was made of, was shining brightly in the slant sunlight.

As he moved his gaze up, he noticed something. There were rusty reddish-brown stains on the shining metal of the tower. And as soon as Mukunda realized what they meant, he lowered his sight and looked towards the guard. The guards nodded in agreement.

'Whose blood is that? Who did this?'

'The very hope of us eastern empires. And the people you call your own did this,' said one of the guards.

'It was one of the saddest days in our history. This, one gruesome act, changed the course of our collective destiny,' said another one.

·◆·

Meanwhile, in the palace in Xarlok, Xardukht was eagerly waiting to hear from for Xandhrin. The workshop was to go fully functional on that day.

He was feeling restless and fidgety in his office armchair.

Xandhrin then appeared at the door to his office.

'Do we have those weapons now? The bigger, better ones?' he enquired.

'We have something much bigger than that!' Xandhrin replied.

'What is that? Tell me that things haven't deteriorated further!' he said.

'Rest assured, everything is good. Rather better than before!' Xandhrin said.

'How so?' he said.

'We have a visitor from a very distant past!' Xandhrin replied.

'A pleasant visitor?' he asked.

'Oh! You won't believe your ears or eyes! He is the guiding light we always sought. He will take us back to the heights we always belonged!' Xandhrin replied with an unreasonably bright smile on his face.

'Who is it that you are talking about?' his voice was now drenched in anticipation.

'Prepare the royal carriage, we will go out into the deserts!' said Xandhrin in a dramatically raised voice.

Two guards came rushing in, bowed and then left to get the carriages ready.

As they reached the workshop, Xardukht was still unsure of who the visitor was.

As they walked past the main door of the facility, Xardukht asked, 'Have I met him before?'

'None of us have!' Xandhrin replied.

'Can this visitor help us win against our troubles?' he then asked.

'Oh! He will help us win the worlds, both the known and the unknown,' Xandhrin replied.

Hearing this, Xardukht grew restless beyond control and held Xandhrin by his arm. As they both halted, he said, 'I need to know? Who is it?'

'My majesty! What you are about to see is divine intervention. Even the greatest of great kings have not been worthy of such an opportunity. I do not want to dilute your moment. This will be a life-changing moment for you. So, please hold your breath and walk with me towards the control terminals,' Xandhrin requested.

Xardukht let go his arm and started walking again. They reached the control panel, but it was completely dark. 'Where is that wise boy now?' Xandhrin said, looking around.

'Chinju,' called out Xardukht.

Chinju came hurrying in from the auxiliary supply room and stood in front of both of them.

'Turn on the Paramganak,' Xandhrin said.

But before Chinju could move even a few steps towards the panel and see why the panel was dark, something happened. The panel started glowing and within the next few seconds, came back to life.

'Paramganak! Is the revered one awake?' Xandhrin said.

'He always is! He sees, listens and knows even while resting,' said Paramganak in a machine-like heavy reverberating voice.

Then suddenly, the voice changed into a more human-like voice, 'Ahaa! The great among Xarnakhts, Xardukht is here.'

'Who are you?' Xardukht said.

'It's baffling that you do not recognize me,' the voice replied.

'I run through your veins and am part of your mind. I am the one who liberated you and can free you from all your troubles again.'

Xardukht was still standing there trying to connect the dots.

'I am the one whose guidance your forefathers have sought,' the voice said.

Now Xardukht's eyes widened and his mouth went dry, but he was still not able to assemble coherent words to speak.

'I am the one who raised the Xar tribe and made them Xarnakht!' the voice announced.

By now Xardukht was weeping with tears of disbelief and ecstasy. With his hands folded in reverence, he fell to his knees.

'I am Kamsa!' finally the voice revealed.

Xandhrin signalled everyone including Chinju to leave the premises, while Xardukht was kneeling, with his forehead touching the ground.

'Rise, my son! For now, your tormentors shall be tormented and your troubles will be dealt with a heavy hand,' said the voice.

Hearing this, Xardukht collected himself and got up from the ground. His shoulder blades were now pulled back and his head held high like a valiant and worthy king.

'There hasn't been a day that we have not been grateful to you. And there hasn't been a day we haven't sought your guiding hand,' Xardukht said.

'And there hasn't been a day when I have not waited eagerly for my liberation. So that I can be back and handhold my children on their path of destiny,' the voice emanating from the computer replied.

'How did you get into this metal box, Great Father?' Xandhrin said.

Xardukht turned towards Xandhrin. 'We should never question the Great Father. He can choose to manifest himself in skies, stones or the metals. He can do whatever he wishes to.'

'I understand, you have your own fair share of doubts!' Kamsa replied.

While Xandhrin thought for a second and shook his head in negation, Xardukht instantly spoke up, 'I can feel your voice. I have heard your voice in my dreams, in times of my desperation. I knew, in my heart of hearts, that this day was bound to manifest. When you speak, it is as if the whole lineage of the Xars before you and the Xarnakhts after you, speak in unison.'

'Aren't you the sweetest of all my descendants! A Xarnakht with a heart of gold!' Kamsa replied.

'I don't want to be sweet! I don't want a heart of gold! For, this world doesn't deserve a heart of gold. It only understands a battle-ready iron fist,' he said.

Hearing this Kamsa laughed. 'They don't! We shall conceal our hearts of gold and bare our iron fists!'

Xandhrin then stepped in. 'Help us out! The kingdoms that feared us eons ago now stand mocking us.'

'They have taken my daughter hostage. And as we speak, one of our most special envoys has gone there to negotiate.'

'That is Xarnakht pride we are talking about. How did they abduct our pride?' Kamsa said in a voice seething with anger and rage.

'They outmanoeuvred us. They have shields which render all our weapons useless,' Xandhrin replied.

'And you have sent a what? Envoy? To secure the release of Xarnakht's pride?' he said in an agitated voice.

'We initially sent a battle-ready troop of two thousand brave men. None of them returned. It was their demand to see Mukunda alone,' Xardukht said.

'Mukunda! The same person who has built this system?' Kamsa said.

Xandhrin nodded.

'He is just 12 or 13 years old and see what a marvel he has crafted. Once he is back, I am sure you will be very happy to see him,' Xardukht said.

'You two do not realize whom have you hosted here. Do you?' Kamsa said.

Xandhrin and Xardukht looked at each other in bafflement and then they looked at the computer and shook their heads in ignorance.

'You were asking me: how did I get into this metal box?' Kamsa said.

Xandhrin nodded his head in concurrence.

'After the Evil-Wise abandoned me in these deserts with my hands and feet tied, my body perished from heat and starvation. But my higher-self got entangled in those sand grains. I lay dormant there for ages, waiting for any possible liberation. Then, it seems, this special boy of yours came along and used the silicon extracted from that sand to make the internal workings of this computer. First, my best friend and companion Paramganak came out of dormancy and gained control of this system. He overrode all the native programmes and commands running on this system. And when the conditions became conducive, he woke me up.'

Then the screen that up until now had just Paramganak written over it started running some scans. Lines after lines of codes started appearing. Then the system pulled up files on Mukunda and everyone in his relation.

'And guess what? A Manava brought me back to life!' said Kamsa, laughing.

'If I am ask: what difference does that make, being brought back to life by a Manava?' Xandhrin asked.

'The people of the Xar tribe found me in the desert, wandering in search of food and shelter. Just like this Mukunda, I too came from a different world,' Kamsa said.

'Great Father! You mean you have visited that Manava's world?' Xardukht asked.

'I came from their world! I too was a Manava. One of the most valiant Manava, who commanded great respect among his people,' he replied.

They both stood there amazed.

'It is a matter of joy that a person from your tribe has brought you back to life,' Xandhrin said.

'This is a matter of amusement…as to how fate plays out!' Kamsa replied.

'We do not understand,' Xardukht said, still looking confused.

'Mukunda's father Krishna banished me from my own land. I was about to become the king, when he tricked me and left me here. I was exiled and left to die,' Kamsa said.

'If you wish we can avenge the injustice meted out to you,' Xandhrin said.

Even before Kamsa could reply, Xardukht chipped in, 'Mukunda is innocent. Even if his father was cruel, he is unlike him. Come to think of it, he made all this for us. Let's not punish him for the deed of his father,'

'You are right! I am not here for vengeance; I am here to help you Xardukht. And if that boy proves to be a useful means to do so, so be it,' Kamsa replied.

'Now I see it too! If that boy has even a fraction of Manava intelligence, let's use that on the ground for the betterment of the Xarnakht tribe,' Xandhrin said.

Xardukht nodded.

'Great Father! I trust that boy. Even as we speak, he is out there trying to save my daughter,' Xardukht said.

'About that! We are letting the enemy set the agenda, we cannot win a war on the enemy's terms!' Kamsa replied.

'My hands are tied. My only daughter is in their captivity. And I don't even know who they are or what they want,' he replied.

'We will do something about it!' Kamsa's voice reverberated through the hall.

Xardukht smiled a little at the assurance.

'When I reached here, most of my life went by in paying back to the Xar tribe. They accepted me and brought me back to health. And subsequently, I taught them every higher skill I knew of,' said Kamsa.

'That's true, Father! You taught us proper language, you taught us tool-making and you taught us the importance of cooperation and coordination. You even accepted the daughter of the then Xar chief in marriage. Your bloodline became our bloodline. Our future generations could now naturally speak and make swords and arrows. You are our god!' Xardukht said.

'I had further plans. I could have built you these sophisticated computers and flying weapons, but those Evil-Wise captured me. They tortured me and cut short my physical life,' Kamsa said.

'And we repaid them in their own coin. We drove them to extinction, Great Father,' Xardukht replied.

'But now someone else, someone viler is tormenting you, isn't it?' Kamsa said.

Xardukht and Xandhrin both nodded in reply.

'Just follow what I say. I shall destroy each and every one of your enemies,' said Kamsa and then those words were followed by his laughter, full of darkness and gloom.

15
The Missing Links

As Mukunda walked through the outer limit of eastern Gurupur, he could see a settlement a few hundred metres from there. It was beaming with life. It seemed like a civilian settlement rather than just an army camp.

'Is this where we are headed?' Mukunda asked, continuing to walk.

One of the masked men nodded in reply.

'Will Xarnika be there?'

The same man nodded again.

There now was a degree of buoyancy in Mukunda's gait. His eagerness to see Xarnika was now apparent. He knew if Xarnika was in a civilian settlement, her chances of being treated right were high.

As Mukunda approached the camps, he could see better the life the residents led there. There was smoke rising from the chimneys. There were kids playfully chasing each other. There were men and women shunting things from one place to another. And there were people huddled in groups, conversing.

Soon, Mukunda and the masked men reached the main entrance of the settlement. Mukunda stopped, turning to speak to the guards, who had by then removed their masks. What amazed him was that they had the same facial features as Xinjhua, after all, they too belonged to the same tribe from Chinjing.

'We will have you meet with our camp commander; he will tell you the further course of action,' one of them said.

Mukunda nodded and then followed them through the camp. After ten to fifteen minutes of walking through the hustle and bustle of the camps, they reached what seemed like the biggest tent house in the whole settlement.

'Commander Xhi shall see you shortly,' the guards said in unison.

As Mukunda faced the tent again, a lady emerged out of it. She was beauty, elegance and grace personified. Her smile and gait were filled with the reassurance of maternal care. As she noticed Mukunda she smiled. Her smile bore a warmth that Mukunda hadn't seen or felt in a long time.

'Please come inside!' she said politely.

Mukunda, without even thinking twice, followed her and entered the tent.

Though overwhelmed by the sound of chuckles of kids inside, his eyes scanned the place and quickly found Xarnika. Her glowing face and vibrant smile gave him goosebumps. His heart was now racing with joy. She was sitting there on a bed amidst what seemed like many toys.

'Xarni! Are you OK?' Mukunda said.

As she smiled and nodded, two kids came running and leaped onto the bed amid those toys. 'I am actually having fun with these two little angels,' she said, smiling again.

Mukunda nodded and smiled in relief too. Before he could speak another word, the lady directed him outside. 'While my kids and I are entertaining this lovely guest of ours, my husband Xhi is putting up in that camp,' she said and pointed towards an unimpressive-looking tent just behind her own.

A man emerged out of it and started walking towards Mukunda. Two guards were accompanying him. His build was average but his persona exuded a charm, one that stems from confidence and surety of purpose.

As he came and stood near Mukunda, the lady said, 'This is my husband Commander Xhi!'

Mukunda smiled and nodded.

'Now I will excuse myself and let you two talk,' she said and left for her own tent.

'Come with me,' Xhi said, pointing towards a bench some twenty feet away.

As they walked, Mukunda noticed that there were more kids in this section of the camp. They were running around in the sun, playing all sorts of games. This place, he guessed from the presence of so many kids, was the innermost and safest part of the camp. *They are keeping their own kids safe, while abducting others*, he thought.

As Xhi sat down and made sure Mukunda was comfortable too, he looked at his guards and signalled them to leave. 'You think of me as a cruel person. I have brought a lot of anguish to your king and people, haven't I?' he said.

'Particularly to the father of this girl! Xardukht is shaken to the core!' Mukunda replied.

'I am sorry for that! What can I say or do that can bring him comfort? How about reminding him what he did to someone else's daughter?' he said.

Mukunda remained unmoved. 'Whose daughter was it? What did he do to deserve such a fate?'

'King Guruk's! Our King Guruk's! She was the hope for the future of the eastern alliance!' he replied.

Mukunda remained silent, not knowing what to say.

'I have been told that you were curious about those rusty stains on that tower?' Mukunda nodded in reply.

'Guruvi was a very lively girl. Though still very young, she was as apt in administration as she was in warfare. She was to lead us eastern empires into a new age. The Xarnakhts treacherously stole a Bhavya and used her and her progenies against us. These wise men of Gurupur had great respect for the big bird of flight; they couldn't hurt her even when she turned against them.'

'No sane voice in Gurupur suggested otherwise?' Mukunda asked.

'Guruvi did! She wanted her father to order a full counter-attack against the Xarnakhts, even if that meant hurting a Bhavya. King Guruk instead went for penance even amid the onslaught. He was conducting a yagna, when Guruvi decided to take matters into her own hands. She, undercover, was heading towards the other military unit posted on the far-eastern end when one of the Bhavya-commanding Xarnakht commanders spotted her. He, without even seeking orders from his higher-ups, swooped in and took her away. He did not stop before crossing the borders and brought her to Xardukht.

'Xardukht should have reprimanded his men for this heinous act, but that coward was instead happy. He knew that war would now be over without much effort.

'He told his men to write pamphlets threatening King Guruk to surrender. And he then made them air-drop the pamphlets all over Gurupur.

'The council of ministers rushed in to meet King Guruk and everyone agreed that the safety of Guruvi was paramount. They thought that surrendering for now would makes sense, as the enemy is powerful. The plan was to bring Xardukht to the negotiation tables and bargain some part of the eastern territory for the release of the princess. The message was then conveyed to one of their commanders, Xanuk, and a time was set for the meeting. The resupply to the fighting forces was stopped and troops were asked to stand down.

'It was morning of the next day when some initial ministerial-level talks were to be held. But just an hour before that, amid the low lights of dawn, a sea of Xarnakht soldiers descended upon Gurupur and started a massacre not seen before in Prithvi history. The city guards were caught unprepared; their morale was already low from the previous news of Gurupur surrendering. By the time they could regroup and mount a counterattack, half of the city was destroyed,' Xhi said.

'Don't tell me that none of them fought back?' Mukunda said.

'You cannot imagine that madness, that hysteria now. Brave men of Gurupur did regroup and mount a counteroffensive and were soon able to inflict heavy losses on the Xarnakht army and were able to save almost half of the town. But then a small party of Xarnakht soldiers was able to breach the Gurupur palace with the objective of abducting the king and his queen. But King Guruk and his queen were nowhere to be seen. Nonetheless, Xanuk's mandate was very clear, annihilate Gurupur and capture Guruk alive.

'Xanuk, seeing his own army suffering losses now, and King Guruk untraceable, went back to Xarmatik. He grabbed hold of Guruvi and flew her back to Gurupur. He announced that Guruk needed to turn himself in or Guruvi would die.

In spite of the council of ministers suggesting otherwise, King Guruk came out on the streets. That part of the city was already under the control of Xanuk's forces. King Guruk was then taken into captivity. He was flown to Xarmatik. Xardukht was waiting for him there; this victory was even beyond his wildest dreams. Xardukht then flew King Guruk to the Xarlok palace, which then used to be King Guruk's winter palace. He used to frequent that along with his family and ministers during his leisure times, mostly during winter.

Seeing the king in captivity, the place guards surrendered too. The Xarnakht forces quickly gained control of the palace and

Xardukht's royal court was quickly set up in the heart of the palace.

The city of Xarlok was annexed by Gurupur to snatch the tactical advantage enjoyed by the Xarnakhts on the eastern border of Gurupur. But now, the same palace had fallen to the Xarnakhts and King Guruk was being tried there.

'For almost half a day, he was insulted there. Finally, by the end of the day, he was executed in full public view.

'King Guruk didn't deserve the kind of treatment he was meted out. But the Xarnakhts, it seems, could not get past the fact that a few military commanders from Gurupur had once killed their founding father and then had usurped their ancestral palace.'

'What happened to the rest? The queen, Guruvi and the council of ministers?' Mukunda asked.

'They all met the same fate; they were massacred by Xardukht's army. Except for Guruvi, her fate was the most gruesome of them all. They flew her back to the city and in front of the now-captured queen and ministers, spiked her on the Tower of the Wise. Her blood dripped over the tower for hours. Then another wave of the Xarnakht army swooped down upon the city and killed every last of the remaining souls,' Xhi said.

'I have been told that even after victory, the Xarnakhts could never occupy this territory. That it turned poisonous. What happened?' Mukunda said.

'Every new ruler of Gurupur had to go through a ceremony, where they had to donate a drop of their blood along with their new council of ministers. The blood of nine ministers and a king would then be mixed and stored under the Tower of Wise. That tower was made as a contingency plan, for if, in the future, any calamity, enemy or disease ever wiped the Wise Men's civilization, the blood was to be used to raise them again,' Xhi said.

'Did it work, did the Wise rise again?' Mukunda said.

'Not exactly, but something happened that day. After Guruvi met that cruel fate and her blood dripped over the tower, something happened. The hull of the tower started cracking. And by the evening, the tower's four edges separated like a blossoming lotus.

'A few minutes after it got dark, the interior of the tower started glowing a magnificent radiant blue. It soon started making a very loud rumbling sound.

Then someone said that the tower is about to blow up and that they would all be buried alive there. The Xarnakht army, which by now had killed everybody in Gurupur, started running for their lives. They ran towards the outer limit of the city and now the ghost town was glowing blue from the radiance of the tower.

The edges then fully separated and another slender tower emerged from inside, growing higher and higher. A blazing blue trail of fire lifted it up skywards. Soon, it rose to magnificent heights while illuminating the night sky.

'The Tower of Wise was still open but the blue glow was now gone. Slowly and cautiously the Xarnakht army again began descending into the city to search for valuables. And then the tower, with a huge booming sound, emanated a blue shockwave, blasted every living being in the city limits. Half of the Xarnakht army was decimated in a matter of seconds. And the city, with its structures intact, turned poisonous from the blue shockwave emanating. The tower closed again. And no one ever ventured into the city of Gurupur,' Xhi said.

'So, what brings you people here? Are you immune to that poison?' Mukunda asked.

'We weren't, that's why the city was left abandoned. But now we have started cleaning the poison from the city limits. It is still not completely inhabitable but we are trying our best to bring it back to its glory. We want to use their military bases and garrison as a defence line against Xarnakht people.' Xhi said.

'That's why you abducted Xarnika. You feared that once the poison waned away, Xarnakht would capture it from you. So, you chose to give them a preemptive message,' Mukunda said.

'We indeed brought Xarnika here to send out a message. But we don't fear them snatching Gurupur from us. We want you out! These wars and conflicts will last for generations; go back to where you came from and stop meddling in our affairs,' Xhi said.

'Please! Do show me the way! I will happily be on my way back home,' Mukunda said.

'What do you mean?' he asked.

'I was chasing an illusion back home when I got sucked into this restless world of yours,' Mukunda replied.

'You were not brought here by the Xarnakhts?'

'They are clueless about my origins,' Mukunda replied.

'So, you are just a wayfarer, an unintentional guest here?' Xhi then said.

'Who got stuck in someone else's battle…' Mukunda added.

'All the more reasons for you to leave and go back to where you belong,' Xhi said.

'Instead, take me as a hostage here and let Xarnika go!' Mukunda said.

'I don't know who your people are. I don't want them coming here and searching for you. I cannot afford to be enemy of someone I know nothing of,' Xhi replied.

'Probably the only reason these Xarnakhts have kept me alive too. And now I am an useful idiot for them, who will do all their bidding.' Mukunda replied with an overtone of helplessness in his voice.

'You will find your way out,' Xhi said.

'Let her go!' he said.

'It's about time you left! But before that, I have a piece of advice for you. I know that you are in love with her. I also know that you are young and impressionable and you are prone to misreading people. Her love is a sugar-coated poison. It's not intentional but it's something that these Xarnakhts inherit. They will turn against you the moment you are of no use to them. Love means next to nothing to them,' Xhi said.

'Somewhere down in my heart I know this. But the strange thing about us all is that we do not respond to facts, we respond to situations. And I am so wound up in my situation, that I control nothing. My situation drives me,' he replied.

'Tread cautiously, you seem like a nice person. Our guards will now take you to the Xarnakhts,' Xhi said, getting up before disappearing into his camp.

As Mukunda walked back towards the guards standing near the tent where Xarnika was housed, he couldn't help but think about what Xhi had just said.

He reached there and one of the guards handed him a paper. 'Please convey this to your king. The message is straight from Commander Xhi,' the guard said.

Mukunda opened the note and read it: 'Close that weapon facility and send this boy Mukunda home.'

Mukunda then turned to the guards. 'Can I see Xarnika just once before we go?'

They nodded and pointed towards the tent. Mukunda then walked up and went inside.

Xarnika was arranging the toys and other trinkets, while the other kids were now sleeping on the bed behind her. She turned around and gasped and smiled. He walked up to her. 'We all miss you there. But be assured that we will come back for you, your father will come back for you.'

Xarnika stepped forward, 'I know! Even if my father doesn't, you will.'

Those words vibrated in his heart while her captivating light eyes were looking deep into his soul.

He stood there frozen when Xarnika said in her now trembling voice, 'Do you love me?'

As soon as Mukunda nodded, she leaned in and kissed him. She then held him as if she never wanted to let him go. Mukunda could now hear approaching footsteps. He held her by her arms and gently pried them away.

'Take me along,' she muttered with tears rolling down her cheeks.

He raised his arms and cupped her face with his palms and looking into her eyes said, 'I will. Soon.'

•

The next day, even before the sun was up, Xardukht and Xandhrin were sitting in the workshop, near the control panel. Paramganak was busy doing calculations and integrating data. It had been almost half an hour since Kamsa had last spoken. He was waiting for Paramganak to complete the assigned task.

Finally, a blue glowing line of text appeared on the screen.

Kamsa broke his silence. 'The deep-surveillance equipment that I got fabricated and installed are now working. I can keep an eye on the surrounding areas, up to hundreds of kilometres.'

'Great, do we now have any information on who abducted Xarnika and how can we get her back?' said Xardukht.

'It is someone called Commander Xhi of an eastern empire of Chinjing,' he replied.

'The Chinjing empire of Emperor Jhuching,' said Xardukht in a tone that was heavily laced with sarcasm.

'Any long-standing enmity?' queried Kamsa.

'Historic enmity! Had it not been for them, we would have established the Rule of Righteous from one end of Prithvi to another,' Xandhrin replied.

'Well then, you have some more problems at your door. Commander Xhi has been entrusted with the task of extending the empire to what once was Gurupur,' Kamsa said.

'That's impossible! Gurupur is uninhabitable. No one can stay there permanently,' said Xandhrin.

'Does this Xhi have the blessing of the Emperor or is he just a breakaway rebel?' Xardukht asked.

'He enjoys royal patronage,' Kamsa replied.

'Tell us how we can rescue Xarnika and teach those hideous beings a lesson too,' Xardukht said.

'At this rate, this workshop will manufacture enough weapons for your entire army in a matter of weeks. I will teach you how to use them effectively. We will crush their empire,' Kamsa replied.

'But, these people have those special shields. Our weapons have already been rendered useless,' Xandhrin reminded.

'Oh, about that! When is your good golden boy going to be back in town?' Kamsa said.

'He was back yesterday! He is not here because his journey was arduous and we asked him to remain in the palace and rest for a day or two,' Xardukht said.

'I have some work lined up for him. Also, he cannot ever come here. He cannot know of my existence. In his country, I am folklore! If he hears about me being here, he will freak out. We don't want that. We need his cooperation,' Kamsa said.

'He did freak out when he saw Paramganak here,' Xandhrin said.

'Also, was he able to negotiate a deal or make any headway in

Xarnika's release?' Kamsa asked.

'He couldn't. They instead have put forth more demands. They now want this workshop shut,' Xandhrin said.

Before Kamsa could say anything, Xardukht said, 'I will never allow that. This workshop and this computer are your abode, Great Father! I will never betray my ancestors, not even for the love of my child.'

'You won't have to choose between either, my child. Just keep them busy in negotiations for a month or so and I will get you everything to defeat them and set Xarnika free,' Kamsa said.

Xardukht smiled and nodded, affirming his trust in what Kamsa just said.

'Great Father, what was that work that you had lined up for Mukunda?' Xandhrin asked.

'You were worried about those shields protecting Xhi's men, right? I ran checks on the site from where they abducted Xarnika. They used some sort of high-energy weapons, which chipped a few molecules and miniscule material out of their shield,' Kamsa said.

'I am not sure if we told you but Mukunda has a machine friend. He calls him Garuda. And that little machine can fly around and shoot those fancy light arrows. He attacked Xhi's men,' said Xardukht.

'All the weapons that we manufactured here, that flying being already has them. Mukunda learned how to make these weapons from him. Earlier, we were wary of that flying being, but then we noticed that he meant no harm. His only concern was Mukunda's safety,' said Xandhrin.

'It's good that you informed me about that drone. Any future plans I have for Mukunda will have to account for that too,' Kamsa said.

'What was there in those shields?' Xandhrin then asked.

'Strangely enough, they are made out of Jaradium,' Kamsa replied.

'We have never heard of that material, but still, what is so strange about it?' Xardukht said.

'I, when I was still in my world, invented this special alloy. I used them to make my own machine army. My men were indomitable and no one could have defeated them. But I lost. I lost because I overlooked a very simple vulnerability in my design. The power source I made for my machine army was unshielded. The Manavas came to know about it and decimated all my men by striking on that point of vulnerability. These men of Xhi are now using that alloy. I do not remember manufacturing that alloy here in this world,' Kamsa said.

'Any chance that the Manavas supplied them with the material or the alloy itself?' Xandhrin said.

'There is a remote possibility. But if they indeed were capable of interfering, they would have gotten Mukunda back by now,' Kamsa said.

'Any chance it was Mukunda who gave them the know-how?' Xandhrin said with a little scepticism.

'I have searched all the files on this computer; there is no mention of Jaradium here. So, it may be safe to assume that Mukunda may not be part of the game,' Kamsa said.

'Does that vulnerability exist in the shields of Xhi's men too? Can we somehow break through those shields?' Xardukht asked.

'Their armour is perfect. We can keep manufacturing higher-grade weapons but those shields won't relent,' said Kamsa.

'There has to be some way to defeat Xhi's army?' Xardukht almost pleaded in desperation.

'There is and that is where Mukunda comes into play. As a

matter of fact, I have been building something which will get us what we want,' Kamsa said.

Suddenly, a rumbling noise filled the workshop. A huge wall of metal in the leftmost section of the workshop started moving. Behind that wall was a very tall structure built of many polished metals. And around that structure was a scaffolding on which many Xarmiks and machines were working.

'Your Mukunda will have to prepare for a long journey,' Kamsa said, breaking into a deep and dark laughter.

16

An Outlandish Sojourn

Mukunda was sitting by the window in Xardukht's office and the midday sun was shining brightly through that big window. Xardukht, meanwhile, was reading and re-reading the note that Xhi had sent him.

'If I give up on Xarnika, I will bring eternal shame to my clan. And if I give up on our workshop, those savages will run over my kingdom and my people,' Xardukht said.

'They also want me gone!' Mukunda added.

Xardukht nodded while still staring at the note. He then stood up. 'I am supposed to be the pillar of strength to the Xarnakhts, but I am at a loss. Being a father, I cannot see my daughter being put in harm's way. And being a fatherly figure to my subjects, I cannot see my people in ruins either. My mind is clouded with fear, doubt and anxiety.'

'I am sure there must be some way out of this,' Mukunda tried to comfort him.

'There is a faint hope. But again, for the sake of my daughter and my subjects, I cannot put my son in peril,' Xardukht said.

Mukunda got a whiff of what Xardukht may be up to, but he kept his calm. 'If I can be of any use to his majesty or the empire, it will be an honour. I am a part of this storm; I cannot wish myself away from it now,' he said.

'We do have a plan in mind but it's far-fetched and will put you in peril,' Xardukht said.

'If you do not mind my asking, who is "we"?' Mukunda said.

'Me, Xandhrin and Paramganak,' he replied.

Mukunda grew wary and it showed on his face, 'Paramganak is still operational?'

'Son, he explained everything to us. He is just an error in your system. He said it was not his choice to reside on your data. He says that he means no harm and he even apologized for his prior master's sins,' Xardukht said.

'If he is just an error, let me wipe him off the system. We don't need him,' Mukunda replied with a stern face.

'That's the thing! He says he is embedded into the system. And no matter how many times we build everything again, he was programmed to manifest. Moreover, trust me, we need him. He is smart beyond our wildest imagination. He figured out everything about that invincible armour that Xhi is using,' Xardukht said.

'What did he find out?' Mukunda asked.

'They are using some alloy named Jaradium. And he says that the only thing that can pierce through Jaradium is Jaradium itself,' Xardukht said.

'How on Prithvi did they manage to get that? It's impossible to manufacture the mineral here,' Mukunda said.

'You know about this special alloy?' Xardukht asked.

'It's a forbidden metal and was only found in my world,' Mukunda replied.

'That's what Paramganak said and my ministers for a brief moment thought that you might have passed on the information to Xhi,' Xardukht replied.

'Is this what I am perceived here as—a traitor? I do not know how to manufacture Jaradium,' Mukunda replied in a cold, steady voice.

'We know that now. Paramganak checked your databases and

concluded that you knew nothing about it,' Xardukht said.

'Trust me, that vile piece of software should not have access to that database,' Mukunda said.

'He accessed them the moment he woke up,' he replied.

'How does that Paramganak suggest we get hold of any Jaradium?' Mukunda then asked.

'I do not want you to jump to conclusions and I want you to take your time to decide. He says that we can manufacture some weapon-worthy Jaradium on the dark side of the moon. He knows the formula and thinks that only you are smart enough to make it in a timely manner,' Xardukht said.

'If it's already decided, so be it,' Mukunda said.

'I know you love Xarnika and would do anything to ensure her safe return, but think it over. If you think anyone else can do the job, tell me,' Xardukht said.

'How do we reach there, the dark side of the moon?' Mukunda asked.

'Paramganak has crafted a special vehicle that can travel to the moon. He will arrange for everything required for the journey,' he replied.

'I have decided, it has to be me. I went to Gurupur for negotiations and I will arrange for the forbidden alloy. I cannot quit this battle midway,' Mukunda replied.

'If this is your final decision, then let me tell you that I won't send you alone. Your safety is equally important, so Xarki will accompany you. He is young and hopefully he will learn fast enough and would be of some help,' Xardukht said.

Mukunda nodded and smiled.

'One more thing, if we slow down our operations at the workshop and you were not to be seen around in the workshop or Xarlok, Xhi might think that we are taking his demand seriously.

We can then prepare for battle under this ploy without alerting them,' Xardukht said.

'Makes sense!' Mukunda said, nodding in affirmation.

'Will there be any training sessions for the journey, some acclimatization exercises?' Mukunda then queried.

'Paramganak has figured that out too. He will have a makeshift facility constructed in a concealed location and train you both,' Xardukht replied.

•◆•

Mukunda was busy packing, when he heard someone at the door. It was Xinjhua.

'Come on in, my friend!' Mukunda said flashing a big jovial smile.

'I got to know from the palace people!' Xinjhua replied with a stern face, still standing at the door.

'Because I am a coward and you are honest to the hilt! I didn't have the courage to face you,' Mukunda said.

'Why are you playing into their hands?' Xinjhua said, walking inside.

'Every morning when I wake up, I do not think about this palace or its people or even Xarnika. I long for my people, my place, and above all, my mother. I do not even know what time zone I am in. There is a fair chance that my people might have aged by hundreds of millions of years...' Mukunda paused, and that silence was filled with an abysmal hopelessness. 'I am doomed here! I thought the workshop and the computer that I built would someday help me find my way back home, but I erred. I got infatuated with Xarnika and even before I knew it, a rogue programme took over my hard work.'

'Can we not fight back tactically and regain control of your workshop?' Xinjhua said.

'Paramganak is already manufacturing weapons, rockets and what not. If we rebel, he will crush us in a matter of minutes,' Mukunda said.

'You can at least refuse to fly to the moon. Why would you knowingly want to endanger yourself?' Xinjhua said.

'Safety isn't an issue. They are sending Xarki along, which means they will not put him and me in any danger,' he replied.

'What is in it for you then? You want Xarnika back here with you?' Xinjhua said.

'In all honesty, I do. But more than that, I have relented control. I have left it all on fate. If I am ever meant to go back home, fate alone will find a way for me.'

'I hope you find your way back amid this chaos,' Xinjhua said, turning to leave the room.

'Just in case if there is any foul play and I never make it back here, try leaving the palace and head for Gurupur.'

'Why?' Xinjhua grew a little confused.

'If they decide to eliminate me, they will come after you too. I wish that day never comes but if it does, just head to Gurupur. I am sure Commander Xhi will protect you,' Mukunda said.

Xinjhua walked towards Mukunda and embraced him. 'My kids were languishing in that desert with me. Your honesty and boldness got us here and gave my kids a life full of opportunity. You are not a coward, never were and never will be,' he said, tearing up and his voice trembling with gratitude.

Mukunda patted him on his shoulder. 'Thanks for being an elder brother to me in this strange land.'

•◆

Mukunda was driven in a horse carriage to a distant point on the western-most corners of Xurabhur desert.

'This Paramganak can now make rockets but could not find the time to design and build cars?' Mukunda mumbled.

'What's that?' Xarki overheard and asked.

'A car! A self-propelled vehicle which runs by itself without smelling like horse crap,' he said.

'All by itself! How?' Xarki asked.

'It runs on fuel like oil, solar heat, etc.'

'Aha! Now, I remember! Paramganak says it is very time consuming to search for oil. Maybe after taking care of Xhi, he can focus on finding oil too,' Xarki replied.

'Priorities!' he mumbled under his breath again.

Xarki's gaze was now fixed on something in the horizon. Mukunda, seeing this, turned to look too. The towering rocket, made out of glittering silvery metals, looked marvelous in the daylight.

Mukunda wanted to gasp in amazement but chose to keep his calm. 'Are you not afraid, even a bit?' he asked.

'Anxious and excited, yes! Afraid, not even a bit,' Xarki said. 'I trust that computer, and I trust you too.'

Mukunda nodded. 'I am sceptical. But keeping in mind the reason why we are here taking such risks, helps.'

'For Xarnika,' Xarki said, grinning.

'For the Xarnakht people and the empire!' Mukunda corrected him.

They were in their spacesuits and the unrelenting desert heat made them very uncomfortable.

'I wish we had those oil-powered cars, it's getting hot and itchy in here,' Xarki complained.

'Absolutely! If not cars, at least have air-conditioned carriages,' Mukunda got up and yelled.

'Mukunda, let's accept the fact that we are both anxious. The moon looks good from a distance, but landing on it is outlandish,' said Xarki.

Mukunda laughed, to which Xarki said, 'What?'

'You said outlandish!' he replied.

Xarki stared at him for few moments and then laughed nervously, and pointing towards the sky, said, 'Aha! Outlandish! Because we will be far away from our land, out there!'

Xarki then turned pale. 'We will be up there? What have I signed up for'

Mukunda patted his back. 'Relax, brother.'

Their carriage, which was now fairly close to the launch site, came to a gradual halt. They both got down and looked at the rocket. There was a small desk, over which a small portable screen was set up. Mukunda walked up to it and glanced at the screen.

'Sir, Paramganak will keep a close watch on the launch. All parameters are good to go. Weather is all clear. If you wish you can recheck the schedule and parameters on this terminal,' Chinju, who was standing next to the table, said, pointing towards the screen.

'If it's good to go, we are good to go!' Mukunda replied.

Chinju nodded.

'How many more minutes till launch then?' Mukunda asked.

'It's ready, sir!' Chinju said.

Mukunda signalled Xarki and they both walked up to Xanuk, who was the only important person from the palace present at the site. It was Mukunda's idea to have neither Xardukht nor Xandhrin there. He wanted to concentrate on the launch and wanted no emotional goodbyes.

Xanuk patted them both on their backs. 'You both are brave and smart. Get there, do the job and be back home soon.'

They both nodded and walked towards the launchpad. There was a staircase next to the rocket, which they had to climb for about twenty metres. As they both reached the top of the staircase, Mukunda pushed open the door of the spacecraft. The interior of the spacecraft was slick and clean. It was a fully functional engineering marvel and yet whatever could be concealed was concealed. There were no wires, no confusing meters or panels and everything was aesthetically designed.

'For once, a good job done by that machine, man!' said Xarki as he peered inside the rocket.

Mukunda, meanwhile, located a glass capsule a few feet away. He held the door lever and leaned in side the capsule, till he reached a red button. He pressed it and a mini door opened.

'Come on in, Xarki, we need to sit in this capsule, this should take us to our seats in the payload module at the top,' Mukunda said.

Xarki nodded and stepped inside the rocket. 'You go first,' Xarki said, pointing towards the glass capsule.

Mukunda then entered inside and sat on the floor. As Xarki squeezed into the capsule, the door closed. It slowly started to rise and went past all the system and circuit boards.

At every few feet, as they ascended, the boards had signs reading: 'Automated! Do Not Try to Open or Operate'.

'It seems Paramganak has taken care of everything,' Xarki said, impressed.

'He has, and that leaves me with one question. If this mission gets into trouble, will we be able to do any kind of manoeuvring at all? I don't like this level of automation,' Mukunda replied.

'I am sure Paramganak knows his art well. He must have planned everything,' Xarki said.

The capsule reached and attached itself to the payload module. The ceiling of the capsule then retracted and a small staircase appeared on the wall lining of the capsule.

Mukunda ascended the stairs and pushed open the little vent

on the module's floor. He squeezed through it and signaled Xarki to follow.

With both of them in the module, Mukunda closed the vent in the floor.

They both took their seats and started looking around the module to familiarize themselves with the craft.

'Hi! This is Xari, I will be your friendly flight support. Kindly buckle your seat belts and remain seated throughout the sojourn,' a female voice announced over a speaker.

They both buckled up and waited for the next instruction. Mukunda, by now, was fidgeting in his seat.

'Mukunda! I see, you are a little anxious. Aren't you?' said Xari.

Mukunda nodded. 'Why is most of this space craft hollow?'

'Do you mean the part of the vehicle you travelled through, in that elevator?' Xari asked.

Mukunda shook his head vigorously.

'We are going very light on fuel. We don't require much. The part you traversed is the mother ship. It shall orbit the moon as long as you stay there,' she replied back.

'What kind of fuel are we sitting atop?' he then asked.

'Mukunda, I know what you are thinking and you are right. We have gone nuclear. I can be to the moon and back a thousand times on the fuel that we are carrying,' she replied.

'Sitting atop a nuclear device, now that comforts me like a lullaby,' he mumbled.

'They weren't wrong, you do have a great sense of humor,' Xari said, making a giggling sound.

Mukunda rolled his eyes. 'Are we on a countdown?'

'We are, and in the next five seconds, for the first phase of the flight, I will have to administer a sleeping pill. This is to save you from the inconvenience of vehicle turbulence,' Xari said.

Even before Mukunda or Xarki could ask or say anything, their suit's visor turned foggy and they both began to feel sleepy.

'They were right again; gas does work faster than pills,' Xari said, laughing. And this time it was not a playful giggle.

A faint countdown could now be heard in the background. And with each sound the rumbling grew prominent. The spacecraft started shaking violently and then it took off with a huge thrust.

•◆

Mukunda and Xarki were now wide awake. Mukunda leaned towards the window by his seat and saw Prithvi receding and the blue colour of the sky changing into ink-black.

'We are now in micro gravity. Always remain seated and buckled up,' Xari said.

'What is our ETA to the moon's orbit?' Mukunda asked.

'Two hours and twenty minutes!' she replied. Mukunda's eyes widened with disbelief.

'Everything okay?' Xarki asked.

'It usually takes days to reach there. We must be cruising at a very high speed,' he replied.

'That is right, Mukunda. Humour as well as intelligence, I love that in a guy,' Xari said, giggling playfully again.

They both found the machine's behaviour a little odd; they looked at each other and shrugged. Xarki then turned towards the window by his side and started gazing at the dark-blue space outside. He leaned in further to have a good look outside. At one extreme corner, on the horizon, he saw the sun. It was glowing bright and the contrast with the deep dark space was mesmerizing.

'We will have to be extra careful. What if we err by a little and drift towards the sun,' Xarki said.

'That won't happen, Xarki. I have each parameter of our flight under control,' Xari replied.

'Meanwhile, Xari, could you please run me through the vehicle details and the parameters for manoeuvres that we will be performing for orbit injection,' Mukunda said.

'Access denied,' Xari replied.

'What? Why?' Mukunda asked.

'Too many cooks spoil the broth,' Xari replied tersely.

Mukunda drew in a sharp breath under his suit and leaned back in his chair.

'ETA to moon…one hour! Control sleep will now be induced,' Xari announced.

'Why?' Xarki asked Mukunda.

'Paramganak doesn't want us to know the details of this flight,' Mukunda said.

'Maybe Paramganak and the palace people too don't trust us. They just want us to complete the mission while letting us know as little as possible,' Xarki replied, with an undertone of dismay in his voice.

But before Mukunda could say anything, the gas released into their suits took effect and they both lost consciousness. The spacecraft then shook violently and the booster rocket swung into action. The spacecraft was now accelerating like a frenzied arrow. At one point, it seemed that the spacecraft would shoot past the moon. But after a few minutes of accelerating, it started slowing down with a less-noisy rumble. The mother ship was still in the moon's orbit when it dropped the payload module, which had its boosters fully functioning.

'Get up!' said a muffled voice, that gradually grew louder and louder, till it became a frenzied scream, 'GET UP.'

Mukunda regained consciousness and looked towards Xarki. He seemed terrified. Xarki was screaming, 'We are crashing….'

Mukunda looked outside the window. He could see the module approaching a desert of silvery sand.

'We are on course and about to touchdown. The reverse booster will fire anytime soon now,' Mukunda said as a soft rumbling picked up.

It grew louder and violent with each passing second and the module started to slow down. Only a few metres out, the module came to a stand-still and started hovering. It then carefully landed on the surface.

'Welcome to the moon! An accomplishment unprecedented in Xarnakht history,' declared Xari.

'When can we get out of the spacecraft and venture on to the moon's surface?' Mukunda asked.

'There is still some time for that. My workers will make a safe habitat for you and then you can venture outside the module,' Xari said.

As Xari completed her sentence, a hatch opened at the bottom of the module and a small team of robots rushed outside. They were no taller or bigger than a couple of dinner plates stacked one upon another, but they all had two sets of hands with two opposing metal fingers on them. When in need of height, they could extend themselves up to a foot and half and when in need of reaching further high, could stand atop one another. As soon as the robots landed on the dusty lunar surface and started looking for a sweet spot for a habitat, another rumbling sound started growing loud. Xarki grew a little suspicious and turned towards Mukunda.

17

A Home Away from Home

'System malfunction! Alien sound detected onboard the payload module!' Xari said.

Hearing this, Mukunda grew a bit cautious, but before he could say or do anything, Xari announced 'Leaving lunar surface in T-10 seconds!'

'Wait!' Mukunda exclaimed.

'Do not start ignition!' he exclaimed, as the background vibrations of boosters grew louder.

'Xari! Stop! Abort the lift-off! This is just…' and before he could finish his sentence, Garuda popped out of his spacesuit.

'Intruder, confirm your ID,' Xari said, while the boosters were still hot.

'This is Garuda. He is with me. He has his clearances to be here, abort lift-off,' Mukunda yelled again.

The vibration started dampening down and the little tremors running through the vehicle started dampening too.

'Master! This place is new. Where are we?' Garuda said as he looked around.

'On a mission! Now power down and let us work,' Mukunda's voice though muffled by his space suit, bore a tone of annoyance and anguish.

'Can I help you, Master?' he instead replied

'Just go back to hibernation,' he now yelled.

'Wait! If he promises to behave, we can use his services here,'

Xari said.

'I will. I will.' Garuda said, his metallic voice brimming with joy.

'But first, let my team make a livable habitat on the surface,' Xari replied.

Garuda blinked his glowing eyes and sat on the module's dashboard, with his camera gaze set on the robots working outside. He was like a kid on the bench, waiting for the coach to call him up for his turn on the field, when he would go out there and out-trick every other kid on the block.

'Where exactly have we landed?' Mukunda then asked.

'We have landed on the Aitken basin on the far side. The terrain is rough, but it is only here that Jara, the key component of Jaradium, can be found,' Xari replied.

'And how much time before our houses get built?' Xarki then asked.

'Look outside the window!' Xari replied.

As they turned they saw a half-finished building made out of a transparent glass-like material. The cylindrical body of the habitat was complete and the robots were crawling up and down its wall trying to build its roof.

'Our new home, Master!' Garuda said, looking at the habitat with his affixed gaze.

'Wow! He is really looking forward to it. How adorably adaptable is he,' Xarki said.

'He has been programmed to do so. He is tagged to me, so he will take an interest in whatever I do. This is all pre-programmed theatrics,' Mukunda replied.

'You may call it whatever, but he is adorable,' Xarki said.

'And my only connection, whatsoever, to my own lost world.'

'The habitat is now complete and has been pressurized with breathable air. You two and your little flying friend can now step outside on the moon,' Xari announced.

They undid their safety belts and pushed open the module's main hatch. It was barely a metre or so from the surface and they both jumped from there.

'I feel light. I think I may trip,' Xarki said.

'Welcome to the moon, my friend!' Mukunda said on his comm line, laughing.

They both then walked towards the habitat. Xarki, though, did trip and tumble once or twice. Mukunda opened the outer door of the habitat. 'Xarki, this is the entrance to our habitat here. But before you open this one, the inner airlock door has to be closed.'

'I have read the manual and we need not care about that. This door remains locked unless the inner airlock is completely shut. And the inner airlock wouldn't open until this is shut,' Xarki replied.

Mukunda nodded and signalled Xarki in. They both now proceeded towards the inner airlock door. As Mukunda tried opening the airlock door, the surface below him and the habitat shook. 'Xari, what was that?' he asked.

'It was a moonquake! They do happen. But this is unusual, as moonquakes, once they set in, last longer. This one stopped,' Xari replied.

'Can this habitat withstand such vibration?' Mukunda asked.

'We knew beforehand and the design already takes care of such exigencies,' she replied.

Mukunda then pulled open the door and entered the habitat. It was like a mini living room. There was a small bunk bed for sleeping, in a corner and adjacent to it there was a compact bathroom too.

Xarki followed close behind, 'This looks exciting!'

'Wait till they put us to work. We have been brought here as metal miners,' Mukunda said.

'That's right! But you both have until tomorrow. The production unit will be up in another eight hours or so,' Xari replied.

'What will our work day be like?' Xarki asked.

'Relax! You will not be working, these robots of mine will do most of the work,' Xari replied.

'Then why were we brought up here?' Xarki asked.

'We, the machines, can design, formulate and manufacture things. We can test and validate too, but what we can't do is feel. And you don't manufacture Jaradium by just mixing few metals and compounds. A piece of alloy is not Jaradium until and unless it encapsulates that eternal glow of darkness in it,' Xari said.

'The eternal glow of darkness?' Mukunda scoffed.

'Check the pockets of your suit. There is a small chunk of Jaradium there. See it from a close range to understand what that glow stands for,' she said.

They both pulled the chunk out of their suit pockets and drew the alloy piece close to their eyes. The metal first seemed like a dull chunk of dark lacklustre metal. But then, within a few seconds that glow became apparent to both of them. It was as if its dull brilliance was a doorway to a dark and cold world.

'Do you now see what I meant?' Xari asked.

The two of them, still mesmerized from the subtle radiance of the chunks, nodded.

'Good, because neither I nor the other machines can ever understand that. We can only run chemical tests on it, but it wouldn't talk to us the way it can to you living beings,' she replied.

'And to be battle-ready it has to have that eternal glow of darkness to it,' Xarki mumbled.

'You are catching up quick, Xarki,' she said with jubilation in her voice.

'Now, you can get out of your spacesuits and breathe in fresh air. Catch some sleep and we will have a great workday tomorrow,' she said.

They both changed and went to bed. There were no moonquakes that night and they slept pleasantly. After an interval of eight hours, Xari woke them up. The facilities were now ready.

As they stepped outside the habitat, they saw an opaque metal tent built about fifty steps away from their habitat. The robots were already pacing up and down the oblong tent. There was extraction, smelting, mixing and refinement all happening under that makeshift production unit.

'Is the first batch ready?' Mukunda asked.

'It will soon be. I will monitor the composition of the final product myself. You both will have to agree on the eternal glow,' she replied.

'Meanwhile, if we are free, can we hop around?' Xarki asked.

Mukunda smiled. 'You can, if you feel like.'

Xarki started jumping from one place to another, he tripped and tumbled many a time and then got up again. Seeing him tumbling on that dusty surface and seeing him struggling to get back on his feet again, was funny. Mukunda stood there smiling.

'I wish the others in Xarlok could see us having fun here. Xinnun and Xarnika will be so jealous,' Xarki said.

Mukunda smiled. 'Come back here. We need to stay in sight.'

Xarki turned and started his way back towards the habitat. He was still halfway when a violent moonquake shook the surface. Xarki tripped and fell. As he got up, he saw a big red light atop the factory tent blinking.

'Mukunda! Look at that,' he said.

Mukunda turned towards the factory tent and saw the light aglow.

'Xari, there was a strong moonquake here and now some

indicator light is glowing atop the factory tent. Is everything okay?' Mukunda said into his comms.

Xari took a few seconds to reply. 'A small mine inside has collapsed, one of my critical robots has gotten trapped there.'

Mukunda and Xarki looked at each other. 'What do we do now?' they asked.

'My other robots are trying to pull him up, but they aren't able to reach him. I fear one of you may have to, very carefully, go inside to the rear end of the factory and rescue that miner,' she said.

'Let me go in there and fix it,' Mukunda said.

'You won't, I will!' Xarki said.

'Let me go in there and fix it. I will get the facility up and running. Let's finish our mission here and go back to Prithvi,' Mukunda replied.

'You have always been at the forefront, protecting the interests of Xarlok. This time I cannot let you go in there. You cannot be the one always risking it for others,' Xarki said, his voice laden with both fear as well as newly discovered valour.

Mukunda then turned and looked Xarki in his eyes. Beneath his helmet's visor, his eyes were glowing with fervour. The gleam of decisiveness left Mukunda speechless. He nodded.

'Xari, I am going in. Guide me through the operation,' Xarki said.

'All right! The mine-pit is located at the extreme end of the factory. Enter the premises and keep a watch out for falling objects. Once you reach there, let me know,' she replied.

Xarki stepped forward and moved towards the entrance of the tent. The outer door opened and he went inside. The set-up and equipment were all in their place and the work robots were on standby. He continued walking till he reached the other end of the premises and saw the pits. The pit where the work-robot was stuck was almost eight feet deep.

'I am at the site. The pit is narrow and deep and the ramp meant for movement has collapsed. I will have to go down and then climb back with that robot,' Xarki said over his comms.

'That's the site. Miner 104 is stuck there. Please bring him back safely,' Xari replied.

'Take a deep breath, Xari. I am going into that pit now.'

But before Xarki could begin his descent, a mild rumbling started growing and the surface started shaking. He could feel the vibrations running boldly through his hands and feet.

'It's a moonquake, again. Abandon the rescue mission.' Xari said.

Xarki turned and was about to get up when the vibrations grew more violent and a piece of metal beam supporting that segment of the tent came hurtling down.

A piece of the beam hit his leg and pierced through his spacesuit. The extreme portion of the tent had collapsed too. Mukunda could now see Xarki trapped under the debris.

'Xarki is hurt. I repeat… Xarki is hurt! He needs to be flown back home immediately,' Mukunda yelled as he entered the factory and saw Xarki lying beneath the debris.

·◆·

It had been ten days since Mukunda was alone on the lunar surface. He, alone, was able to restart the mining operation and under his supervision, a considerable amount of Jaradium had been produced and shipped to Xarlok.

Xarki, though still recovering, was doing better and was with his loved ones in Xarlok.

But something was still perturbing Mukunda; it was a constant annoying tremor that lasted eight days on the lunar surface. The tremor was too soft to interfere with the mission but it constantly occupied Mukunda's subconscious mind.

And when they peaked a little, they interfered with his communication with Xari, in the orbit above. It was his bedtime and the tremor had peaked a little again. Mukunda was tossing and turning in his bed and was about to scream out of annoyance when he instead said, 'Xari, How long will these tremors continue?'

He waited for a reply but got none. 'Xari! Xari!' he tried again.

'Garuda, get up!' he said, still lying in bed.

Garuda, who was resting on a coffee table, did not respond. Mukunda then yelled 'Garuda!'

Garuda blinked his glowing eyes twice, 'Yes, Master!'

'Can you also feel these constant tremors?' Mukunda said.

'Yes, Master, I can. But they are not constant; they have very subtle peaks and lows to them. Also…' he said and paused midway.

'Also, what?' Mukunda asked, a little angrily.

'Also, the tremors do not annoy me the way they do you!' Garuda said.

'Extremely funny! A machine is now telling me how cool he is,' Mukunda said.

Garuda flickered his glowing eyes twice, unaware of the slur just directed at him.

'Is it really not constant? Does it have a pattern to it? Can you try decoding those patterns for me?' Mukunda then asked.

Garuda got up from the table and settled on the floor. He sat there for a minute and started humming those vibrations. After a full minute of humming, Garuda said, 'Its Morse code, the simplest of them all.'

'Does it say anything?' Mukunda was now baffled.

'Master! You won't believe me though!'

'What does it say?' he said.

'Hello, Mukunda!' Garuda replied.

'What?' Mukunda hollered.

'The moonquakes are greeting, you!' Garuda replied.

'Listen! This is crazy, but we cannot talk to Xari or anyone else about this ever,'

Garuda flickered his eyes in agreement.

Mukunda started pacing up and down the habitat and after thinking for a while said, 'Can you reply back in Morse code?'

'How do I reply, Master?'

'Encode the word "hello" and vibrate at the frequency of the incoming message.'

Garuda flickered his eyes and used his internal motors to generate vibrations. 'I have conveyed your message,' he then said.

'Now keep listening. See if there is any relevant message is coming back.'

'The vibration says, "Welcome to the moon, Mukunda. It is fate that has brought you here",' Garuda spoke.

Mukunda eyes widened and his mouth went dry. 'Ask him who is this speaking,' he then muttered.

Garuda relayed the message and upon receipt of reply, spoke 'Your distant brother, Mukunda.'

Mukunda was finding it hard to follow. He yelled, 'Ask him who he is?'

'I am Grutvator,' Garuda read the message.

'Why are you here in this barren land? How do you know my name?' Mukunda then said and Garuda translated it into vibrations.

'The fact that this land is barren brought me here. From here, I keep an eye on the whole solar system. I know who you are and who sent you here,' the reply read.

'Who sent me here?' Mukunda spoke back.

'The same people who forced me towards these barren lands,

they have exiled you here,' Garuda read the message.

'Exiled? I am on a royal mission here. No one has exiled me,' he replied and chortled in disbelief.

'Xandhrin will not let King Xardukht bring you back to Prithvi,' the vibrations replied.

'Why will he do so?' Mukunda asked.

'Xandhrin is the upkeeper of Xarnakht dharma, he and his predecessors have always made sure that a Xarnakht king's thinking and action never get clouded by weaker forces of love, compassion and kindness. In the beginning, they both had kind feelings for you but the reappearance of Kamsa changed everything.'

'Kamsa!' Mukunda exclaimed. It was now too much for him to process in a day. 'So, it was not Paramganak alone who resurfaced. That was a façade to conceal Kamsa. I have been taking orders from the evil incarnate?' Mukunda said after a while of silence, his voice heavy with gloom.

'It was not only you who got fooled by him. Kamsa is fooling both Xandhrin and Xardukht and he is also fooling every person on Prithvi. He is the one who sealed my fate too,' the vibrations replied.

'Again, what is he up to? And who are you?' Mukunda asked.

'As I said, I am Grutvator. I was not supposed to be invoked under normal circumstances. But Xarnakhts, following the commands of Kamsa, drove the whole of the race of Guru people to extinction. And as a result, I was invoked and brought into being.'

'You are the Evil-Wise?' Mukunda asked.

''One of the many names they called me by. When Kamsa met the people of the Xar tribe, my kingdom was the biggest, the finest and the richest kingdom on Prithvi. Kamsa married into the Xar tribe and taught his progeny finer skills. He turned a simple, forest-dwelling Xar tribe into an organized fighting force. He turned them against us. After he was killed, his descendants were preparing for war. Then, one day, by deceit, they got hold of our beloved friend and the guardians of the eastern empires, Bhavya. One thing led to another and they overran us,' the reply message read.

'They overran you because you were weak and much too attached to a dumb bird,' Mukunda replied.

'Maybe we were or maybe it was something else. Kamsa lifted the Xar tribe from their primitive living ways. He, in a way, took care of them and gained their loyalty. In this matter, he was better than us. When we, the Guru people, formed the most affluent kingdom on earth, we forgot to take care of the less privileged. A little help from Gurupur could have changed the fate of the Xar tribe. They, with their rudimentary hunting skills, used to depend on the forest for food. They were living in poor conditions; famines, wild animals and diseases often troubled them. And we, from our high chairs, thought that this was nature at work and we need not interfere. They needed help and we overlooked and refused to be the supporting people that we could have been. Meanwhile, Kamsa showed up and helped them with all honesty. He thus, won their trust and unwavering loyalty. He became a god to them.'

'So, you were guilt-ridden for not helping the tribal people around you?' Mukunda asked.

'In a sense, we were! When the Xar people became Xarnakht, it is then that we realized that thousands of years of our arrogance had brought unspeakable suffering upon those people. A little help could have saved them from the clutches of Kamsa,' the vibration replied.

'You can still stop the Xarnakhts. Shake away any feeling of guilt that you have and rebuild and repopulate Gurupur,' Mukunda said.

'We are way past that point. After everyone in Gurupur, including the royals, was killed, I was invoked. I am not a person, I cannot repopulate Gurupur or bring back its glory.'

'Then what are you? A computer programme?' Mukunda asked.

'I am the unified consciousness of each and every Guru person who ever lived on Prithvi,' Grutvator replied.

'If you cannot reinstate Guru people or Gurupur, why were you made in the first place?' Mukunda asked.

'I was made to guide a world devoid of the Wise. I was made as a last beacon of hope for times when darkness and despair of evil would take over Prithvi. I was made to be the guardian of Prithvi.'

'But how do you plan to do that sitting here, in the farthest side of the moon?' Mukunda asked.

'As I said, I am a beacon of hope. And people in need are drawn to hope. Look at you, you are in distress and you found me,' Grutvator relayed.

'I am not distressed.... And what do you mean *I found you*?'

'You are distressed and you came here looking for answers, not to help the Xarnakht kingdom,' Grutvator relayed.

'I am not distressed. What do you even know about me?' he replied with a little anger in his voice.

'A lot, younger brother.'

'Why have you been calling me "brother", anyway?' Mukunda said, and it was now apparent that he was perturbed.

'Because I am your brother! Son of Krishna!'

Mukunda stood up, 'Who are you? And how do you know his name?'

'A son, no matter where he is, never forgets his father. Why wouldn't I know his name?' Grutvator replied.

'My father was trapped on Bhoomi. You are lying. How can he be father to the voice of bygone people?'

'Your father was, indeed, father to all Guru people. And I am their collective mind and voice, so he is my father too,' Grutvator replied.

'He had another family that we never knew about?'

'Your father designed Prithvi and made it inhabitable too. During the Jurassic era, he visited Prithvi through a computer simulation. But Kamsa used Paramganak to push Krishna's conscious self on to Prithvi. Krishna got trapped here and, in a scuffle with wild beasts, got injured too. Krishna was able to go back to his world but his blood ran through the rivers here and made the riverbeds fertile. Along those riverbeds, we, the Guru people, evolved. That was the reason we had a head-start compared to other people and had intellect much beyond our time and place,' Grutvator relayed.

'My father created all these wonderful worlds and people, but he abandoned me,' Mukunda said in a sombre voice and misty eyes.

'He hasn't abandoned you. It's just that you haven't been able to find him yet!' Grutvator replied.

'I left my family and my world in search of him. I thought I will seek him and will ask him all the whys that had been bothering me,' Mukunda replied.

'You were not looking for him for answers. You were seeking him, because you love him. You want to be by his side,' Grutvator relayed.

'Then why could I never find him? Where did I go wrong?'

'We both are children of the same father. But your love is laced with anger and bitterness. I, on other hand, have only gratitude for him and I know that he loves me and thus he is always by my side,' Grutvator replied.

'My people say and believe that he got trapped on Bhoomi and his fate was in peril. I believe that he could have accompanied us along. For some reasons known only to him, he stayed behind,' Mukunda said.

'He couldn't have accompanied other Manavas. He could never

have stepped on Prithvi or in this Universe–1408. He visited Prithvi once through simulations and all equations changed. His physical presence here would have been dangerous,' Grutvator replied.

'What do you mean dangerous? And is he still alive on Bhoomi?'

'He created this world. And when he did, he knew he could never be here. For us this is the real world and the real universe. For Krishna, this is a figment of his thoughts, a dream. His presence will make this whole place, this whole world collapse,' Grutvator replied.

'Just tell me this, is he still there on Bhoomi? Does he still survive?'

'Bhoomi, a few thousand years after the Manavas left, collapsed. There is no Bhoomi now. He could have travelled to other worlds, but that would be too optimistic,' Grutvator replied.

'How do you know about the fate of Bhoomi?'

'Have you ever wondered why I am causing these tremors for conveying my messages instead of speaking to you directly?' Grutvator said.

'Because sound doesn't propagate well here on the moon, I guess!' Mukunda said.

'Fair point! But no,' Grutvator said.

18

The Fabric of the Universe

'Get prepared to hear what no man has ever known and what was later known but withheld even from the Manavas,' Grutvator relayed.

'How to cause quakes?' Mukunda replied, not sensing the magnitude of what he was about to hear.

'How to alter gravity itself,' Grutvator replied.

Mukunda's eye widened. 'You are causing these moonquakes by playing around with gravity?' he asked.

'I indeed am.'

'You can collapse the moon, if that is what you are doing,' he exclaimed.

'I can hear gravity, I can see gravity, I can sense gravity, I can taste gravity, I can smell gravity and I can alter it up to the smallest fraction,' Grutvator replied.

'That's impossible! These tremors are your spoken words?' Mukunda said.

'They are. And if I raise my voice, I can make this very moon collide into Prithvi.'

'I know you won't! That was not what Guru people stood for,' Mukunda said. 'They stood for betterment of the world. That is why they concealed the knowledge of gravity altering, right?'

'They created a module called Grutvator and kept it for doomsday. They knew that if ever any power strong enough to uproot the Guru people arises, that power would be catastrophic for the world too. So, they made me and kept me dormant. They never gave me other senses, lest I get detected and destroyed too. They made gravity my language and marked moon as my abode. Near home and yet hard to detect. The day the last Guru kingdom was uprooted, a basic rocket catapulted me to the moon. And then the Grutvator module was invoked and I was planted here,' Grutvator replied.

'How do you perceive gravity? How do you alter it?' Mukunda asked.

'Under normal circumstances, I would not have revealed it to you. But you need to know now in order to gauge the depth of the storm that is brewing. But still, you cannot pass this information on to anybody else,' Grutvator warned Mukunda.

'I promise, your wisdom shall stay safe with me alone.'

'Gravity is not a force but an aftereffect of an endless cosmic play. The whole universe is made up of a space fabric, constituting of a field and an array of particles connected by that very field. The wise Guru people used to call the field Gurutva field and the particles Gurutva particles. The field is unique and has no measurable mass of its own. However, it interacts with the matter so that we can see or observe and lend them mass. The particle–matter interaction is rate sensitive. For a matter to move in space, it has to cleave its interaction with surrounding Gurutva particles and move on and interact with the next. This very interaction is rate-sensitive. In the absence of external force, a matter having mass can stay still forever and the same matter, when set in motion, can keep on hopping from one interaction to another at constant rate, which is measured as constant velocity. To change this rate of change of interaction, and hence accelerating a particle through Gurutva particle-field web, needs external force,' Grutvator relayed.

'That's conservation of momentum that you are talking about.

This proposed field of yours causes the inertia?' Mukunda asked.

'It's not a proposed field. It exists and I can see it too. I, as a matter of fact, manipulate its density to play with gravity,' he replied.

'But this energy field, you said, governs momentum. Then what effect will its manipulation have on gravity?' Mukunda asked.

'Gravity, as I said before, is not a force but an aftereffect. This momentum web created by matter–particle bonding generates gravity. This web, for instance, treats Prithvi and all its occupants as one mass-momentum system and then will not allow any object on it to fly off; until and unless objects develop a considerable momentum of their own, by gaining enormous mass or great speeds. A person standing on Prithvi belongs to the mass-momentum system of Prithvi. Prithvi belongs to the mass-momentum system of the sun and the sun belongs to that of the Milky Way and so on and so forth. The Gurutva force indirectly generates gravity by limiting the rate of change of matter-particle bonds,' Grutvator relayed.

'And the upper limit on this rate of change of matter-particle bonds is the speed of light, isn't it?' Mukunda said.

'It very well is. The Gurutva field-particle web prevents any interacting matter from accelerating beyond that speed limit. Also, what you see as time dilation for very fast-moving objects is, in reality, distance dilation. A very fast-moving object increases the matter-particle interaction exponentially, causing same distance to effectively seem longer and same object effectively seems heavier. And thus giving an impression of time dilation,' Grutvator explained.

'Is this a one-way interaction, or does matter also affect the field-particle web?' Mukunda asked.

'Beyond a critical mass, matter also starts affecting this web,' Grutvator replied.

'I knew this one! Massive object bends the space-time around them, too!' Mukunda said.

'It doesn't bend anything. What a massive object does is it increases the packing density of the Gurutva particle around them. That's why light bends as it enters a denser medium and also takes longer to make it's way through this denser medium,' he replied.

'So, even as I speak, I am bound by this field-particle web, this Gurutva field?' Mukunda asked in amazement.

'Yes, you are! And as you speak, the very minute subatomic particles that make you up are renewing their mass from the energy drawn from this field,' Grutvator replied.

'You said that this knowledge was withheld from us Manavas. Who among us knew this?' Mukunda asked.

'Do I need to point out such an obvious fact to a Manava of such intelligence?'

'My father did, Krishna did! He concealed everything worthwhile from all of us!' Mukunda said.

'He concealed this fact because broadcasting this one small, yet important, piece of information could have placed universes after universes in danger.'

'So, he feared that a person like Kamsa might take hold of this info and bring the Manava order to its knees?' Mukunda said.

'But, alas, that is what is about to happen now. And this time, your father is not around to prevent it. You will have to stop Kamsa all by yourself,' Grutvator replied.

'He now knows about this field-particle web too?' he asked.

'Not only has he gained access to this information but is developing an intergalactic missile to disrupt this field and end this whole galaxy and several others,' Grutvator replied.

'An intergalactic missile to end all galaxies... The only way he can accomplish this insanity is by spotting the centre of gravity of the Milky Way and the inbound Andromeda galaxy and shifting that. He wants to expedite the long, pending collision of these two galaxies. Doesn't he?' Mukunda spoke, even as he got goosebumps from both fear and excitement.

'At the current rate, Andromeda will start smashing the Milky Way in the next four billion years, but he wants to manipulate the Gurutva field to generate new mass. This will shift the centre of gravity of the Milky Way and the Andromeda system and make them collapse in a couple of decades,' Grutvator said.

'How do I stop him from destroying this world?' Mukunda said.

'Simple solution to a complex problem, dislodge Paramganak. Unplug him,' Grutvator replied.

Mukunda kept quiet for a few second before speaking. 'It won't be that simple. Kamsa must have enough provisions in place to keep the Paramganak computer system plugged and alive.'

'So, you do get the gravity of the problem?' Grutvator relayed.

'I do and it seems like a job beyond my capability,' Mukunda replied.

'I could have done it myself but for a problem. There is this small town midway, a town you people call Ksharanpur. If I direct a gravitational shock wave towards the Xurabhur desert to shatter that facility where Paramganak is housed, it will play havoc on that town of yours too,' Grutvator replied.

'Do you mean Ksharanpur is orbiting Prithvi?' Mukunda asked.

'And is protected by the Gurutva force field too. Krishna was running out of time, so he created a world, insulated from the outside world. But he forgot to account for the glitches in the field. And you escaped out of Ksharanpur,' Grutvator relayed.

'And then I brought Kamsa back to life. My father made all these beautiful things and I invoked the evil,' Mukunda lamented.

'You did not. Your discontent did. Your father sacrificed

everything for your future and built you a safe and wonderful world. But you were discontent with it all and mistrusted the intentions of your own father. That discontent was the soil on which Kamsa grew back,' Grutvator relayed.

'I need to pay for this deed of mine. I resurrected Kamsa and I will have to bring him to an end,' Mukunda said.

'And how do you plan to do that?' Grutvator asked.

'I will go back to Prithvi and forge an alliance of all kingdoms and will dislodge that very facility that I built,' he replied.

'Your plan on paper sounds good. But first, how do you plan on getting back to Prithvi? You can try asking but they won't let you back. Second, there isn't much time left,' Grutvator relayed.

Mukunda paused for a moment and then spoke. 'The Jaradium that I have been making here was never meant to raise an army? It was required to build a heat-shield for the intergalactic missile?'

'Heat and impact shield, yes indeed,' Grutvator replied.

'So, they never had any plan to rescue Xarnika?' Mukunda then said.

'Xarnika is already back home. As soon as you left, they sent out word. They thought sending you on exile and concealing the facility will convince Commander Xhi to set Xarnika free. But Xhi insisted on waiting for three months, to make sure that you were indeed gone. This irked Kamsa and he directed the test missile on the small kingdoms south of Chinjing. The mountains flattened, farming fields grew into hills, lakes and rivers threw their water thousands of feet away and wind patterns changed. The topography and weather changes inflicted unspeakable hardship on the people living there. Many perished, many migrated and quite a few who never had anywhere else to go, stayed back. A cold wave started covering Prithvi, from the east to the west. Xhi, fearing that this could be the fate of his people soon, released Xarnika,' Grutvator said.

'How do I go back then? Can you fix something?' Mukunda asked.

'Can I catapult you back to Prithvi? I can but not without crushing you to your bones? Can I plan an escape for you, tacitly? That I very efficiently can,' Grutvator relayed.

'For a being with no voice, you speak very complex words. Tell me in few simple words, what escape plan do you have on your mind?' Mukunda said.

'They are fuelling up the Intergalactic missile. So, within a couple of days, they should be launching it. They plan to circumambulate Prithvi and then this moon to gain enough velocity for the intergalactic journey ahead. We have just one chance to grab the bargaining chip. I will trap the missile in my gravity net and keep it orbiting here. You will then proclaim this as your work and ask them to give you a safe passage back to Prithvi. You will also promise them to return to your abode, but you won't. Once you are there, you shall reach that facility of yours and bring it down,' Grutvator replied.

'What if he doesn't give in and sets the warhead here in orbit?' Mukunda asked.

'This is a causal world that we live in. The effect can only follow the cause and can never precede it. We have to take this calculated risk,' Grutvator replied.

'What if I talk sense into them, rather than blackmailing them,' Mukunda said.

'I have shown you your options. The decision of which path to opt for, is yours. But remember, your action as well as your inaction will have consequences. You will have to choose the action or inaction whose consequence you can live with,' Grutvator said.

'Allow me some time before I decide to blackmail the most powerful and most evil of all empires on Prithvi,' he replied.

'Weigh your options well, my brother. Also, I will have to phase out and reinstate your communication lines with the command module orbiting above us. Any further blackouts will make Paramganak suspicious. I will reach out to you again when you are prepared. I am now lifting the communication blockade, it should be up in the next ten minutes or so,' Grutvator relayed.

With messages from Grutvator falling silent, Garuda now spoke, 'Master! Are we trapped here? Are we sure this new alien being won't plan against us too?'

'We were already trapped in a world away from our own. I am more worried about all those people on Prithvi and all the Manavas back home.'

'Master, the day we leaped across our world, times have been difficult for us,' Garuda said.

'It's all about cause and effect. The actions we pursued lead us to these consequences. And the manner in which we act now will lead to future consequences. We will have to be very cautious about our next step,' Mukunda replied.

Garuda blinked his glowing eyes in agreement and support. Mukunda raised his eyes and looked into the dark space above. It was haplessly empty and mercilessly endless. The only specks of hope were those far and few glittering stars spread across the space. Before Mukunda could realize, his eyes were moist. Those specks of hope on that abysmally dark sky were now blurry at best.

Before Mukunda could clear his throat, a voice grew on his communication line.

'Mukunda, hope you are fine down there,' Xari said.

'We are good. Why do you ask?' he said.

'I had some trouble connecting to you for a good hour or so,' she replied.

'Hey! Can I ask you something?' Mukunda then said.

'Go ahead, Mukunda,' she replied.

'It's quite lonely down here, plus work hours are indeed long. Can I go back to Prithvi for a few days?' Mukunda said.

'I am afraid, Mukunda, this is one thing I am not authorized to do for you,' Xari replied.

'Why would that be so?'

'These are complex matters. Our enemy is holding Xarnika hostage. If the enemy spots you on Prithvi, he may inflict harm on our little princess. And I suppose, no one wants that. Not you at least, of all the people. Am I right?' she replied.

'I understand and I wish only the best for Xarnika. But I cannot be stationed here forever. Someday, I will have to go back,' he replied.

'Trust me, that day will arrive soon. But times are not right for your re-entry. Moreover, everyone is so focused on securing Xarnika's release. You may just complicate what is already very complex,' Xari replied.

'Well, let me know when they secure Xarnika's release,' he said.

'For sure. As a matter of fact, I will make sure that you get ample time to spend with Xarnika, once the tides turn in our favour,' Xari replied.

'Xari, have you figured out what is causing these communication blackouts?' Mukunda asked.

'Paramganak and I are analysing the nature of these disturbances. But for the moment, they are beyond our understanding. Why do you ask?' she replied.

'The very idea that my only link to you and Prithvi is vulnerable makes me anxious. What if I need your assistance and am not able to contact you?' he said.

'Relax, Mukunda. These are passing interferences; the whole command module is at your disposal. Please stop being anxious. I am here for you. We will find some way around these blackouts,' she replied.

'Thanks for the assurance,' Mukunda replied.

'On a similar note though, four Prithvi days from now, the command module will be shut for a whole day for maintenance. I will check on you before going offline. Hope you won't mind,' Xari replied.

19

The Subverted Systems

'Any reply?' Mukunda scribbled on a piece of paper.

Garuda flashed a message on a little display on his front, reading: 'None, whatsoever.'

'Keep on sending messages, I need to speak to him.' He then scribbled below the prior one. Garuda read the message and blinked his eyes in agreement.

Mukunda, meanwhile, kept pacing up and down. He was steadily running out of patience. He reached for the piece of paper again and scribbled: The missile launches soon. Garuda read it too and relayed. But there was no reply in return. Mukunda mumbled some curse words and finally wrote on that paper: I have made up my mind. Garuda relayed the message and waited eagerly.

A noise grew over Mukunda's communication line to the command module and then the line felt silent. They were now in a comm blackout.

The surface shook a little. 'Good!' the inbound message read.

'They say that the command module will be offline for maintenance, but I know what they are actually up to,' Mukunda said and Garuda relayed.

'Good! Now you understand,' Grutvator relayed.

'I have a suggestion though. Can you trap the missile here and catapult it on an unretractable path, away from its course?' he asked.

'Sure, I can. And then instead of two galaxies smashing into each other, many galaxies would be set on a path of collision. Kamsa will then thank us for doing what was beyond his capabilities,' Grutvator relayed.

'Why is he hell-bent on destroying Prithvi and the people he calls his own sons?' Mukunda then asked.

'He realizes that he can vanquish the whole of Prithvi in a matter of minutes. He is about to run out of enemies. And for him to exist he always needs one.' Grutvator replied.

'He wants to destroy this world so that he can transition to the next,' Mukunda said.

'His idea of fun!' Grutvator replied.

'Will Ksharanpur survive the blow?' he asked.

'The gravitational reshuffling will rip apart its protective shields even before Prithvi. Manavas won't have a chance,' Grutvator replied.

'So, four days from now, you intercept and take hostage that devil's weapon and I will go for Kamsa's jugular,' Mukunda replied as he clenched his fist and his eyes grew wide.

'Deal! Till then do or say nothing. Comply with whatever they ask you to do. I shall speak again once I have this Xari of yours by her neck,' Grutvator said and then fell silent.

After a good ten minutes, the comm lines resumed.

·◆·

It was 8 p.m. and Ksharanpur already sported a deserted look. The lake had been turbulent of late and the weather unusually cold. The colder-than-usual wafts of air were keeping people indoors, especially once nightfall engulfed the island city.

Kanha was in the lab that evening, covering for Mohan, who, meanwhile, was busy in a meeting with the empowered councilors. Kanha was supposed to be monitoring an ongoing assignment in Mohan's absence. But that was not what he was doing. He, on the very chair he was supposed to sit and monitor Samganak, was sleeping like a baby. His head was sliding to his right and resting on his own drooping shoulder. He was completely unaware of the automated code getting executed on Samganak. After all, he had had a long and tough day at school.

Samganak, meanwhile, was throwing up codes and figures and whatnot on its screen. But then, a glowing red line of text started appearing on the screen repeatedly. It could not have been a part of the project as all it read was: 'Danger!'

Samganak was repeatedly displaying that text, but Kanha was fast asleep.

The text, after a dozen repetitions changed, to: 'Dangerous times ahead. Press any key to know'. But the text displays kept flashing without a response. It was then that Samganak started chiming. But that too fell on deaf ears.

Then suddenly, the chiming and messages stopped. And, the glass full of water, placed on the table beside Kanha's chair started trembling. Then, the table that it was placed on started shaking too and the glass tipped over and shattered into pieces. Kanha now moved and was drifting in and out of his slumber when his chair started trembling violently.

He woke up and jumped from his seat. He looked around and the whole building was shaking. He raised his arm and was about to issue a public warning to be transmitted to the whole of Ksharanpur through his wrist-phone, when the red blinking text on the screen caught his eye.

'This is not a Prithvi-quake. This is a warning message for Manavas!'

Kanha read the text and muttered, 'Who are you?'

But his words bore no answers. He then lowered his arm and moved towards the panel. He typed in, asking for the identity of the person flashing those messages on the screen. But then instead of messages, a voice emanated from Samganak:

'I am Grutvator.'

'Kanha hearing that heavy reverberating voice, asked, 'Grutvator who?'

'I am the voice of the Guru people, who lived on Prithvi ages before you. I am here to warn the Manavas of Ksharanpur about the imminent danger that they face,' Grutvator said.

'This system and all its access lines are highly secured, how did you gain access to them?' Kanha instead asked.

'Of all the things that I have said so far, this is what caught your interest?' Grutvator replied.

'You have hacked into our lifeline, so yes, this is what interests as well as concerns me,' Kanha replied.

'I need to talk to Mohan. I suppose he is not here; will you be a charm and have him brought here?' Grutvator replied.

'He is somewhere important. I wouldn't call him for you. Tell me whatever message you have for us.'

'You are too young and naïve to handle it. You don't understand anything that goes on around here. I will deal with Mohan alone,' Grutvator replied.

'I perfectly understand everything around here,' he shot back.

'You don't know how I hacked into this Samganak. That's the level of your cluelessness. Now summon Mohan or…' Grutvator said.

'Or what? You freak!' he replied, his voice trembling with anger.

'Wait! Just wait!' Grutvator said. And after a couple of seconds, he said again, 'Or, I will summon him myself,' he said and Kanha's wrist-phone started shaking.

He turned his gaze towards the shaking wrist-phone and saw it dialling Mohan. Even before, Kanha could move and disconnect the call, Mohan answered. 'I am a little busy right now, Kanha. Anything urgent?' Mohan said.

Kanha was shell-shocked enough and he kept quiet. Seeing his pale face and eyes filled with anguish, Mohan exclaimed, 'Kanha! What's the matter?'

'Kanha is fine. I need to talk to you. Head for the lab now,' Grutvator said, disconnecting the call.

The screen meanwhile was displaying images and texts about Gurupur and its bygone people. Kanha knew that Mohan was on his way, so he pulled up his chair and sat staring at the screen.

'This doesn't bode well for us. Last time someone hacked into our systems, we had to abandon our home planet. We can't afford that now,' he murmured to himself.

'You don't have to be afraid of me. It's not me that poses a danger to you people,' Grutvator replied.

Kanha sat in silence and tried to focus on the images and texts being displayed on the screen, to keep his nerves in check. After a good ten minutes or so, he was completely submerged in the imageries when the lab's main door opened.

Mohan rushed in, accompanied by Shyam.

'What's the matter? Are you okay?' Shyam yelled as Mohan rushed towards the erratically behaving Samganak.

'I am fine. But we have a guest here,' Kanha replied, pointing towards Samganak.

Shyam looked up and said with his voice raised, 'We have been through this several times. Why can't we fix the Samganak once and for all? How come people just waltz into our systems?'

'This is not a hack attack. Not some rogue codes trying to interrupt Samganak. This is a complete takeover,' Mohan replied, trying to regain control of Samganak.

'What do you mean?' Shyam yelled.

'This is not the Samganak we nurtured. It is now under complete command and control of this unexplained force. I am trying everything to break into it. They haven't just changed the lock; they have changed the damn door!' Mohan said, dark clouds of helplessness engulfing his voice.

Samganak's screen was now flooded with endlessly flowing encrypted messages. But then the messages suddenly paused and the room reverberated with Grutvator's voice, 'Are you done panicking?'

'Not until I get back control of my machine,' Mohan yelled back.

'I cannot relent control until I am done talking with you. I do not have a voice of my own, so I am using the very architecture of your Samganak as a vocal chord,' Grutvator replied.

'To subjugate Samganak on the architecture level, one needs to know its architecture. Even I do not know it thoroughly. Who are you?' Mohan replied.

'I am Grutvator, the collective consciousness of the people of Gurupur—the people who descended from a single drop of Krishna's blood. They are now gone, but they left me behind. I am all of them. I am Krishna's other son!' Grutvator replied.

'What are you doing to our systems?' Shyam said, his voice subdued and eyes widened in disbelief.

'I have overridden all its learning and have implemented my schema on its hardware itself,' Grutvator replied.

'What is he talking about?' Shyam said, looking towards Mohan.

'Samganak learns like a Manava. He remembers each input like an experience and then his future decisions stem from those experiences and their previous outcomes. Neural learning, if you will,' Mohan replied.

'He erased all of Samganak's memory and gave him a new personality? He destroyed eons' worth of work that we did?' Shyam murmured.

'I did not. I have just subdued his original personality and given him a new identity for a while,' Grutvator replied.

'Like the epicortex part of our Manava brain! You have found the ultimate override switch in Samganak!' Mohan said, his face pale with astonishment.

'And I promise I will give you your Samganak back, as it was. But listen to me first' Grutvator said.

'But we will need to know how you did it to begin with. We don't want to be in such a vulnerable position in the future,' Shyam said.

'That is what my message is about. You people, unless you act fast and decisively, have no future,' Grutvator said.

Shyam looked at Mohan, but said nothing. They were both perturbed but kept quiet, processing all that they were listening to.

'And, I will let you know how I took over your Samganak. Because the methods I used are the exact ones that will tear Ksharanpur apart in a few months from now. And you have just four days to avert it all,' Grutvator's voice echoed in that high-walled hall.

'We are listening,' Mohan said.

'Krishna withheld the architecture because had it been documented, there could have been a chance that some person with mal-intent someday could have gotten access to it. The threat was not the Samganak's architecture per se but what was hidden inside its deepest corners,' Grutvator said.

'What is in there that even we don't know about?' Shyam said.

'The one secret that can destroy this world and others. The one secret that I have used to control your Samganak,' Grutvator said.

'Do we now get to know that one secret? Or are we still out of bounds from this elite knowledge of yours?' Mohan scoffed.

'You were kept in the dark for your own good. But now that one secret, kept safe for millions of years, has fallen into the hands of darkness. And those hands are hell-bent on using that sacred knowledge for devastation. But to understand that one secret, you must know what it can do and what it actually did to Samganak,' Grutvator said.

'Oh! Gentle being, please do tell,' Shyam said, his voice now mellow and his brows a little less arched.

'When Krishna took over the reins of the technologies used by the Manavas, there were only two computing technologies. They both were fighting for dominance, while being oblivious of their own shortfalls. Transistor-based technology had an intrinsic upper limit on packing density and the quantum coupled systems, as it turned out, were unreliable on large scales. Krishna then took it upon himself and built a more humane computer based on a technology which no one ever thought could be used for such purposes—Piezoelectric Effect. He fabricated such nano-sized cubes, which on application of physical pressure, generated electric charges. He made a whole matrix of them, millions of such cubes, one after another in a network, which were inter-joined by nano-tubes. As and when pressure was applied to a nano-cube, it would generate electricity and, that in turn, was fed to the fragile network of reverse piezoelectric nano-tubes. Those fragile nano-tubes, under the influence of the piezoelectricity, would extend laterally and apply pressure on further nano-cubes. The more the application of charge on nano-tubes, the more they would strengthen with time, owing to a special organic dye applied on them. And the tubes which were rarely used, over the period of time, were snapped by that very special dye,' Grutvator said.

'He made a neural network out of nanoparticles?' Mohan said.

'And trained them to compute real-life scenarios,' Grutvator replied.

'No wonder, Samganak always had a personality of his own. He was always like a friend…' Shyam said.

'He is still your friend and will always remain so. As soon as I relinquish control over his neural networks, he will be back to his usual self again,' Grutvator assured them.

'How did you, pardon my words, subvert such a beautifully designed system?' Shyam then asked.

'I, as I said, have no voice. I can only speak through gravity. I can modulate gravity. I use it to monitor Prithvi from a safe distance. And I am using it to use your Samganak to relay my message,' Grutvator said.

'You have managed to pinpoint gravity-induced pressure changes on the nano-cubes?' Mohan said.

'The easiest way to just waltz into your systems,' Grutvator replied.

'Gravity is a force of nature, how on Prithvi can you modulate it?' Shyam said, his voice wobbling in disbelief.

'Krishna knew that, he discovered the secret of doing so. He found a new force field which, when altered, could modulate gravity. The Wise People of Gurupur found this out too. And they, just like Krishna, kept this knowledge a secret. But now there is someone quite special, you would never expect who, who now has access to this secret. And he has no qualms about using it against whole Prithvi,' Grutvator replied.

'Who?' Shyam asked.

'We sent him to Prithvi to wither and die. How did he survive?' Mohan said, aghast.

'He survived that day but only to be killed at my people's

hands,' Grutvator replied.

'Then who?' Shyam asked again.

'Him!' Grutvator replied.

'How? If he got killed eventually?' Mohan asked.

'He was resurrected. He rose from the desert, like a phoenix and now rules over those deserts. He will not stop unless he vanquishes the whole of Prithvi and destroys it completely,' Grutvator replied.

'Who brought such a wretched creature back to life?' Shyam said.

'Your grandson, son of Krishna and Radhika did!' Grutvator replied.

'Mukunda! You know about his whereabouts?' Kanha chirped in.

'I do. He is here with me. Under my protection and at a safe distance from the storm that he helped brew,' Grutvator replied.

'And where are *you* right now?' Shyam said.

'On the moon. On the farther side of it,' Grutvator replied.

'I don't believe this! I need my grandson here, with me. Send him back, right now,' Shyam yelled.

'Would you rather spend four-odd days with your grandson or a fulfilling worthy life with him?' Grutvator asked.

Shyam sank into a nearby chair and holding the chair's arm said, 'I just want my grandson back. My daughter-in-law needs him too. Mukunda needs his mother. Please release him and I will pay any price,' Shyam said in a helpless voice.

'I have not held him here in captivity, Kamsa has. He now resides in a computer system that he calls Paramganak. He planned everything and sent your grandson on the moon on the pretext of acquiring Jaradium. I am here to help and avert imminent disasters. If we don't act in time, no one will survive; me, you, your dreamy city and your grandson—all will be sacrificed at the altar of Kamsa's megalomania!' Grutvator replied.

Shyam was about to yell in frustration when Mohan looked at him. 'Let me talk to our guest.'

'What kind of a catastrophe are we talking about here?' Mohan said.

'Now we are talking! Kamsa has gotten hold of the secret of gravity modulation. He has built an intergalactic nuclear-fueled missile and has equipped it with a gravity-bomb. He has pinpointed it to reach a conclusive distance and there he will set it off,' Grutvator said.

'Big deal, some firecrackers in deep dark space!' Mohan scoffed again.

'By the way, when I told the same to Mukunda he figured it out, without me prompting,' Grutvator said.

Mohan brows arched and fine lines began to appear on his forehead as he scrambled for an answer to the riddle.

'He wants to expedite the collapse of Andromeda unto our Milky Way. We will be bombarded by the stars from afar,' Kanha said, jumping at his place out of sheer anguish.

'See, the kids are way smarter than you folks from Madhavpur,' Grutvator said.

Shyam nodded vehemently. 'They indeed are! And that's why I just want a safe and secure future for them.'

'How much time until the launch?' Mohan said.

'Just four days,' Grutvator replied.

20

The Nandaki Arises

'So, this Universe 1408, planetary position-wise, is an exact copy of our prior universe. If he does succeed, how many days until first impact of the blast?' Shyam said.

Before the rumbling from Samganak could grow into a voice and Grutvator could reply, Kanha yelled, 'Few months at the most, for a missile to travel to a favourable blast spot and within another few months, the gravity shifts will start tearing us apart.'

'He just needs to place the missile from where he can shift the centre of gravity of two galaxies and nature would do the rest. He has chosen three points for the blast. First is near Prithvi and takes less time to travel but the impact would be low. Second one is a bit farther but an optimal mix of distance and blast impact. The third is still farther to travel but the impact will be beyond all imagination,' Grutvator said.

'How do we stop him from doing so?' Shyam said.

'We can't stop him from launching the missile. All preparations have been done, he can set it off any minute now,' Grutvator replied.

'Can he be launching the missile as we speak?' Shyam said.

'He has some last-minute double checks to perform, so, no, he won't, for another four days. But the point is, he can!' Grutvator replied.

'How do we stop him then?' Mohan said.

'We will not try stopping him, but we can always entrap him and buy us some time. See, the journey the missile has to make is enormous and using nuclear blasts as propulsion fuels alone wouldn't cut it. He plans to take a quick sling around the moon. I will then capture the missile and keep it in orbit, while we get boots on ground and try dislodging and destroying Paramganak. If we take down Paramganak then, it will be the end of Kamsa,' Grutvator said.

'What happens to the missile then?' Shyam asked.

'I will release it and let it travel into deep space. Hopefully without Paramganak in the picture, the warhead won't be triggered. If you wish, I can also impart it enough momentum away from both the galaxies,' Grutvator said.

'Why are we risking it, what if the warhead is pre-programmed to detonate? Can't you hold the missile in orbit for, let's say, a few decades to come?' Mohan said.

'Mohan! Can you lift a twenty-kilo boulder?' Grutvator said.

'I very well can!' he replied.

'And for twenty days at a stretch?' Grutvator then said.

'We get it, keeping that missile in orbit forever will drain you out,' Shyam said.

'What if he detonates it here, in your moon's orbit?' Mohan said.

'He very well can but that would destroy only a tiny segment of this solar system. Prithvi, though, will be completely devastated from the impact from both the moons,' Grutvator replied.

'What do you mean by both the moons? Whose moons?' Mohan said.

'Prithvi's moon, what else?' Grutvator replied.

'Is this moon as old as the one you are lodged on?' Shyam asked.

'It is a fairly recent one, it formed a few million years ago,' Grutvator replied.

'Are you sure it formed recently?' Shyam again asked.

'Affirmative! Its gravity signature suggests it was formed fairly recently,' Grutvator replied.

'You talked about Krishna, by any means do you know about his whereabouts? I mean, is he still there on Bhoomi?' Shyam asked.

'I am glad you asked. I was avoiding this very topic, as it entails the pleasant and the unpleasant, both,' Grutvator said.

Shyam nodded. 'We are ready for both.'

'When the Guru people discovered the secrets of gravity, we started scanning our known universe. We found the signatures of his existence all over. He started communicating with us. He wanted to talk to you people too, but the gravitational shield around Ksharanpur wouldn't let him do so. For him, the safety of Ksharanpur was paramount, so he never compromised the shield. When the Guru people perished, it made him sad. But when I materialized and reestablished contact with him, his happiness knew no bounds,' Grutvator replied.

'Go ahead, share the unpleasant part too,' Shyam said.

'In the last signals that I picked, he talked about Bhoomi imploding unto itself. The whole universe he said was collapsing. He planned on leaving for a younger universe,' Grutvator replied.

'By any chance, was he planning to come visit 1408, our Universe?' Mohan said.

'He cannot enter into this realm; it would cause the collapse of this universe,' Grutvator said.

'Is this why he never accompanied us?' Kanha asked.

'He chose loneliness and despair for the sake of the Manavas,' Grutvator replied.

'He could have mentioned something, at least Mukunda wouldn't have wandered in search of answers,' Kanha said.

'He did what he deemed right, Kanha. Now, gentle being, finish what you had to say,' Shyam said.

'He probably left his home realm; I am not sure what happened afterwards. But I had no contact with him after that. This silence is baffling; I fear if the journey bore any fruit. If he made it out of Bhoomi safely...' Grutvator said.

Shyam nodded. 'The planetary object you refer to as second moon, is it visible on Prithvi's sky all year round?'

'It appears once every two years, it has a very long orbit around Prithvi,' Grutvator replied.

'Mohan, how many dust bodies used to orbit Bhoomi?' Shyam asked.

'At least two,' Mohan replied.

'Prithvi has no dust bodies encircling it. Am I right?' Shyam said.

'They should be there but they aren't,' Grutvator replied.

"Krishna is safe and knows about the danger. He did those little tricks and made those orbiting dust bodies join and formed this moon,' Shyam said.

'What purpose will the second moon serve?' Mohan asked.

'It will cushion the impact of the great collision of galaxies that is about to happen,' Grutvator replied.

'Does that mean Krishna is safe?' Shyam said with jubilance in his voice.

'I don't want to dampen your spirits, but the second moon was formed when he was still on Bhoomi. I have tried everything possible and he is untraceable. We will have to act on the assumption that Krishna did not make it safely out of his abode. We will have to be ready for doomsday,' Grutvator said.

'I may be out of line here, but if Krishna couldn't contact us because of our shield, is it compromised now?' Kanha said.

'I made a vent in it to communicate with you people; I will close it once we are done. But before that, here is the rest of the plan. I will capture the missile and use that as a negotiation chip to send Mukunda back to Prithvi. Once on Prithvi, Mukunda will head for Xarlok, an army of Ksharanpur soldiers will meet him there and try to destroy Paramganak,' Grutvator said.

'He is just a kid, let Mukunda go back home to his mother. We will go and liberate Xarlok,' Shyam said.

'Mukunda has seen Xarlok, he is familiar with all the threats there. Moreover, he is not a kid now; he is all grown up and intelligent,' Grutvator replied.

'How does he look now?' Shyam said in a mellow tone.

'I have no conventional vision, but I have read his gravitational signature. He is almost six feet tall and built like a war machine,' Grutvator said.

'His journey has taught him well,' Shyam said.

'I cannot keep the shields channels open any longer, I will have to go,' Grutvator said.

Shyam nodded. 'You open the routes to Xarlok and we shall reach there on the fourth day from today. Goodbye now, gentle being,' Shyam said.

'Also, I have a gift for the people of Ksharanpur. Actually, Krishna crafted this small present with his own hands. You shall receive it once I relinquish control over Samganak. Bye for now,' Grutvator said and the sound from Samganak fell flat. The befuddling mystery codes running across Samganak's screen vanished too.

Then as soon as Samganak returned to normal, its screen read: 'Loading Module Nandaki.'

•◆

Samganak's chassis split open and it was shining bright blue. They all looked at each other in amazement and while Mohan and Kanha stood their ground, Shyam finally mustered the courage to peep inside the chassis. His eyes were struggling to see what was beyond that vision-blurring bright light. He tried harder and saw a glistening sword lying underneath the light. He stretched his arm and grabbed the hilt of the sword. He tried picking it up, but it was way too heavy to be moved. As he pulled harder, a message written in bright red light appeared adjacent to the sword.

'What is it?' Mohan asked as Shyam struggled and grunted.

'There is a very heavy sword inside it. A big bright sword, but it is either fixed to something or is very heavy to move,' Shyam replied and backed off from the sword.

'Should I try?' Mohan said and leaped forward.

'It says something, some sort of instructions I guess,' Shyam said.

'What does it say?' Mohan said loudly as he reached the bright light.

As Mohan extended his arm to grab the hilt, Shyam mumbled, 'I can't read it!'

Mohan's face flushed as he tried lifting the sword. 'It is beyond me too,' he said while still trying.

Kanha then stepped forward and peeped. 'It's written in Brahmi script,' he said.

'What does it say?' Mohan said, letting go of the hilt.

'It says: "May the worthy one possess the Nandaki sword",' Kanha replied and then tried lifting the sword, but to no avail.

'It seems none of us are worthy of this gift,' Kanha sighed.

'Call all military commanders first thing tomorrow morning and let's see for whom it was carved,' Shyam said.

As the sun ascended the Ksharanpur skies, the gates of Café Evolution were thrown open and all the commanders of the Narayani Sena—senior policy makers, generals, senior commanders, unit commanders and junior commanders—lined up to try their luck with the sword. Each one would approach Samganak and would try lifting the glowing sword. Few gave up in a matter of minutes and few grew adamant, trying very hard for hours.

Shyam was growing impatient and he signalled Shriram to keep the line moving.

Shriram then made sure that no one was allocated more than five minutes to pull the sword up.

The line grew thinner and the overall morale of the aspirants was getting damper. Minutes became hours and hours soon culminated in dusk.

'Each one of us has tried. Young, old, naïve and veterans! This sword was not meant for us,' said Shripathi, a senior advisor on strategic matters of the Narayani Sena.

Gopal walked up to Shyam and Shripathi. 'Either of you mind if I try my hand at this thing?' he asked.

'Go ahead!' Shripathi replied and Shyam nodded in agreement.

Gopal started taking firm steps towards Samganak, while Shyam followed him there. Everyone was eager to see if the old man could raise the coveted sword.

Gopal stood beside Samganak and said, 'Krishna, wherever you are and whatever condition you are in, know that I have always wished well for you. Did I misunderstand you often? I did! Was I ever jealous of you? Maybe, sometimes. Did I ever doubt you? Never! I always considered you as young hope that would steer Manavas clear of every storm. I have been made to understand that fresh trouble awaits us. That this is a lull before the storm. When you were among us, you were completely committed to Manava welfare. And now, I have been told, even in your absence, you have left us with a divine sword. A sword that will cut through the oncoming storm and deliver safe havens of freedom to us. I, now, in the name of your selfless dedication to the might of Manava society, proclaim this sword.'

He then bent a little and extended his arm to grip the hilt. He firmly secured the hilt in the palm of his right hand and pulled it. But the sword didn't relent. Gopal now gripped the hilt with both his hands and pulled vigorously. His face grew red and the blood vessels running from his neck to head swelled. Unable to move the sword for even an inch, he placed his right foot against the Samganak panel and pulled harder. He kept on pulling till his face and neck got completely drenched in sweat. Shyam moved forward and after placing his hand over Gopal's shoulder, said, 'It's not meant to be. Let the sword go.'

Gopal nodded and rose up. Shyam then turned towards Shripathi. 'Let's forget about the sword and plan for our days ahead,' he said.

While Shripathi nodded and turned to signal dispersion to all military commanders, Shriram stepped forward. 'Wait! Where is Raghav? Has he tried his hand at this?' he asked.

'I placed Raghav in charge of the event. I think he skipped his turn here!' Shripathi replied.

Shriram turned and called for Raghav, who came rushing.

'Go! Lift the sword!' Shriram instructed.

Madhav walked towards Samganak and saw the glowing light. 'This light emanating from this device is a beacon of hope. I am sure this sword, whosoever it will obey, will bring peace and prosperity to Ksharanpur,' he said, smiling. He looked back at Shriram, who signalled him to lift the sword with all his might.

Raghav grabbed the hilt and pulled it with all his might. But the sword wouldn't relent. He tried a few more times and then loosened the grip.

'It isn't in a mood to obey you or anybody! This is a riddle beyond all of us,' Shyam said, this frustration apparent in his voice.

Turning around, Shriram announced, 'Gentlemen! Let's vacate this facility and let these good folks at the lab get back to work!'

But before the people could disperse, Raghav turned to say, 'It's not over! We are forgetting someone. We missed out the fiercest commander of ours.'

Mohan smiled and raised his left arm. He dialled on his wrist-phone and said 'Come to the lab, now!'

The crowd dispersed into smaller groups and started conversing.

'They believe Raghav on this?' said a young soldier amongst his group.

'They have gone crazy in desperation!' replied another young soldier, while everyone nodded.

In other groups of older veterans, there were voices too, feeble but audible. 'They cannot accept that an alien voice misguided them. Who knows who planted that shimmering sword in there?' A decorated old soldier mumbled softly.

'Even if they manage to get that sword picked, what will a single sword amount to? We, over the years, have designed and crafted majestic weapons of war! What will a showpiece of sword exactly do?' said another veteran in a muffled-up voice.

'She is here!' Shriram suddenly said.

'The Commander of the Vaishnavi Sena, who once fought and captured Krishna too!' Raghav said.

Even as Radhika walked past the gathered gentry, the voices refused to die down. 'Why her of all?' murmured a young jealous soldier.

'I will be surprised if she so much as manages to grip the hilt of that majestic sword properly!' said another veteran, under his breath.

Shyam was able to hear all this and was losing his patience at a fair pace. 'What have you all brilliant Manavas descended to? If a sword rejects you, will you start blabbering anything?' he yelled.

The voices died down and Radhika kept walking forward with her unwavering gait. She walked right up to the Samganak and peeped into the abyss. 'Krishna made this?' she said, pointing towards the shining sword and light.

'He did,' Shyam replied.

'This is all he left behind for me?' she said, glaring into that brilliant light.

'That is yet to be decided. If you can pick it up, it will be all yours,' Shripathi said.

She turned her gaze towards Shripathi and smiled. She then in a blaze turned towards the abyss and picked the sword by its hilt. She raised it above her head and waved it in the air. It was glowing with a blue radiance and its edges were shining with an ambient light. 'Does anybody doubt my capabilities now? Anyone?' she roared.

'We never doubted your capabilities! My men's only contention was that you haven't been in active services for a while now. They see you as an administrator and not a warrior,' Shripathi replied.

'So, are we together in this now? Will you follow my commands to the end of the worlds? Will we walk and strike under a united command? For Manavas?' she then yelled.

'For Manavas!' Shripathi yelled in ecstasy.

'For Manavas!' the lab reverberated with chants as young recruits and veterans raised the slogan alike.

'On the third day from today, we will cross this realm into enemy's land. We will not only free Prithvi of all malice but will finish the evil once and for all!' Radhika yelled with rage colouring her eyes red and the sword piercing through the air above her.

'For Manavas!' the crowd chanted in unison.

'All commanders, report to your unit. Plan and prepare, as our gentle friend from the moon will open the realms for us. And we will have to be prepared for this mega war,' Shriram announced.

'For Manavas!' they all replied.

The crowd then dispersed and Raghav was also about to leave along with his colleagues when Shyam signalled him to come back.

Shyam then walked up to Shriram as Raghav drew close.

'What have you done?' Shyam said to Raghav.

'I knew she was worthy of the sword!, he replied.

'I already knew exactly for whom Krishna may have left a gift behind. The gift of power!' Shyam replied.

'Yet you never mentioned it? You don't want her to lead, do you?' Shriram said with his brows arched.

'I don't want her to go through more suffering. You have encumbered her with the fate of Manavas. She has virtually lost everyone she ever cared about. I don't want her walking on burning embers again,' Shyam replied.

'I understand! But what you have forgotten is that she is much braver than what you accredit her for!' Shriram replied.

'Had I been in her place, I would have gone mad by now. She, on the other hand, never thought twice before bearing the weight of this sword. Brave she is, but are we so ruthless and selfish to put her in this position, time and again?' Shyam replied.

'I understand your concern. But look at it this way, Krishna believed in her too, that's why he left this Nandaki sword for her,' Shriram said.

'I lost my son. I lost my grandson. Pardon me if I see a daughter in my daughter-in-law. Pardon me for caring for her!' Shyam said, his voice heavy and his hands trembling a little.

Shriram held his trembling hands. 'She is a fierce warrior. She will set everything right. You have to trust her!' he said.

Shyam nodded in agreement.

Mukunda got up from his bed in the habitat and looked outside. 'Today is the day!' he thought.

He scribbled on his notepad, which Garuda read and replied in text, 'I haven't heard from him yet.'

Mukunda smashed his clenched right fist into his left palm. He started pacing up and down the habitat, while his feet were pressing hard against the moon soil.

'Calm down!' Garuda displayed in text.

Mukunda raised his gaze and read the flashing text when the ground beneath him vibrated. As he looked down, the glass dome above him started shaking too.

Before he could look up, a dark shadow started covering up the surface around him. He raised his gaze and saw a huge space ship passing very close to the lunar surface. It was a huge spacecraft crafted out of a titanium-like metal, with edges of its wings and fins coloured deep red. As it approached and began to occupy the space above Mukunda, the surface and habitat started shaking violently.

'Is it him?' Garuda started flashing the message sensing the vibrations.

'Look above!' Mukunda yelled in reply.

As Garuda turned his gaze towards the space above, his eyes glowed bright with amazement. 'The missile is here in orbit!' he then displayed.

Mukunda started his comm lines and spoke, 'Xari, am I audible? What is this just above us?'

After a lull of about ten seconds, Xari spoke, 'That's a rocket making some quick manoeuvres around the moon. Nothing to worry!'

'Why is it here? What's going on?' Mukunda asked.

'Just a deep-space communication satellite launch. To resolve our communication-link breakdown! You see, I become restless when I cannot get through to you,' Xari bantered with a playful chuckle.

'It's too huge and too low! My entire habitat is shaking like a twig!' Mukunda replied.

'It is going around for some low-orbit manoeuvres. We will raise its orbit in a day or so and then it will fly off in another couple of days,' she replied.

'It is tremendously huge for a satellite launch vehicle! What payload is it carrying?' Mukunda enquired as the whole habitat shook.

'Just a communication satellite… Stop being paranoid,' Xari said, with haste in her voice. As she completed her sentence, Mukunda heard a crackling sound. The glass on a habitat wall started developing cracks.

'I think my habitat is developing cracks from the vibrations!' Mukunda yelled.

'Put on your suit then,' Xari replied tersely.

21
A Good Thing Going

Mukunda got dressed and put on his suit helmet before the air could get thin inside the habitat. The spacecraft had now advanced and was not visible. Mukunda scribbled on the notepad: 'How will we know when Grutvator takes over the spacecraft?'

Garuda read the message and flashed a text saying, 'He will ensure we know!'

Mukunda nodded and started pacing up and down the habitat. After a good twenty minutes or so, the habitat started picking up the vibrations, but nothing was yet visible on the horizon.

'One more pass and this habitat will shatter. Just saying!' Mukunda said on his comm line.

'We will find a way to mend it,' Xari replied in a flat voice.

Then the spacecraft started appearing on the horizon behind Mukunda. He turned as the vibrations intensified and spotted the oncoming vehicle.

'We can see it approaching, Xari!' Mukunda spoke into his comm line again.

'Xari, this is a very low orbit! Have you calculated well? At such a low orbit, the moon's gravitational perturbation can pull down this spacecraft of yours!' Garuda spoke.

'The calculations were carried out by Paramganak. Master ensures correctness of every fine detail,' Xari replied.

'Xari, we are just worried about the safety of our project down here on the surface!' Mukunda spoke.

'Safety…all…lunar…paramount…!' Xari mumbled as the comm-lines started growing noisy and choppy.

Mukunda looked up again and noticed that the spacecraft was now passing at an accelerating speed. 'Xari, are you there?' he spoke into the comm-line. But she didn't reply. The comm lines were now completely silent. 'Keep an eye for any seismic activity and any noise or voice over the communication line,' he instructed Garuda.

Garuda didn't reply and kept hovering without blinking his eyes.

'Garuda?' Mukunda said, seeking an affirmation.

'Wait, Master! I am listening!' Garuda then replied.

'Then why aren't you replying?' Mukunda frowned.

'I meant, I am listening to the seismic activity. He is saying something!' Garuda replied.

'What does he say?'

'He is unclear, the vibrations from this annoying spacecraft are interfering with his seismic messages!' Garuda said.

Mukunda nodded in agreement and started pacing up and down again. A loud noise started reverberating through the habitat. Mukunda looked up but the spacecraft was yet to reach the zenith. The voice started growing louder, it baffled Mukunda but Garuda seemed unperturbed.

'What is this additional noise?' Mukunda finally broke his silence.

'What noise? Are you hallucinating? Are you okay, Master?' Garuda said.

Mukunda shook his eyes in disbelief and kept pacing up and down. The noise grew a little louder and Mukunda started grinding his teeth. The noise grew deeper and he clenched his fists too, still pacing up and down the habitat.

The voice then suddenly started gaining character and grew a little less noisy. Mukunda loosened his fists and his eyes narrowed. The voice was now saying something, albeit with substantial background noise. He stopped and tried focusing on the voice and then it all made sense.

'The missile is under my control and command!' the voice said.

'Who are you?' Mukunda said.

'I cannot keep on answering the same question again and again!' he replied.

'So now you have a voice?' Mukunda said.

'It's your mind, Mukunda!' Grutvator replied.

'I am picking up those vibrations, is that what you are suggesting?' Mukunda said with a certain degree of disbelief.

'I am your elder brother. I took the liberty of changing certain specific structures in your brain. Your skin is picking up the vibrations and your somatosensory cortex is relaying them to your auditory lobe,' Grutvator replied.

'I am hearing the vibrations? You rearranged my brain's neural connections using gravity? Your being my remote brother doesn't give you that right!' Mukunda replied with a stern face under the space suit.

'It absolutely doesn't! But believe me, you will need to hear my voice once you are back on Prithvi. I cannot rely on Garuda redirecting my messages to you,' he replied.

'Can he hear you?' Mukunda asked, pointing towards the hovering Garuda.

'He has no brain to rewire!' Grutvator replied.

Mukunda looked at Garuda again and noticed his clueless yet cute glowing eye and he then smiled.

'He has no brain. But he has a heart, a heart of gold!' Mukunda replied.

'I understand he has been there for you since you left

Ksharanpur,' Grutvator replied.

'So, you have the missile now. When do we start negotiations with Xari for my return?' Mukunda said.

'I just want to know again that you are ready for this. The journey will be long and the battle will be bitter. But you need to bring to an end what you unknowingly started,' Grutvator said.

'I should have known better, but I do now. I am on board, get me back to Prithvi,' Mukunda replied.

'I could not pick any intelligible signal from him, Master!' Garuda meanwhile, complained.

'He spoke to me directly!' Mukunda said.

'Is he disappointed in me, master?' Garuda said.

'Don't you ever think that! You have gone way beyond your duties. You are a brave machine, a true friend,' Mukunda replied.

Garuda hearing this, lovingly and slowly blinked in gratitude.

Mukunda's comm-line came alive again and Xari's voice emanated from the other end, 'Mukunda, I got your message. Are you sure this is what you want?'

'Read it aloud to me. The lines were cracking up, I need to know that you got my words right,' Mukunda said as he wondered what message Grutvator relayed to the ship above.

'This communication ship of yours is now under my command. Get me back on Prithvi or I will bring it down,' she read the message.

'And?' Mukunda asked.

'And you have no clue who you are rubbing the wrong way,' she replied.

'Then go on, snatch back control of your ship and raise its orbit. Andromeda is still far away for this communication ship of yours!' he replied.

'So you knew all along?' Xari said.

'I created that facility where that Paramganak hides and squats.

I can see beyond all your childish plays,' he replied.

'Then you do understand that this communication payload can be set in motion here in orbit too. You won't get to survive it,' Xari replied.

'Go ahead! Why wait?' he replied back.

Xari fell silent for a few seconds but then replied, 'I will have to talk to my higher-ups. I do not have authorization to put you back on Prithvi.'

'Your higher-ups!' he said and laughed. 'I know your higher-up is right now eavesdropping on each message of ours. You are just trying to buy some time to gain access to this missile,' he replied.

Xari replied after a brief delay, 'Yes we are trying. And if I do not get access in the next ten minutes, Paramganak will override me and bring the rogue missile back under his command. You have ten minutes, after that he will free the missile and you may not like whatever will follow.'

'Do it. Call your daddy, let's see what's he got?' he replied.

Xari went silent. Meanwhile, the missile was again reappearing on the horizon. This time its orbit was raised and speed lowered.

'The missile now flies higher. Congrats on your orbit-raising manoeuvre!' Mukunda said.

Xari kept quiet for a while and then she spoke, 'I thought we had a good thing going. We grew a little distant and you started mocking me already!' she said.

Mukunda sighed in relief. He was now sure that Grutvator was in full command of the vehicle and was raising it to the optimum height.

'I thought so too! But then you left me here on this barren land to rot. Had I been you, I would have come running to your rescue,' Mukunda said.

'Right, this is what makes us different; you are a free Manava, I am a subordinated Xarnakht who has orders to follow,' Xari replied in a flat tone.

'Duty before love!' Mukunda said, keeping an eye on the passing by missile.

'You get me. That is the very reason I like you!' she replied.

'Are we done with this sham? I know you are just buying time to get hold of the missile. Tell me when you are ready to talk,' Mukunda said and turned off his comm-line.

Garuda, meanwhile, was staring at Mukunda with his glowing bright eyes wide open, to which Mukunda said, 'Oh! Don't give me that look, I know what I am doing. She will talk. They will talk. We are going home.'

Garuda took his time but eventually blinked in agreement too.

Mukunda again started pacing up and down his habitat. 'I know! I know! If Xari or Paramganak get back control of the missile before I reach Prithvi, they will crush me to my bones!' Mukunda said, pacing up and down.

'I wouldn't even let them hover around you, master!' Garuda replied.

Mukunda, not expecting any reply, looked up and smiled. As he rushed up and down the length of the habitat for another twenty minutes, the missile showed up again on the horizon. It was still low enough to be visible but the vibrations and the trembling were now completely gone.

As the missile approached, Xari too started speaking over the comm-line, 'Are you happy now, darling? My boss just got a whiff of our secret affair and now he wants to talk to you. I fell for your boisterous behaviuor. Never knew it will get me in trouble,' Xari said.

'Put him across,' Mukunda said.

'Hello! Mukunda, this is Paramganak! I command the NEAR:

Natural Explorations and Research programme for the Xarnakhts,' a male voice now spoke over the comm.

'I know! I built the facility that you now call NEAR and I built that computer that you are living in rent-free!' he replied.

'Fair enough! We have worked hard in making that big spacecraft for deep-space explorations and your actions are hindering the advancement of science. Let it go!' Paramganak said.

'By all means, go about your deep-space explorations, I have nothing to do with it. But before that get me home,' Mukunda said.

'We have no idea where your home is. If we had known, we would have sent some exploration teams there too,' Paramganak said.

'My folks know how to defend themselves! Just don't go there!' Mukunda said.

'I then wonder why they never came to your rescue?' Paramganak said.

Mukunda heard that but had no answers. He remained silent.

'The point is, neither you nor I know your way back to home. Why do you even want to come back here? Stay there and enjoy the view,' Paramganak said.

'I haven't met Xarnika for a while. And I have heard she is back home too. I will meet her; we have some catching up to do,' Mukunda replied.

'She is indeed home and happy. But here is the party buster. For lack of better words, let me say, she has grown close to Xarki. They are now good friends. If you know what I mean... She never even enquires about you!' Paramganak said.

Mukunda was using Xarnika only as an excuse for reentering Prithvi, but with this additional information his heart started pounding. A feeling of abandonment and betrayal gripped him. His mouth went dry and he felt a little dizzy too. 'I risked my life for her! And it took her just a few months to get over me? Women, huh?' Mukunda said sneeringly.

'Life! Not women! Life will always backstab you when you least expect it to. You just experienced your fair share of life,' Paramganak replied.

'Well! Good luck to her with her life then. Let's talk terms of my return, shall we?'

'First, I need to know how you have overridden all our controls over the spacecraft,' Paramganak replied.

'That's proprietary and I would rather not disclose that,' he replied.

'Then what assurances do I have that you will not disrupt its flight even after reaching Prithvi?' Paramganak replied.

'You have to take my word for it, I won't!' Mukunda said.

Paramganak didn't reply and after a few moments, Mukunda instead said, 'You are holding me up here against my will. You do not have a moral high ground to mistrust my intentions. What assurance do I have that once I let go of your spacecraft, the royal army will not chase me and hunt me down?'

'That we are willing to assure you. You reach Prithvi and disappear. We are willing to look the other way,' Paramganak said.

'I shall not disrupt your space explorations and you shall not disrupt my life. Deal?' Mukunda said.

'Sounds good to me, let me instruct Xari. She will fly you home,' Paramganak replied. The comm-line then went silent.

'Congratulations! I have intercepted his lines. He is instructing for your return,' Grutvator's voice grew.

'Now you are speaking. I was running out of words. You could have prompted me back when I was talking to the evil incarnate,' Mukunda said.

'First, you can't hear me while your mind is busy processing conversation with others. Second, he is just the first officer. You are still to meet the evil incarnate,' Grutvator replied.

'Will you guide me, when I will have to really face him?' Mukunda said.

'I will direct you towards the right goal! I cannot win your fights for you,' Grutvator replied.

Mukunda nodded.

'You don't really have to speak out aloud, just think and I will pick it up from there. You never know if they are eavesdropping on you,' Grutvator again said.

When will they arrange the pick-up? Mukunda thought to himself.

'From what I am able to decipher, that will happen in a few hours from now. Relax and prepare for the long journey ahead,' Grutvator said.

Mukunda nodded and sat on his bed. Garuda seeing this, took a little flight and came close to Mukunda. 'Let us once reach Prithvi, I will take you home, my master!' he said, hovering a few inches from Mukunda.

Mukunda smiled and nodded.

◆

Mukunda had been sitting in the surface module for ten minutes now. He was waiting for Xari to command a lift-off. But the comm-lines were silent.

He was growing restless when Xari finally announced: 'We will be lifting off in under a minute. The module will not try intercepting my ship. It has enough fuel to orbit the moon and then move onward to Prithvi on its own. You reach a safe landing zone on Prithvi and then, as agreed upon, you disappear, never to show up again.'

'Agreed!' Mukunda said.

The engines started revving up. The module started vibrating a little too.

Grutvator, are you there? he thought.

'I am right here. You're a little scared, aren't you?' Grutvator replied.

"I want to see my family! It has been ages!" he replied.

'Would you like to hear a little poem your father wrote for his future son?' Grutvator said.

Where did you get that from? Did Krishna actually ever think about me? Mukunda thought.

'I found it in the archives of Samganak. He indeed did think about you. Would you like to hear the poem? I think it will comfort you,' he said.

'He called it "The Fade",' Grutvator said.

'Recite the poem to me,' Mukunda yelled as the module vibrated violently and the engines started roaring.

The sunsets are not that bad,
But what if, along you set?
The last evening of the year,
Will the perceptions still be clear?
If the sun ever knew his going was due,
Is this a fact that he ever will rue?
If it's all you have, what will be more dire.
The possibility that you set with ire?
The horizons will soon fade,
The senses you once cherish will degrade?
Though the majestic maybe the sun,
But what if Bhoomi never spun?
But the sun would still be there,

Though his glory would grow rare?
On horizons unknown he may shine,
Those new home, will he call them mine?
For tides come and tides go,
Not an ounce deducted from the flow?
Worry not for the canvases change,
Worry not for what impressions remain?
Worry not for once the tree was a seed,
Worry not for it will be all that will remain?

The module's engine was now spewing enormous fires and the module started ascending onto the moon's sky, far out of vision.

22

For Vishnu

The morning was yet to make firm its grip over Ksharanpur, but a multitude of brave men had already gathered by the lakeshore to hear their commander speak. Radhika walked in from the right side of the battle formation and went up to the head of the formation. She was wearing a red saree with yellow borders in Nauvari style, with its long far end tucked in the back. Her glistening hair was tied in a bun and adorned with fresh jasmine flowers. Gold bracelets bejeweled her wrists; they were all made of solid gold with the exception of the first one on the left wrist. It was a Mani-Bandhika, with a jewel-studded shimmering gold bracelet that Krishna had gifted her after unification. 'This will always connect you with me,' he had once said.

Her nose was ornamented with a big gold nose ring, shimmering reflections from which cast lights on her left cheek. Her big black fish-shaped Meenakshi eyes were adorned with rage of vengeance and war.

As she took her position close to the lakeshore, winds started picking up speed and waves on the lakefront started waking up. She turned and glanced at those churning waves.

Taking a deep breath, Radhika turned to address the congregation. 'In the era before Vishnu, when the world was vast and diverse, we were all good and just people. Yet, the world order imploded and collapsed. It collapsed not because of the few people who considered the world to be their playground. It collapsed because good and just people chose silence over rebellion. We followed what was told to us and we gave up on everything that we loved and cared for. We flocked to Ayudhpur and Madhavpur from all quarters of a sinking Bhoomi. We organized and laboured and together we ushered in a golden era of Vishnu. We took new names; we accepted new identities and chiselled a new glorious Swarnim-Yuga with utmost love and care. Likewise, when our two-million-year-old Bhoomi order was threatened we let a single Manava strive to protect the order. It was a rogue amongst us who thought he could rule over us. He, for his personal ambition, brought our world to the ground. We did not rebel; we did not make the evil accountable.

'We had to leave behind that beautiful handcrafted world of ours too. We migrated to this beautiful town of Ksharanpur on Prithvi. And, it's no wonder, we once again handcrafted this beautiful world under the aegis of Vishnu.

The sword of the brave, it is said, forges history. For the meek and voiceless, history, particularly the unjust times, keeps repeating itself.

The same enemy is again knocking at our doors. He is much more powerful than before and has desires darker than we can imagine. One mistake and he wouldn't hesitate wiping out our history and us forever.

'Do we wait for a chosen one this time too? Or do we stand up and bring our swords up to the jugular of our enemy? Do we sit back and let a few brave men fight on our behalf or do we stand up and make our enemy regret his very existence?'

'This time do we obey or do we rebel?' She yelled, staring at her brave men in the eye.

'We rebel,' shouted the formation in unison.

'Do we return if an ounce of Kamsa remains recognizable?' she then shouted.

'We shall not return,' was the reply of the Narayani Sena.

'We will strike the enemy in his home turf!' she shouted as deep, dark clouds encumbered the skies above.

'We will strike him down,' said the formation.

She then lifted Nandaki and pointed it towards the dark overcast skies above.

The metallic sword started glowing bright blue and sparks rose from it. The sparks climbed up to the skies and were met with thunderbolts from above.

'What war cry do we unite under this time around?' she asked as her eyes grew red with rage.

Shripathi stepped forward. 'We have always fought for preservation of the Manava order. For Manavas, we shall fight!'

'For Manavas,' chanted the troops.

But neither did her widened eyes mellow nor did her jaw bulge as it started raining heavily. 'We have always fought for Manava existence and this is where it has brought us. We will not fight for mere existence this time. We will fight for the rule and era of justice. We will fight for the ultimate good. We will fight for the ultimate truth,' she said as thunderbolt flashes glowed on her face and raindrops trickled down from her forehead.

'Who would that be?' Shripathi said.

'We shall fight for Vishnu!' she yelled and her voice echoed and rumbled through the cloud-covered Ksharanpur.

'For Vishnu!' chanted the troops in unison.

As the chants reverberated through the lakeshores, the Eye started developing across the horizon.

'The realms should open any minute now,' said Shriram.

The winds were combing through the luscious golden wheat fields. For a moment, they would be cold and blow from the east end of the fields and sweep snow along with them. And another moment, they would reverse and become very hot and start blowing sand from the west end of it. The wheat crops that the winds were ruffling were clinging to the snow-clad toppled mountains. And the mountains were balanced on their tips while their bases hung skywards.

The thick, dark smoke from the wreckage was dancing with the changing winds. A few sparks were still flying off the metals parts, all spread across the desert sand below.

Mukunda, as he regained his consciousness, tried raising his head. But his head and neck were still hurting and he gave up midway. His left cheek was firmly placed in the warm sand below. Even with his eyes closed, he could sense blood trickling down his face. He wiped the warm fluid with his palm and opened his eyes. He wiped the sand off his face and looked up to his right. His vision was blurry at best and the wind was hurting his already hurting face. He closed his eye and sank his face in the sand again. *How did I get here?* he mused.

Then it all started coming back to him. He was on his way back to Prithvi on that lunar module. He was reentering Prithvi's atmosphere when the parachutes deployed before final landing. But this didn't answer his question. *How did I get here? Why am I in a crash wreckage?* he thought to himself.

He lifted his head and half opened his eyes to see around. It was still blurry at first, but as he exerted, he could see to his right. He could see, but believing what he could see, was a question for another day. A toppled mountain, a few hundred feet from him was what he could see at first. But as he narrowed his eyes to make more sense out of the scene, he saw a blue vibrant lake on the summit. The lake, just like the mountain, was upside down too.

This is a concussion, I am hallucinating, he thought. He again closed his eyes and sank his head back in the sand. He lay there for a good five minutes and then raised his head to look towards his left. He saw more sand and gusts of winds blowing, but the sand, a few feet from him, was engulfed in some sort of darkness. He then realized that it was a shadow of some sort. He looked up and what he saw left him speechless.

A huge mountain was hanging above his head. The peak of the toppled mountain was pegged into the ever-shifting sand some thirty feet ahead of him.

What kind of sorcery is this? he thought, raising his head further.

There were golden wheat fields growing upside down on the steps made on that mountain. And the field was covered with thick layers of snow. Not an ounce of it dropping down. He then felt the fast-alternating winds. One waft would bring along sweat inducing heat and the other, shivering cold. He then looked around and noticed the wreckage. *Did I crash into one of these weird mountains?* he wondered.

Mukunda's eye then caught a glimpse of a bright-blue parachute burning in flames, some feet away from him. A memory flash occurred to him. 'The parachutes... They got deployed fine for a soft landing and then one of them malfunctioned,' he murmured.

'The module was built to take the impact, that's why I survived,' he said in a more jubilant, louder voice.

'I am glad you survived,' said a person squatting some ten feet away from him in the direction of Mukunda's feet.

Startled, Mukunda sat up.

'Whatever the reason, I am glad you survived, my friend,' the man said, a broad smile covering his face.

Mukunda looked back and saw the face of that familiar voice.

'Xinjhua! Are you really here or is this all a dream?' Mukunda said.

Xinjhua rose up. 'Well! Here you are and so am I.'

'We are in the Xurabhur desert, aren't we?' Mukunda asked.

'We are in Greater Chinjing.'

'Who did this?' Mukunda said, looking towards the toppled mountains.

'If you have to ask, maybe you were not ready to return,' Xinjhua replied.

'No one can be ready for this,' he yelled, pointing towards the landscape.

''Kamsa unleashed some sort of weapon on Greater Chinjing to set an example for all other,' Xinjhua replied.

'You escaped?' Mukunda asked.

'They let me and my family go. They said that it was the payment for all the good things you did for them,' Xinjhua said.

'They let you free so that you could narrate the tale of these horrors to me. They made me land here to scare me away!' Mukunda replied.

'You had some plans of retribution?' Xinjhua asked.

'I am not here for any retribution. Kamsa is about to do to the whole of Prithvi and beyond what he did to this place. I need to stop him,' he replied.

'Why? That will kill him too,' Xinjhua asked.

'He believes that total destruction will set him free from that machine. Destroying this world would let him rule other new world,' Mukunda asked.

'What about his people, the Xarnakhts?' he asked.

'He doesn't care about any of them. He seeks glory in destruction,' Mukunda replied.

'How do you plan to stop him?' he asked.

'I don't have the details yet. I have a friend who will guide me through,' Mukunda replied.

Xinjhua clasped his hands and chuckled like a kid. 'Mukunda has new friends. I am happy for Mukunda.'

Mukunda got up, dusted the sand off his suit and walked towards him. He placed his hands over his shoulders and asked, 'Are you okay? Are you happy here?'

'We all are happy here. I mean the winds blow hot and cold; the rice won't grow. But we make good of whatever works,' he said, pointing towards the wheat fields.

'I uprooted you and your life, didn't I?' Mukunda said.

'Don't ever blame yourself, my friend. It is better to live free in this dry land of sand and snow than to live in plenty as a Xarmik, an outsider.' His eyes were glittering with hope.

'If I am unable to stop Kamsa, all this would get destroyed in the next few decades. If I fail, I will come back here to take you to safety,' Mukunda said.

'In the next few decades, my children and I would have spent a fulfilling life in our motherland. I don't want to leave Chinjing ever again,' he said.

'I am responsible for this mess. I cannot leave you behind,' Mukunda said as his throat choked.

'You are not responsible for anything. They fooled you, you were a kid.'

'I should have known better,' Mukunda said, shaking his head.

'I am happy here. My family is happy here. We are free now. Had it not been for you, they would have kept us as voiceless Xarmiks forever,' he replied.

Mukunda nodded while clearing his throat.

'When do you need to reach Xurabhur?' Xinjhua asked.

'Right now! But I don't know the way. How far is it? How do

I reach there?' Mukunda asked.

'This is the farthest point on land from Xurabhur desert. And it will take you weeks before you reach there unless ...' Xinjhua said and then whistled aloud.

'What is it?' Mukunda asked.

'Turn around,' Xinjhua said.

Mukunda turned and noticed nothing for a while. Then he spotted a speck on the horizon, in between two distant toppled mountains. He observed for a while and then turned to say, 'Where did you find a Bhavya?'

'On my way back from Xarlok. She was left abandoned in the middle of nowhere. I raised her,' he said, smiling.

Bhavya was now flying very close to them. She rushed in and tried to land but skidded and fell beak first. Seeing which they both laughed.

'She is young and fumbles, will she be able to fly so far,' Mukunda asked.

'She is learning. She will take you there and fly back,' Xinjhua replied.

'What do you call her?' Mukunda asked.

'Just Bhavya! Original name of her kind,' Xinjhua said.

'I wish I could stay longer and meet Chinjhi and the kids. But I have to reach there. I am sure, I won't receive a kind welcome there,' Mukunda said.

'You won't. But you will find your way,' Xinjhua said.

Mukunda stepped forward and hugged him. Xinjhua patted him on his shoulders. 'Go and finish what you unknowingly started.'

Mukunda stepped back, smiled and rushed towards Bhavya.

'Bhavya! Take my young friend to the forbidden deserts!' Xinjhua said and waved as Bhavya lowered to carry Mukunda.

As Mukunda held on to Bhavya firmly, she raised her long

slender neck and blurted a shrill sound. As she started flapping her wings to generate lift, Mukunda looked towards Xinjhua, who was wearing his usual nonchalant childlike smile. Mukunda waved him goodbye as Bhavya took off and started gaining height rapidly. Xinjhua waved back as Mukunda grew distant.

Soon, Bhavya was gliding amid toppled mountains and Xinjhua was out of sight. He started looking around and found Bhavya flying too close to the topography. He feared the proximity to those weird mountains, but then extended his arm in a bid to touch them. But before his palm could touch past those mountains, he withdrew his hand. *What if the touch tipped us over*, he thought?

Bhavya flew past the confusing topography of Greater Chinjing and headed westward. Mukunda could already see gravity-compliant mountains, lakes and rivers. *Grutvator! Are you there? What next?* Mukunda wondered.

23

Some Familiar Faces

The lakeshores were filled with ankle-deep water and the rocks and boulders adorning the shores were wet. The rain had stopped a long time ago and the skies had cleared. The Narayani Sena had long left for Xarlok and a lull persisted.

Rukmini was sitting atop a small cliff, on a rock. Her armour and sword were glistening in the evening's slant sunshine, and her face was wet, either from the long-gone rains or from her tears, it was difficult to say. Every few minutes, she would clench her teeth and sob a little. Her eyes were red but the fine lines beside her eyes were curled with worries.

'We tried our best, they found us at the last moment,' Madhav said, but she kept staring at her sword.

'See, we exercised all possible options. They wouldn't take underage kids along with them. What more could we have done?' he said again.

'We should have tried harder. Letting them go alone was not an option,' she replied in a sombre voice.

'They are seasoned warriors, they will handle this,' Madhav said, in a bid to placate her.

'They have not read what we have. They don't know what they are walking into,' she said in a muffled voice.

'I tried that too! I told several senior commanders that they are walking into a trap and we are not well prepared. But no one was in a mood to listen. They overlooked Samganak's report,' Madhav said.

'As soon as they approach the realms of Kamsa, he will render all their gadgets useless. He will deploy machines against the Manavas. And once he overruns them, he will turn towards Ksharanpur. All the young and old who stayed behind in Ksharanpur will have to pay the price,' Rukmini said, gliding her fingers over the blade of her sword.

'We cannot let that happen,' Madhav murmured.

'That is the reason I wanted us to sneak in, we could have cautioned them,' Rukmini replied.

'I meant we cannot leave the young and the old here defenseless,' Madhav said.

'What do you mean?' Rukmini said.

'We have to build defenses,' he murmured.

'What do you have in mind?' she asked.

'I saw a module called Airavata. It is an automated weapon system that Samganak has the design maps for. I saw those while browsing through Samganak with Mukunda, way back,' he replied.

'If Samganak has preloaded design maps, it means it can mass manufacture it without any Manava intervention,' Rukmini said.

Madhav nodded.

Rukmini held him by his arm. 'Get up! We need to go to the lab right now.'

'Kanha wouldn't allow us access without permission,' he replied.

'Oh! He sure will,' she said as she lifted her sword from the ground.

Madhav was looking through Samganak as Rukmini stood guard with her sword.

Kanha was sitting in his chair. 'Mohan will be here any minute. Then show this sword to him. You both are up for some good thrashing.'

'We needed the access codes to Airavata and we have them now. Keep yelping, you poor little boy!' she replied.

Mohan flung the door open and rushed in. He looked around and saw Madhav and Rukmini. He then turned his gaze towards Kanha, 'These two have taken you hostage, Kanha?'

'She has a sword and I have a fear of sharp objects,' Kanha replied.

'Okay, what are you two doing here?'

'We are installing the Airavata system all across Ksharanpur,' Rukmini replied.

'Whose idea is this?' Mohan asked.

'Your son's; he is a genius,' she replied.

'Madhav! Who gave you the authority to manufacture weapons?'

Madhav's face turned pale.

'Authority can never be granted or bestowed. You have to assume it,' Rukmini replied, lifting her sword.

'Enough of this crap! Put down the blade,' Mohan yelled with his fists clenched.

'Rukmini, lower the sword,' Madhav said and she complied.

'We have a good explanation for all this,' Madhav said, proceeding to explain in detail the incoming attack.

'Fine! I will send the Narayani Sena your message, again! And as a precautionary measure, we will install some Airavata system at a few critical installations,' Mohan replied after hearing them both out.

•◆

The sun was about to set over the Xurabhur desert and the winds were growing cooler by the minute. The whole of the Narayani Sena was lying face down in the warm desert sand. They were spread over many dunes. A strong wind blew and shifted the sand from beneath. The small dust storm brought many of them back to consciousness.

Raghav jolted Shripathi, Radhika and Vallabha back to consciousness.

'Ask every battalion leader to run a headcount, make sure that no one is missing,' Raghav instructed Shripathi.

'Start setting up uplinks with Grutvator and ask him to put us through to Ksharanpur too,' he then said to Vallabha, who had communications and navigation under her command.

Raghav turned towards Radhika to discuss further course of action but saw her walking away.

'Radhika, where are you headed to?' he said.

She turned around. 'There is somebody over there.'

Raghav looked towards the distant horizon and he too noticed somebody fast approaching them. The person was on a horse and wearing a black robe. His horse stopped near Radhika and Raghav.

The stranger was about to speak when Raghav said in an authoritative voice, 'First, get down from that thing and then speak.'

The person got down and declared, 'I am Xarmik. I hereby declare you a prisoner of Xarlok. You all must accompany me and our King Xardukht may let you live.'

'What is a Xarmik?' Radhika said.

'Slave of Xarlok!' he replied without even batting an eyelid.

'A slave! Your king has sent a slave to capture us?' Raghav said.

Xarmik nodded.

'You alone will capture all of us?' Radhika asked.

Xarmik nodded again.

'What if we do not turn ourselves in?' she asked again.

'They will descend upon you like black clouds. This is your only chance, surrender and come along,' Xarmik announced.

'We will not surrender, let your king know,' she said and turned a little to walk back.

Xarmik drew his sword and placed it on her neck. Feeling the blade of the sword, she stopped and turned back. Her eyes turned red and her jugular vein swelled with anger. She looked him in the eye, when Xarmik blurted, 'Surrender!'

In a matter of seconds, she clenched her fist, raised her right leg and kicked him in his face, throwing him to the ground. 'Prepare the Sena for movement, *now*,' Radhika told Raghav.

As she spoke, Xarmik got to his feet and rushed towards her with his sword. She noticed the rustling of the sand under Xarmik's foot and saw his shadow approaching too. She turned and drew her sword, Nandaki. As soon as Nandaki came out of its sheath, it started glowing with a brilliant blue light.

She took a few steps forward and lept in the air. Seeing her move, Xarmik raised his sword further and shouted, 'Surrender or else!'

As she reached closer to the oncoming Xarmik, she swung her sword and with a single strike cut him into half.

•→•

Mukunda looked back and caught a glimpse of Bhavya flying back home. 'How far from here on?' he said.

'An hour or so of walking only, exactly from where you stand,' Grutvator replied.

'Only? If I walk that much, what would be left of me for fighting?' he complained.

'I have strategically placed you here, so that you reach there when they do.' Grutvator replied.

'They who?' he said.

'The Narayani Sena! I was able to reach them.'

'Really? How many Manavas?' he asked.

'Around ten thousand,' Grutvator replied.

'The Xarnakhts will outnumber them any day. They should have gotten more,' he replied.

'Ksharanpur has not been the same. The new Bhoomidium-1008, the elixir which helped Manavas survive for so long, is more stable but has its own limitation. Population has dwindled, they could only gather so many young able people,' Grutvator replied.

'Who is leading the charge?' he then asked.

'Your mother, Radhika,' Grutvator replied.

Mukunda didn't reply.

'Did I just hear you cry?' Grutvator asked.

'Just a lump in the throat,' he said in a muffled voice.

'I understand, you haven't seen her in ages. But, first liberate Prithvi of Kamsa.'

'Do you think they haven't kept a tab on my movements?'

'I was more worried about the Narayani Sena's movement. Paramganak has built some very sophisticated radars for Kamsa,' Grutvator replied.

'And since you are so unperturbed about it, you have disrupted the radars?'

'I have taken care of them. The less they know about me, the more it will play in our favour,' he replied.

It was dark and Mukunda could now see a few lights on the horizon.

'I think I am almost there,' he whispered.

'They are there too. I can see them ten dunes to your right. In the next five minutes, Paramganak will send a drone swarm. Hide when you hear their noise,' Grutvator replied.

Mukunda nodded and start crouching towards his right at a

good pace. He was unable to see anything ahead, let alone an army. And he was happy about it, as it meant that Manavas were using enough stealth. He was counting each passing dune. He was past five of them when a buzzing sound started growing. He stopped and looked up. He then shifted his vision towards the dark skies on his left. Faint red lights were fast approaching towards him. He first ducked and then lay on the cold sand. The drone swarm started descending and moved towards him.

'They have sensed me, now what?' he murmured in desperation.

'Let me take care of this,' Grutvator replied.

Mukunda raised his eyes and saw the approaching drone army when the space above him first wobbled and then shook violently. A gust of sudden shock-wave hit his face. The next moment, the drone swarm was thrown hundreds of feet towards Mukunda's right. Quite a few drones lost their balance out of the sudden disorientation and smashed into each other. And the rest flew headward as if nothing had happened.

'Thanks,' he whispered, relieved.

'Keep moving,' Grutvator replied.

Mukunda paced up. He ran, instead of crouching across the last two dunes. As soon as he reached past the tenth dune, he looked around but saw nothing.

He wanted to yell at Grutvator but instead dropped to the ground out of fatigue and dismay. As he dropped with a thud, a few feet ahead of him, the sand moved.

And suddenly hundreds of Manavas got up from their camouflage in the sand.

Few of them rushed towards Mukunda and surrounded him. They were now pointing swords and energy-weapons at him. He looked up and saw Raghav and Vallabha amid other partly familiar faces.

'Who are you?' Vallabha said, thrusting her sword forward in an intimidating manner.

'Of all people you don't recognize me?' he blurted out. 'Aunt…' he then added.

Vallabha lowered her sword and lowered Raghav's sword blade down too with her hand. She then extended her arm and Mukunda held it.

As soon as he got up, she hugged him. 'Mukunda, I am so happy to see you. We were all so worried. Let's get you to your mother as soon as possible. Come along.'

Raghav placed his hand over Mukunda's shoulder and patted him twice. 'Very brave of you to have weathered this difficult terrain amid such hostile people.'

Mukunda nodded.

'Will they shoot at you if they see you here?' Raghav then asked.

Mukunda nodded. 'Many times over.'

They both laughed and then Raghav pressed a small button on the left flank of his armour. It loosened and came off. 'You now have grown almost as tall as me. Wear this, young man,' he said and handed the heavy armour to him.

Mukunda looked towards Vallabha and she looked with anguish in her eye towards Raghav. Raghav smiled.

'What? Don't you both worry about me. My skin is thicker than this armour.'

Vallabha looked at Mukunda and nodded with a smile. Mukunda caught hold of the armour and put it on.

'Now let's go find your mother. She won't believe her eyes,' Raghav said.

They trekked to the next dune and seeing them coming, Radhika got up from the sand. She dusted herself and walked towards them. 'Everything under control, Raghav?' she murmured.

Raghav smiled. 'Look who came looking for us!'

'Who is…' she stopped, a thousand subtle smiles brewing at the corners of her lips.

Her steps quickened and she rushed towards Mukunda. But as she reached within arm's length of him, she froze. She looked into his eyes and she started tearing up. Tears of joy and ecstasy started rolling down Mukunda's face too.

But they both stood frozen without batting an eyelid.

Then Mukunda's lip parted as he swallowed the lump in his throat and he finally said, 'Maa…'

Radhika rushed and embraced him. She cried for many minutes while tightly holding onto Mukunda. She then loosened her arms and held him by his shoulders.

'Do you know how much it hurts to realize that I have missed a whole phase of my son's life?' she said, her voice laced with intermittent sobs.

Mukunda nodded, his eyes still brimming with tears.

'But the joy of having you back has overpowered and erased all other sorrows of mine,' she then said.

Mukunda nodded. 'I was willing to give up anything to just have a glimpse of you! I have spent years repenting my foolishness of leaving you behind.'

Radhika nodded and wiped his tears off his cheeks. 'I never imagined that you would grow up to look exactly like your father,' she said.

Mukunda smiled. As he spoke, his attention shifted to a growing buzzing sound and he looked towards his right. The drone swarm was fast approaching and was at a distance of a few dozen feet from them. 'Get down, everyone! Get down!' he shouted.

Raghav was taken aback. 'What are those?' he said, ducking a little.

'Those are enemy drones. Get down, Uncle,' he said, falling onto the sand along with Radhika and Vallabha.

Raghav ducked and raised his gun to shoot them down when Mukunda grabbed his arm. 'Don't! Just ask everyone to lay low.'

Raghav raised his head and shouted, asking everyone to duck. The drone swarm picked up the sound and turned towards the Sena.

'It's late! They are unarmed reconnaissance drones, just take cover!' Mukunda shouted and everybody ducked.

The swarm flew in and hovered above them for a good minute or so and left.

'They are gone now. Let us regroup,' Raghav stood up and announced.

As Mukunda stood up, he heard Grutvator's voice. 'Your cover is blown. Party of thousand armed-men is advancing towards you.'

'They know we are here,' Mukunda announced.

'I can see them,' Radhika said, looking ahead. The rumble of men advancing towards them grew apparent now. 'Let's retreat and find another way to the facility ahead,' Raghav said.

'We will not retreat, let them come,' Radhika said.

'Hurry! Get into formation. Those whose service weapons are still working, lead the formation,' Raghav instructed.

As the Manavas assembled, Mukunda turned towards Vallabha. 'Are the energy-weapons malfunctioning?'

'They were functioning well earlier in the day, but as we advanced, they stopped working,' she replied, working on her hand-held communication device.

'They have deployed some sort of interfering field. I feared that. Now what, Aunt?' he said.

'We will make the best of what we have and fight the good old way,' she said. Vallabha then shut the lid of the communication device and sighed.

'Your communication with Ksharanpur too?' Mukunda asked.

'They were patchy and now they are completely down. If this interference field is not taken down, I will not be able to contact Samganak and get us any help when required,' she said.

Mukunda was now looking ahead as the enemy formation grew closer. What he saw next left him speechless. Radhika was pacing up to them, leaving everybody behind.

'What does she think she is doing?' Mukunda murmured and was about to rush to her when Vallabha held him back. 'She knows, what she is about to do,' she said.

Radhika increased her pace and started running towards the Xarnakht formation. As she drew within twenty steps of the oncoming enemy, she drew her Nandaki from the sheath and waved it. The sword started glowing with a bright blue light and then blue thunder bolts started emanating from it skywards. She could now see the faces of the approaching men.

She leaped in the air and with a single stroke of her sword slashed the head of the leading man. She landed on her feet and turned towards the others, as they stood in horror seeing the decimated head of their leader. She leaped forward and with another stroke of her Nandaki, decapitated three more Xarnakht soldiers. The remaining soldiers gasped in horror. They dispersed and ran away.

'What just happened? Why are they running away?' Vallabha gasped.

'The first person she slayed was one of their finest and senior-most commander. She has killed Xanuk, this won't go down well with Xardukht,' Mukunda replied.

24

A Familiar Foe

'The Manavas are here!' Kamsa's voice reverberated from within Paramganak.

'You said they were locked behind some kind of a stealth. You said they would never find their way here,' Xandhrin said, his voice overladen with haste.

Xardukht stared at Xandhrin in a reprimanding way and then said to Kamsa, 'Great Father, have we gone wrong somewhere? Have we, pardon me, miscalculated?'

'This is my foresight. I felt a connection with Mukunda. I once was Manava too, just like him. And, he unknowingly resurrected me too. For old time's sake, I went easy on him. I assumed a ten-year-old kid to be harmless. I forgot that he would grow up to be a Manava, a strong Manava. I should have factored that in. But my generosity blindsided me,' Kamsa replied.

'And now he has summoned his people too,' Xandhrin murmured.

'Enough! We have to stay strong and counter these malevolent forces,' Xardukht yelled.

'I will take care of them. I know these Manavas well. What I am more worried about is the dark forces from beyond the stars. Our missile is still held hostage. We need to finish those dark forces before these wretched Manavas summon them too,' Kamsa said.

'Mukunda promised that he will let go of our missile if we set him free,' Xardukht murmured.

'We shouldn't have trusted him,' Xandhrin said in a muffled voice.

'We exercised our best option. Mukunda has literally jammed all our accesses to the missile. It's orbiting the moon wildly,' Kamsa said.

'What do we do now?' Xardukht said.

'Paramganak says the second moon is approaching our skies soon. It may turn the tides in our favour and we may get access to our missile back,' Kamsa said.

Xardukht nodded and smiled, when a soldier came running to him. He stood there with his head hung low. Xandhrin sensed something was up. 'What is it?' he hollered.

'A large contingent of enemy is headed our way,' the soldier said and fell silent.

Xardukht nodded and asked him for further information.

'General Xanuk first noticed them and moved swiftly, but…' the soldier was trembling, his voice was now betraying him.

'But what?' Xandhrin shouted.

'They mercilessly killed the great general,' he finally mustered enough courage to break the news.

Xandhrin's face grew pale and he looked helplessly towards Xardukht.

Xardukht saw the fear in his eyes, he then turned towards the soldier. 'Ask each commander to prepare his men. Send down the last man and kill every Manava.'

Xardukht was fuming.

Paramganak, by now, was displaying some messages on the screen.

'Have we found some solution, Great Father?' Xardukht said.

'We have found a bargaining chip. Paramganak has discovered the portal through which these Manavas have entered our world.

I will send armed drones to strike them where it hurts the most,' Kamsa replied.

'But please maintain enough deterrence for the facility. All senior administrators and families are here now. I couldn't trust our palace and have entrusted their security unto you. Please maintain enough deterrence,' he said with his voice concealing anguish.

'I am sure that your men will return victorious. Yet, I have a welcome surprise for the Manavas, just in case,' Kamsa said, and soon a loud roar and rumble filled the entire building.

A shutter at the end of the facility went up and one after an other, robots started emerging from there. Built in Jaradium, they stood at a towering six feet and with each step they took, the grounds below shook.

Xardukht saw the lines of robots and smiled.

'Let them come!' Xandhrin shouted, laughing.

•◆

'Mother!' Mukunda murmured as he walked through the desert along with the Manava formation.

Radhika raised her gaze and smiled at him. 'How are Rukmini and Madhav?'

'They have grown into cheerful Manavas. They are very bright and we are all proud of them, especially Rukmini. She has grown to be a very strong yet caring girl,' Radhika replied, smiling and looking towards Vallabha.

Vallabha smiled and nodded.

'How about Kanha? None of this was his fault,' Mukunda then said.

'We know! He is a very sweet boy. And sharp too. He now assists Mohan in running the lab. He is doing a good job at it,' she replied.

'What? I stand corrected. It was his fault. He planned and

abetted my exile. He always had an eye on that lab. I want him out,' he yelled as his face turned red with anger and jealousy.

Radhika chortled, seeing which Vallabha too chipped in. 'You were gone. Somebody had to step up. He assisted us a lot in tracking you,' Vallabha said.

'I want him out as soon as we are back home,' Mukunda demanded again.

'Grow up, Mukunda. Kanha is a bright boy and after all that he has done, he isn't going anywhere,' Radhika reprimanded him.

Mukunda fell silent and calmed down. After walking along for a few hundred feet, he broke his silence. 'My apologies!'

Radhika nodded and smiled at him.

'Five thousand Xarnakhts are advancing your way,' Grutvator warned them.

'Again? Why are they coming in waves?' Mukunda muttered.

'There is no wave. They are left with limited men and what you faced earlier was a forward patrol party. This is their last batch and they will try everything in their power to defeat you now,' Grutvator replied.

'This is good news, that this is their last defense. But where have all their men gone?' Mukunda asked.

'You do not set a gravity bomb on your neighbours and not suffer its consequences too. The weather change has engulfed the northern bounds of Xarlok. All their troops stationed there froze to death. Many Xarmiks saw this as an opportunity and made good their escape. They are literally running out of men,' Grutvator replied.

'That's good in a way,' Mukunda muttered.

'Tell Radhika about the advancing enemy. Tell her that they are around five thousand and they will flank you from both sides,' Grutvator replied.

'I think my mother has got it covered. She will handle them.

You should see the way she goes on a rampage with her sword,' Mukunda said, smiling.

'That's Nandaki, a special sword designed by your father. She derives all her power from that celestial sword. Now forewarn her of the enemy,' Grutvator replied.

Mukunda paced up and caught up with Radhika. 'Mother, there is enemy ahead. They are fast advancing towards us and planning on encircling us from all sides,' he said.

Radhika smiled. 'They will be dealt with.' She turned towards Raghav, 'There is enemy incoming, alert all your people.'

Raghav nodded and as he was about to turn to talk to other divisional commanders, he heard a faint but growing rumble. He then turned towards Radhika instead. She turned her gaze in the direction of the noise and saw sand getting stirred and ruffled in the distant horizon.

'They outnumber us, but I hope we will have this under control,' she then said to Raghav.

Raghav smiled. 'The weak rely on numbers. The brave rely on their determination.'

Radhika nodded and Raghav then rushed towards his commanders.

'How are our communication lines?' Radhika said turning towards Vallabha.

'They are long dead. The enemy has very tactfully severed them,' she replied.

'We might need backup. Convey to them to send more robust guns and some drones, if possible,' Radhika said.

'I will drop them a message but I cannot say if they will ever get here in time,' Vallabha replied.

'What else are our options then?' Radhika murmured.

'Mukunda has been talking to Grutvator. Can he ask him to

relay our messages?' Vallabha suggested.

Radhika nodded and called out to Mukunda. He was walking a few steps ahead of them and came rushing. 'Ask Grutvator to tell Samganak to send reinforcements,' Radhika said.

'This is the last batch of their men. We need not worry...' he replied.

'Do as I say,' Radhika then said.

Mukunda nodded and started muttering words to reach out to Grutvator.

'He says that it shall take time. But he will relay the message,' Mukunda said.

Raghav came rushing back amid the growing rumble of advancing Xarnakhts.

'They have already started splitting. They will flank us from all sides. Two of our commanders, Shripathi and Raghunandan will hold them off on the other sides, while I will hold them off in the front,' he said.

'Good! Let me then hold the centre of our formation. I want Vallabha to get us supplies,' Radhika replied.

The Xarnakhts soon broke into the Manava formation and close combat ensued.

Shripathi was holding the enemy on the right while Raghunandan was struggling to hold them off on his left. Seeing Raghunandan struggle, Radhika drew her sword and turned to Mukunda. 'Stay here with your aunt.'

She then rushed to Raghunandan's help. The brilliance from Nandaki lit the dark deserts for some moments. She broke into enemy ranks and started slaying one Xarnakht after another. On many instances, Nandaki was able to pierce through the Jaradium armour of the Xarnakht commanders. Brilliant red sparks flew from the impact of Nandaki on the hardened armour, cutting it to pieces.

'Aunt, do you know, all those dark glossy armours those Xarnakht are wearing, I mined them. On the moon,' Mukunda said.

Vallabha looked up. 'Not a good time for chit-chat, sweetheart.' She then went back to work on her communication device. Squatting on the cold sand, she was trying to reach Samganak. Mukunda placed his hand over his knees and stooped forward. He peeped into the communication device, when he heard some footsteps fast approaching. As he turned, a Xarnakht struck him with his sword. The blade of the sword impacted him on his armour and shook him a little. Vallabha, seeing this, tossed her device aside and stood up.

Before the Xarnakht could strike again, Mukunda reached for Vallabha's sheath that was tied to her waist and pulled her sword from the hilt. He turned towards the Xarnakht and struck his neck. The Xarnakht fell to the ground bleeding profusely.

Vallabha looked at him. 'Are you okay?'

'There are many more coming our way. Stay here, I will get them,' he replied.

As Vallabha saw hordes of Xarnakhts advancing their way, she turned to her left and called out for Radhika, who upon hearing her voice turned to look at the oncoming enemy forces. She then saw the left flank of the enemy formation that she was fighting with. It had grown thin and she knew that Raghunandan would now be able to handle them. She rushed back to Vallabha.

Mukunda, meanwhile, was in a close combat with two Xarnakhts. He was struggling against the consorted attacks when Radhika arrived and slayed both the aggressors.

'Thanks, Mother,' he said, sighing with relief.

Radhika then engaged five more Xarnakhts and Mukunda shielded Vallabha from two other Xarnakhts advancing from the right. Each time he faced more than one adversary, he started struggling. He was shielding blows from the sword of one Xarnakht when a swaying blade of the other one touched past his left arm. He blurted out a huge cry of pain. His left hand was bleeding profusely.

Hearing him yell in pain, Radhika rushed towards him and slayed both the Xarnakhts. Vallabha stepped forward and pulled out a solution and bandage from her bag. She drenched his wound in Bhoomidium and tied a cotton bandage over it.

'This will ease the pain in a matter of minutes,' Vallabha told him, cupping his cheek with her right palm.

He nodded and seeing him relieved Radhika turned and unleashed her full fury on all the Xarnakhts around them. Their numbers soon dwindled and the last few Xarnakhts, seeing Radhika heading for them, dropped their swords and fled.

Soon, all the commanders, including Raghav, increased the vigour with which they were fighting, driving most of the Xarnakhts away from the battlefield.

Gradually, the clinking of the swords decreased and the battlefield started growing silent.

As Raghav turned and reached for Radhika, he heard a whooshing sound. He turned his gaze to his left and saw a barrage of incoming arrows. He ducked, covering his face with gauntlets and yelled at the top of his voice. 'Take cover, arrows inbound.'

Most of the Manavas ducked in time, but many were struck by arrows on the exposed parts of their arms and legs.

'Maintain cover, they will reshoot,' Radhika yelled.

'All Manavas with functioning weapons shoot at will,' Raghav shouted.

Soon, a handful of Manavas got up, drew their energy weapons and activated night-vision rangefinders.

'We have a clear vision of the enemy archers. There is a dozen of them hiding behind the dunes,' one of the weapon-yielding

Manavas at the forefront shouted.

'Take them down,' Raghav commanded.

They took multiple shots at them and within half a minute, the same voice hollered back, 'All clear, sir.'

On hearing that, they all got up and looked around for the injured.

'Quite a few of our men have been injured,' Raghav updated Radhika.

'Administer Bhoomidium to them all and let's wait the night out here,' she advised.

'Let me update Grutvator. Also, let's see if he can get us the much-needed backup and medical assistance,' Mukunda said.

Radhika nodded and Mukunda started muttering words under his breath.

'This can't be true!' Mukunda then hollered.

'What?' Radhika enquired.

'Grutvator says that we cannot stop now. The second moon is fast approaching the horizon. He is fatigued from holding that massive missile and the additional pull from the second moon will make him relent,' Mukunda replied.

'What does that mean?' Raghav asked.

'We have four hours to unplug Paramganak and take down Kamsa,' Mukunda said.

'Everyone who is injured will stay here and a small party will advance towards the weapons facility. We will take them by surprise under the Dark's cover and uproot Kamsa as quickly as possible,' Radhika announced. She then turned towards Mukunda and looked at his injured arm. 'You will have to stay here, Shripathi will take care of you,' she said to him.

'Mother, I have to be there. Grutvator will have to guide us through all this. I am his voice; I will have to be there,' he said.

Radhika kept quiet for few moments as she weighed her options and then nodded. 'Mukunda will accompany us,' she said to Raghav. 'But ensure that he remains inside the security circle. They will surely target him.'

'Don't worry, Radhika. No harm shall cross his way,' Raghav replied.

She nodded. 'Ten minutes, we regroup and we move.'

•◆•

Shriram was pacing up and down the length of the lab. Shyam was leaning over Mohan's shoulder as the latter was checking and rechecking Samganak.

'Trust me, I saw an inexplicable reading. There is something lurking over that lake,' Kanha said, turning restlessly from one side to another in his chair.

'Let me check. The visuals are clear, but there was an energy spike an hour ago,' Mohan murmured.

'What about the Narayani Sena, were we able to establish contact with them?' Shriram pitched in.

'They are in the middle of the conflict zone. There could be jammers,' Mohan replied, still working on Samganak's panel.

'What does that mean?' Shriram protested.

'Calm down, Shri! He means that we don't have any clue of the Sena's whereabouts right now, but we hope to establish contact with them soon,' Shyam replied.

'How is one supposed to calm down upon hearing such words?' Shriram said, clouds of agitation engulfing his voice.

'Relax, Shri! Vallabha messaged me about this when her connections started growing weak,' Mohan then said.

Shriram nodded.

'We have something or someone knocking at our doors,'

Mohan then said, still staring at the data on Samganak's screen.

'What is it?' Shyam said, curious.

'These are signatures of some sort of machine or machines trying to breach into our city. They are aggressively looking for a passage,' Mohan replied.

As Shriram rushed towards Samganak for more information, the room shook a little. The Samganak panel then vibrated. Soon the lab's room was filled with Grutvator's voice saying, 'The Narayani Sena is in war zone. They are battling thousands of enemies as we speak.'

'How are they faring?' Shyam said.

'They must have overwhelmed the enemy by now,' he replied.

'You don't have eyes on them?' Mohan asked.

'I am watching them constantly, but there is a lag of a few minutes. The second moon is fast approaching my horizons and with so many variables, it's getting too much for me to process,' he replied.

'We haven't been able to contact them for a while. Did you get to talk with them?' Mohan asked.

'As a matter of fact, that is precisely why I have reached out to you. They need backups: guns and drones,' Grutvator replied.

'We will send that once we can locate them. Here is another thing; we are sensing some weird machines lurking around the corner. Can you see anything from up there?' Mohan asked.

Grutvator went silent for a few moments. Mohan turned his gaze towards Shyam and Shriram. They both were clueless and a little perturbed over the deafening silence.

'There is a swarm of armed drones hovering on the periphery,' Grutvator then said.

'Shouldn't we be shutting all the communication channels and seal the city?' Kanha said as he rushed towards the Samganak.

'It's too late. Any open channel will take at least two hours to shut completely and at the rate that they are searching for an entry, they will breach it in the next hour or so,' Grutvator replied.

'Shouldn't we initiate a lockdown now?' Mohan said, his voice now trembling with haste.

'We need to get supplies and reinforcements to Radhika before that,' Shyam interjected.

'I would suggest an immediate and complete shutdown now. Keep those additional guns and drones for yourselves. Trust me, you will need them,' Grutvator replied.

'But the Narayani Sena needs those supplies, we cannot leave them helpless,' Shyam said.

'They have skilled warriors by their side. You are the ones helpless here. If the inbound enemy destroys Ksharanpur, he will not stop at that. Emboldened by his victory, he will crush the Narayani Sena too,' Grutvator said.

'Thanks for your input. We shall weigh all our options. We are initiating an immediate closure of all channels and portals. Don't worry if you don't hear from us in a while. Take care and keep an eye on all those brave Manavas out there in the battlefield,' Mohan said and initiated the lockdown.

'I will assist Radhika in whatever way I can. Take care,' Grutvator said and then his voice fell silent.

Mohan got up from his seat. 'I have run an inventory check. We have Airavata system to shoot down any inbound enemy. We have spare energy guns too. But getting it to Radhika will be a challenge. I will have to stop the lockdown and search frantically for her location,' he briefed.

'The final word shall be yours, Shri. Radhika and Mukunda are out there and most of the warriors in the Sena belong to Ayudhpur. We shall all agree to whatever you decide,' Shyam said, turning towards Shriram.

'She is your daughter-in-law and that's your grandson too. What do you say?' Shriram instead asked.

'Those are indeed my beloved. That's why I am leaning towards opening the channels and helping them,' Shyam replied.

'You know we cannot do that. We, for our daughter and grandson, cannot risk thousands of young, old and helpless here,' Shriram said.

'I cannot think through this clearly. Your word shall be final,' Shyam admitted.

Shriram turned towards Mohan. 'Lock down every channel and deploy all our defenses. Arm everyone capable of holding a weapon.'

Mohan raised his left arm and made a call. 'Rukmini, get Madhav and reach your school. Get as many classmates as you can.'

Rukmini and Madhav were standing in the school grounds as drones were digging trenches and installing Airavata systems in those trenches.

'There will be three layers of defenses. One by the lakeshore, it is fully automated and completely functional. Second line of defense will be here. Wear your armour and stay in the trenches, because you and your friends will operate this. You are young and fearless and above all, have excellent response time. If our automated defence line fails, you will have to shoot down the enemy drones,' Mohan said and every youngster on the ground cheered.

'I know you are too young for combat, but the old Manavas are bound to be blunt and slow due to their age,' Mohan then said.

Everybody giggled and laughed. 'Don't worry, Uncle, we are all very restless and trigger-happy. None of those junk machines will get past us,' Rukmini said.

'Again, wear your armour at all times and do not leave the trenches and you will be safe,' Mohan said.

25

Beyond the Perceptible

'Garuda!' Mukunda whispered, waiting for a response but the silence prevailed.

The Sena was now some fifty feet away from the facility, taking cover behind the planted trees and shrubs around the perimeter. He then yelled in a muffled voice, 'GARUDA', but still nothing. He reached into his pocket and drew out a shiny metallic cube and holding it in his left palm, kept uttering Garuda's name.

Exhausted from trying, he looked towards Vallabha. 'The interference field is strong,' she replied.

Mukunda turned his gaze back to the cube and then placed it back in his pocket. 'I wanted Garuda to fly over there and do a reconnaissance for us,' he said, feeling disappointed.

'We have no means to know about preprations being made by the enemy. None of my intelligence or communication devices work,' Vallabha replied.

'There is an upside to this too. Under such strong fields, they won't be able to use any energy weaponry on us,' Mukunda said.

As Vallabha nodded in accordance, Radhika stood up and faced Raghav. 'We are all of five hundred now, half of us will enter that building and the rest will guard here against any reinforcements,' she said.

'This should work. Crowding the building may work against us. We will move lightly and take them by surprise,' Raghav added.

Raghav then started suggesting alternate routes to enter the building. He was betting on breaching the building's security from the glass roof patches on the slant corners of the building. 'We will reach there in batches of ten and then ascend onto the building wall from the two sides,' he said.

Radhika nodded.

Mukunda tightened his armour and Vallabha secured her devices as they made a move towards the facility.

'Have your sword ready at all times. Stay safe, Aunt,' Mukunda said to Vallabha.

'You too! And if by any chance Kamsa deploys his metallic army, go for the backs of their necks. That's their weakest spot,' she said, smiling.

Soon, the Manavas started crouching towards both sides of the building. As they gathered on both flanks, looking for points to ascend, they could hear a creaking voice grow louder. Raghav signalled everyone to halt. He hopped nimbly towards the front of the building. As he reached the corner of the building, he saw a growing burst of light emanating from the main doors. Two soldiers came out of the doors and stood at the entrance with their swords lowered.

'Commander Radhika!' a heavy metallic voice reverberated through those now open doors.

Raghav leaped back to take cover.

'Commander, you don't have to storm the building and waste your precious sweat in this desert heat,' the voice said again.

Radhika stood up and started walking towards the doors, when Raghav held her by her hand and stopped her.

'I am your Krishna's old friend and you are all welcome here. Walk in and my people will not obstruct your way,' the voice roared again.

'Is this Vasudevan? What happened to his voice?' Radhika asked.

'He is Kamsa. Vasudevan was just a host, just like this computer that he now resides in,' Raghav replied.

Vallabha handed a microphone to Radhika, into which she spoke, 'I will talk to Xardukht, the rightful ruler of this land. Let him speak.'

'I am his Great Father and protector of this Xarnakht kingdom. I have his best interests in mind. You have my word,' Kamsa replied.

Radhika turned her gaze towards Raghav and Vallabha. 'We should hear Kamsa out,' Raghav said and Vallabha nodded in agreement.

'Let us sit down like rational people and talk,' Kamsa spoke.

'We will talk. But if you inflict any harm on my people, you alone shall be liable for the consequences,' Radhika announced into the microphone.

'I would never mess with the brave mother of the ever-brave Mukunda,' Kamsa said, laughing.

'He is bluffing. We cannot just walk into the trap,' Mukunda protested.

Radhika lowered the microphone, and looking at him said, 'At least the element of surprise is no longer there. This way, we can get into the building without any resistance.'

'I trust you, Mother, but not him,' Mukunda said again, albeit in a muffled and weak voice.

'Have faith, Son,' she replied, signalling the attack party to approach the door. Even before Raghav could make a move, both Shripathi and Raghunandan sprang into action and took position on both sides of the main doors. They peeped in and found nothing suspicious. Even all the guards and soldiers inside were empty-handed.

'All clear!' Shripathi told Raghav.

Radhika stepped forward to enter, but Raghav leapt forward,

and he along with his other divisional heads, made a cordon around her. Radhika stopped, standing there for a moment. She then called out for Mukunda, who came rushing to her. She leaned in and hugged her son and whispered something in his ear. Mukunda stepped back and looked into her eyes. 'Thank you for trusting me, Maa,' he said. His eyes were glistening with tears and he had a lump in his throat.

Radhika then turned to face the main door, walking amid her royal cordon. Mukunda too followed her closely.

As the Manavas walked into the facility, the walls on either side started glowing. They were emanating lights of vivid colours. As they moved forward, those colours started forming a pattern, which then turned into images. Radhika tried hard to remain focused but her gaze kept scrambling from one image to another.

'You know what those images are?' Kamsa said.

Radhika finally gave in and turned to have a long and hard look at the images. 'I couldn't care less,' she replied as she noticed swarms of drones gliding, passing by a mirror-like spherical surface.

'You probably will, once you are told what it is,' Kamsa said, laughing as the main doors to the facility closed behind Radhika and her troops.

Radhika heard the thumping sound of the closing doors but kept walking.

'Those are my machines, loaded with calibre 95 cosmic-guns, about to breach the guardian walls of Ksharanpur,' he said, laughing again.

'Those brave Manavas behind those walls, they are very capable of dealing with these,' she said as she kept walking towards Paramganak.

'Brave don't hide behind stealth walls. Those are helpless people who you left behind, unguarded, for the love of your son,' Kamsa said.

'He is not bluffing; defenses of Ksharanpur are fast falling. They have prepared something but not for this scale of attack,' Grutvator's voice reverberated in Mukunda's ears.

'Maa will handle,' he murmured back.

Radhika and her entourage were now walking at a consistent pace and they could see Paramganak clearly. The computer system was behind a three-feet- high steel wall and was lined with innumerable guards at every inch. Beyond them stood the royals of Xarlok, on a slightly raised platform.

'That's quite a distance. Stay there and we shall talk,' Kamsa said and Radhika signalled her troops to halt.

'I cannot wait to see Mukunda. He has been long gone. I miss that guy,' Kamsa said, laughing sarcastically.

Radhika turned to look back a little and Mukunda stepped forward.

'Ah! The first among equals—Mukunda. Tell them my boy how generous and… What you call it? Ah! Fair I have been to my people,' Kamsa said.

'Far from fair… is the word you should seek,' Mukunda replied curtly.

'The bitterness prevails. I thought distances would mellow it, but so naïve of me,' Kamsa said, sighing.

But Mukunda was preoccupied. Everthing else that was happening around him faded into the background. His mind was seeking something, his gaze was searching for something. He could literally feel it, even from such a great distance. *What can it be?* he thought to himself. It was then that his eyes found what his heart so wildly sought; a face radiant with youth and adorned with that wicked charm of betrayal. It was her, Xarnika, standing in the extreme right corner, along with her family. She had grown tall and blossomed like a pink lotus immersed in full moon's light. Her face was radiant like the rising sun and her deep dark-blue eyes held oceans divine. Her flowing deep lilac-coloured satin robe caressed her body, hugging her at some places as the winds flew.

Mukunda couldn't take his eyes off her. For once, he had to curb a strong urge to walk up to her and embrace her forever. She, too, was looking back at him.

'Let go of my space mission and save those innumerable innocent Manavas, Radhika,' Kamsa's voice reverberated through the hall, pulling Mukunda out of his reverie.

Mukunda blinked and saw her again, those beautiful eyes looking back at him. He suddenly realized that they were radiant as ever but that glow of love was missing. He shook himself out of the hold of Xarnika's gaze and turned to his left.

Xarki was standing to Xarnika's left. As soon as Mukunda caught his eye, he smiled astutely. His smile was laced with slander and his eyes looked down upon Mukunda.

Mukunda lowered his gaze for a moment as a burning sensation gripped his chest and a cold sweat ran down his spine. His heart was beating at a pace he was finding difficult to cope with. Darkness soon grappled his vision. He clenched his fists in a bid to draw up the last shreds of his inner strength. He clenched his fist harder until the dark cloud of dismay started growing thin and the burning sensation of distress subsided.

'We know what that intergalactic missile is intended for. We will not let you jeopardize the future of Prithvi for your petty gains,' Radhika said.

'You sit securely behind those guardian walls. It's not your war to fight. Thank me for keeping your son safe and go back home to your world,' Kamsa replied.

'I surely will take my son back home. But what about your sons?' Radhika said.

Kamsa remained silent.

'Do they know that the voice they call their Great Father plans on ripping their homes apart too?' Radhika said.

While Kamsa fumbled for words, Xandhrin and Xardukht looked at each other, confused. He sensed the fear among both. 'It's for their best,' he said hesitantly.

'You were buried in those sands for eons and now suddenly you wake up and know what's best for them?' Radhika roared back.

Many unintelligible lines of codes started flashing across Paramganak's screen as Radhika spoke again. 'What has your Great Father told you? Let me guess: that missile is meant for the aliens of deep space, isn't it?'

Xandhrin, Xardukht and all other prominent Xarnakhts stood there baffled.

'There are no deep-space aliens conspiring against you. He doesn't even have any imgination. He uses the same script over and over again and gets away with it. But not this time,' Radhika roared.

'What is that huge missile supposed to do then?' Xandhrin finally spoke.

'Prithvi, the planet we live on, is a part of a bigger galaxy. And then there are numerous others galaxies too. The missile he so desperately wants back is meant to put all these galaxies on a colliding path. Distant stars and moons will start colliding with each other, wrecking havoc. Prithvi too shall evaporate in a matter of years,' Radhika spoke.

Xandhrin gasped, but Xardukht held his arm and stared him down. 'You are lying,' Xardukht said.

'Ask your Great Father what happened to all your troops stationed in the northern reaches of Xarlok,' Radhika said as silence gripped the room. 'They all froze to death. And it was a small gravity bomb. That missile contains weapons a million times bigger than that. Imagine what it is capable of…'

Xardukht loosened his grip of Xandhrin's arm and looked at him with concern.

Xarnika stepped forward. 'She is lying, inciting us against our Great Father. Great Father confided in me. We shall remain safe and he promises us many great and abundant worlds to rule,' she said. 'He showed me glimpses of the worlds that he promises us. Yes, there is a slim chance of Prithvi getting harmed but that missile will annihilate our enemy and Great Father will take care of us.'

'He will never share his power with anybody ever. He cannot think beyond his own good. You are like my daughter, help me stop this madness or none of us will remain,' Radhika said, her voice laden with both care and concern.

'I am *not* like your daughter!' she yelled. 'Your coward son abandoned me in a ghost town. It is my people who saved me. You mean nothing to me,' her voice reverberated amid the high walls of the hall.

'Enough of this!' Kamsa said. 'My machines have found the port of entry. They will breach the wall in the next twenty minutes. You have this much time to release the missile and leave,' Kamsa offered.

'What if I really never cared about the Manavas we left behind? What if I do not relent your missile?' Radhika said sneeringly.

'Here is how it will go down, lady. In the next twenty minutes, my machines will burn your city to the ground, and in the next thirty minutes, the second moon will appear on the horizon. I will get back my control, your trickery will fail,' Kamsa said.

Radhika kept quiet.

'I do not have forever. I am extending this goodwill gesture because I once walked amongst you people. Turn around and you shall live. You have twenty minutes,' Kamsa reiterated.

'And in those twenty minutes you will be dead,' she hollered at the top of her voice and drew her sword.

As soon as Nandaki came out of its sheath, it enveloped the hall in its radiant blue colour and the thunderbolts emanating from it filled the hall with blinding lights.

'We will see ...' Kamsa roared as he let open the shutters at the back of the hall.

One after another metallic robots started queuing up by Paramganak's side.

'Jarasandh legion! Annihilate the enemy,' Kamsa shouted.

The bots moved forward.

Raghav signalled Shripathi and Raghunandan to get into a Padmavyuha formation. The Manavas assembled in the shape of a fully blossomed lotus, with each divisional commander at the middle of a petal. The formation grew around Radhika and she now stood in the exact centre of the Padmavyuha. She looked around and saw around two hundred metal beings standing in front of the formation. Before she could think further, the bots drew their swords and charged. Radhika hurriedly made her way through to the front of the formation and then leaped into the air.

She raised her sword and drove it right between the eyes of the leading bot. She fell to the ground and along came the bot. The loud thud of the bot's fall filled the other bots with rage and they started rushing through the Manava formation.

'They can be killed!' Vallabha exclaimed. 'They don't work on cosmic cell. Just a fatal blow and they collapse,' Mukunda said in consonance.

Radhika got up and wanted to run for a good leap, but the

whole hall was now either filled with Manavas or the bots. She kept to the ground and started striking blows at the mid-sections of the metallic bots.

•◆

Madhav raised his head out of the trench and looked around. 'The skies are clear,' he yelled, still maintaining his finger on the trigger of the Airavata anti-drone system.

Rukmini relayed the message to Mohan as she stayed put in the trench.

'There is a huge energy signature making the radars go crazy. Something is brewing. I will keep the coastline Airavata systems ready. You keep a sharp eye on the sky,' Mohan said to her.

'Do we aim and shoot or just go all out on them?' Rukmini then enquired.

'If they are hovering above you, it means our first line of defense has failed. Go all out then,' Mohan said.

'Are we sure those kids belong there, in those trenches?' Shriram hollered, his voice laced in anger and concern.

'There is still time, we can pull them out of there,' Shyam too joined Shriram in his concern.

'Who will then man those guns? You will? I have this medical report of yours. You people, and pardon me for being blunt, it says are too slow for that,' Mohan replied.

'We are slow? And what about those kids? Vishnu forbid if anything ever happens to them...' Shriram revolted.

'You know they have ample armour on them. Will the enemy spare the kids if he runs over the city unchallenged?' Mohan said.

Shriram sighed and shook his head in helplessness.

'Have some trust, Shri. I think Mohan knows what he is doing,' Shyam said, signalling Shriram to sit and relax.

'Guys! A big port is opening up on the western frontiers,' Mohan yelled.

Shriram and Shyam both got up from their chairs and rushed towards the Samganak.

'What next?' Shyam said.

'I am activating Airavata system for a full go. It sees, it locks and it fires. It will be a grand welcome,' Mohan replied.

They were now all fixated on the screen. And before they could bat an eyelid, the inevitable happened. A few drones appeared on the horizons above the lake, from nowhere. Suddenly the nozzles of all the Airavata systems involved, moved in unison and showered the drones with lethal rays. The inbound drones vaporized, not even a shred of them remained.

'It's working,' Shyam exclaimed.

But then a few signatures appeared on the screen and the system indicators started blinking and bleeping like crazy.

'It's too early to celebrate! They are all around us, pouring in like swarms of bees,' Mohan said, his eyes widening in disbelief.

The Airavata systems realigned and readjusted their azimuth and altitude parameters. Soon, they were firing incessantly towards the swarm.

The drone swarm, which was larger than the previous one, first tried deflecting the guns by flying in a zigzag manner. And once they evaded a few gunshots, they started retaliating. The evening sky was lit with a multitude of bright beams piercing through.

Soon, the number of drones dwindled to half and the beams shot by the drones grew thin. But then, a shot from an inbound drone struck an Airavata system and it blew up, taking two adjacent systems with it.

'They are retaliating. They are hitting us back,' Shriram said, his eyebrows arching and his palms sweating in agony.

'The enemy's strength in number is dwindling. They couldn't get past our coastline defenses,' Mohan said, trying to sound reassuring.

He would have succeeded too had Shriram not noticed another anomaly on Samganak's screen. 'What is that?' he pointed out.

Mohan leaned in to take a closer look.

'Unbelievable! Another portal is opening up,' Shyam murmured.

'It's much bigger than the earlier one,' Mohan said as his jaw dropped.

'Can you run a count check on the inbounds?' Shyam said, his hands trembling a little.

Mohan ran his fingers over the control panel and within a few moments, the data popped up on screen.

'Hundreds of thousands of them,' Mohan said as he sank into his chair.

'We are bound to be overwhelmed,' Shyam gasped.

'There is an upside to it. Our people down there on Prithvi are safe,' Shriram said and then squirted out a muffled but frantic laugh.

'What do you mean?' Mohan asked.

'They are sending all their assets up here. I am happy that this will shift the burden from the Narayani Sena in the field.' Shriram replied.

'He is holding us hostage as a bargaining chip. Isn't he? We shall endure this too,' Shyam said.

Mohan got up from his chair and spoke into the microphone protruding from Samganak's panel. 'My young warriors, prepare yourself for some action.'

Rukmini received the message on her communication device and relayed it to each one in the trench. Mohan turned and looked towards Shyam and Shriram and gave them an affirming nod.

Meanwhile, drones started pouring in and soon their sheer

number covered the entire Ksharanpur skies. They moved like clouds and brought along with them a scary darkness. Coastline defenses went hot again and started shooting at will. But the drones were a lot more organized this time around. Several inbound enemy drones were hit, but many managed to sneak through the chinks in the defenses and flew inward towards the city.

'Rukmini, they have breached the coastline. They will head towards you. Drop everything and get to your gun. Shoot them hard and shoot them relentlessly,' Mohan said into his microphone. He then left the system and rushed towards the stairs.

'Where are you heading?' Shriram said.

'I am going to the terrace to man the rooftop Airavata system. Under no circumstances can we let them breach the lab,' Mohan said, dashing out.

'We are coming along too. Let's put these lazy fingers to some good use,' Shriram said and Shyam nodded in consonance.

They then rushed, along with Mohan.

Rukmini meanwhile dropped her communication device and headed for her gun.

'Don't bat an eyelid. Shoot them as soon as you see them,' she said to Madhav.

'We cannot let them overrun us.'

Madhav turned and looked behind. 'If we miss, the school will be next in their line of fire,' he murmured.

'Stay sharp and aim,' Radhika said, firmly gripping the manual trigger of Airavata.

Initially, only a fraction of drones breached the coastline and the shots from the trenches were enough to take care of them. A few drones retaliated, but either they missed or the armour rendered their shots useless. But then the number started growing and inbound drones started hitting the trenches hard. The concrete, steel panels and the mud started flying around. Many young ones got injured by shards of debris and their guns fell silent.

Madhav grabbed a gun lying next to him and started firing with that too. Rukmini saw him and followed suit. As the number of drones grew in number, they started breaching the second line of defense too.

'They are over-running us. Let Kanha know that soon the school will be in the range of these drones,' Madhav said.

'I am not leaving my guns unattended,' Rukmini protested.

'There are little kids there, leave the gun and relay the message,' Madhav yelled. She got up and rushed to her communication device.

Kanha, as soon as he got the news, started instructing every kid and teacher to vacate the ground and rush to the library. 'Those who have attended archery or shooting classes, volunteer now,' he yelled at the top of his voice.

Around twenty kids broke the line and rushed towards him. 'These are my improvisations,' he said, handing out catapults to them. 'Their pellets are loaded with explosives, so handle with care. Aim at those evil drones. But remember to remain behind some cover while shooting,' he then instructed.

As the drones flew within range of the school, they started shooting the empty buildings. The glass facades shattered to pieces and a few sections of the building blew up. When the drones almost reached the open grounds, Kanha aimed at one of the drones and took it down with his catapult. Others followed suit and soon a barrage of exploding pellets brought many drones down to the ground.

Meanwhile, Mohan noticed the drones hovering over the school and he reached for his trigger. Shyam and Shriram also armed themselves with a gun.

Soon, the drones hovering over the school started dropping out of the sky.

And within a few more minutes, thousands of drones sneaked past the coastline defense again.

Shyam looked up and saw the fresh batch of inbound drones. 'They are increasing by the minute. They will outrun us,' he said.

'I don't think we have enough ammunition to take each one of them down.' Shriram said.

Mohan looked at them. 'We are in for some serious trouble. Only Vidhvans can save us now.'

Shyam looked at him in despair and nodded.

Mohan raised his arm and spoke into his wrist-device, 'Samganak! Activate Vidhvans.'

⋅◆

The number of metal bots had dwindled to half. Radhika was slaying them before they could strategize and respond. Some of Xardukht's royal guards had also joined the battle. However, the Manavas were still fending off the attack well.

But as was apparent now, decimating the bots or the guards was not on anybody's mind. They were more interested in moving to the head of the facility.

While the bots and the guards were successful in holding everybody else back, two people were quietly but consistently making a headway. Mukunda was jostling with bots as he inched forward. Radhika gave him cover.

'Your mother told you, didn't she?' Grutvator's voice rumbled in Mukunda's ears.

'She did,' he mumbled.

'Scared?' Grutvator asked.

'Excited. I started it, so I should be the one cleaning up this mess,' he mumbled again as he rasied his head to take a good look at Paramganak, which was some forty steps ahead of him.

'Only the one who resurrected him can kill him for good. Otherwise, he will be back in no time, in one form or another,' Grutvator said.

'I understand,' Mukunda mumbled, struggling with the engaging bot.

'The second moon is almost up in the horizon. We have just a few minutes,' Grutvator added.

'Don't worry. I have got this,' Mukunda said as he kicked the bot obstructing his way. He looked back and signalled his mother to pace up.

Radhika raised her sword and decapitated the bot obstructing her way and leapt forward. Raghav rushed to Radhika, providing her cover. They both rushed towards Mukunda and as Mukunda grew closer to the perimeter protecting Paramganak, he looked back. Radhika, who was some ten steps behind him, flung her sword Nandaki towards Mukunda. She then bit her lip and closed her eyes for a second. She was not sure if Nandaki would accept Mukunda. She prayed that it would.

Nandaki swung through the air and finally landed hilt first in Mukunda's right palm. Radhika saw this and breathed a huge sigh of relief.

Mukunda held Nandaki and raised it above his head. The sword started glowing bright blue again and a thousand thunderbolts started emanating from it skywards. He turned his gaze towards Paramganak and noticed the perimeter around it. Meanwhile, all the bots and the royal guards started closing in on him.

He drew in a long breath and ran forward. When he was five steps away from the perimeter, he jumped. The two bots and several guards standing behind the perimeter, protecting Paramganak from either side, swung into action.

Mukunda leaped towards them and with a single stroke of his Nandaki decimated a bot and three soldiers. The other bot approached Mukunda from behind, but he turned around and with a swift stroke of his sword, cut the bot into half. The rest of the soldiers fled the perimeter.

Mukunda took a step forward when Xardukht drew his sword and stepped ahead. Mukunda, hearing Xardukht approaching, stopped. He turned his gaze to his right and looked at him with rage-filled eyes. He then raised his sword and pointed it towards Xardukht. The blue brilliance of Nandaki illuminated this part of the hall.

Xardukht retracted his step as Xarnika shook her head in disbelief.

Mukunda stepped forward and as he reached Paramganak, he could hear Xarnika say, 'Great Father, do something.'

Mukunda gazed down into Paramganak's display.

'You know where you placed the mother processor, it's still there,' Grutvator's voice echoed in his ears.

Mukunda raised Nandaki and drove it through Paramganak's screen. The display started blinking and then it totally blacked out. Mukunda pulled Nandaki back and kicked the computer, shattering it to pieces.

He was still seething with rage when he heard Xarnika murmur, 'You shouldn't have done that.'

Then he heard the sound of a sword being drawn out of its sheath. He was still looking down, anticipating Xarnika to charge at him with her father's sword. But he instead heard footsteps receding. He looked to his right, but Xarnika was not there. He looked back, and there she was, rushing towards the Manava troops. Baffled, he stood there, frozen. Suddenly, he caught a glimpse of the only person without a sword or a shield, standing right in the middle of the hall. He leaped into action and rushed towards the centre of the hall. His vision was blurred and his legs were shaking. Cold sweat ran down his temple to his neck, when he saw Xarnika making her way forward, to the middle of the hall, unchallenged. But before Mukunda could skip over the perimeter, Xarnika had already made her way to her destination. She stopped there, her eyes and face red with rage. She was a few inches away from Radhika, when she said with her voice trembling with anger, 'You should have left with your son.'

She then raised her sword and drove it through the two-inch gap between the upper armour and the lower armour around her midriff.

Even before Radhika could say anything or react, the cold blade of Xarnika's sword pierced through her veins. She gasped for breath as her vision blurred and a sharp pain started growing in her stomach.

Xarnika rushed back towards her father.

Shocked, Raghav and Vallabha rushed towards Radhika and caught her before she could hit the ground.

'Get some help,' Raghav yelled.

Seeing Xarnika trying to escape, Raghav signalled Shripathi to intercept her. Shripathi rushed towards her with his troops. She was only a few feet away from the perimeter when she crossed Mukunda, who grabbed her by her arm and looked at her with tear-laden red eyes.

'I did what I had to do for my people,' she said, her voice trembling.

'You are evil. You attacked the one whom I held dear the most,' he murmured, his mouth trembling with rage. He raised Nandaki and drove it through Xarnika's stomach.

She gasped, looking him into his eyes. She slowly lifted her hands to touch her wound. She placed her blood-soaked hand on Mukunda's face, still struggling to hold her consciousness together. 'I always loved you!' she murmured, falling to the ground.

Mukunda retracted his sword and rushed back towards his mother. He held her in his arms as she lay in a pool of blood. 'Maa…' His voice reverberated through the halls as tears rolled down his cheeks. 'Get up, Maa,' he pleaded.

'We just been reunited after so long. I have missed you for years. This cannot be happening…' he murmured as he burst into tears.

Meanwhile, a whirring sound arose. It was Garuda, who had come back to life and leaped out of Mukunda's pocket. He stumbled a little and then unfolded himself, after which he started hovering around.

'The interference field is down. We need help,' Vallabha murmured.

'Garuda, let Ksharanpur know that we need help.'

Garuda blinked his eyes and started raising his elevation. When he finally got hold of some strong signals at an elevation of ten feet, he said, 'Samganak, this is Garuda from Airborne Division 4. Radhika is down. We need immediate help. I repeat, Radhika is down. We need help.'

Additional Read: The Theory of Gravity

Starting from the observed facts, let us see if we can explain what actually causes forces of gravity to exist. Here, instead of representing the space-time fabric of the universe as a four-dimensional entity, we shall try to keep it confined to three dimensions. We do so by assuming that the universe is made up of quantized space (such that measurements can be made only on these discreet quantized points and the distance between these fine points is of Planck length scale or its multiples). We can thereby represent the whole universe by a three-dimensional coordinate system.

Now, as observed by Georges Lemaître and Edwin Hubble (collectively called Hubble–Lemaître law), we assume an ever-expanding universe. Such expansion of the universe is facilitated by comoving coordinates, causing constant drifting apart of the coordinate points representing the universe. Assuming such an expansion started at the beginning of the universe, the rate of change of distance between the adjacent coordinates is a fair measure of the passage of time. Thus, we may represent our space-time fabric of the universe with three spatial dimension and one temporal dimension represented by the drifting apart of the aforementioned spatial dimensions. Assuming a homogenous and isotropic universe, we may say that the passage of time can be measured by the rate of change at any point of the spatial axis and it may hold in all direction (thus allowing a single value of temporal dimension).

The expansion of universe was inferred by Lemaître and Hubble by observing the drifting apart of the galaxies from one another. The underlying assumption of such inference is that the expanding space-time tugs the mass-bearing bodies along with it. So, there is some kind of force that acts between the space-time fabric of the universe and any mass-bearing body. Since space-time of our model is made up of quantized coordinates, the force exerted by each coordinate on the mass-bearing object can be surmised as Fundamental-Interaction.

Delving into the fact that the universe is constantly expanding, let us assume that energy is being added to the universe and such energy is being added as potential energy via expansion. Therefore, the greater the drifting apart of the coordinates or the passage of time, the higher the potential of the space-time.

Since, our universe is homogenous and isotropic, this value, which we shall call Hamiltonian of the universe, remains constant throughout.

In a homogenous universe we assume that this Hamiltonian function (summation of all energy, but principally kinetic and potential energy) is conserved throughout the expanses of the universe.

Though this Hamiltonian is changing (increasing) its value with further expansion of space-time, we can safely assume that at any given time, its value remains constant at $H(t)$ (Hamiltonian function at time = t). And as time passes and the coordinates drift apart a newer $H(t+n)$ (Hamiltonian function at time = t+n, where n is units of time elapsed from reference time = t) shall replace the value of the previous $H(t)$.

However, the point under consideration is that to keep a universe homogenous and isotropic, $H(t)$ at a given moment 't' is constant and conserved across all of the universe.

As surmised earlier, in the presence of a mass-bearing body, fundamental interaction takes place between the space-time fabric and the mass. And these interactions provide enough force to slow down the very expansion of coordinates, which is obvious from the fact that while galaxies are drifting apart, they are not increasing in size due to the expansion of universe.

It is as if the space-time fabric of the universe is expanding like an elastic sheet, with mass-bearing areas clamped down. So, while the expanding universe witnesses an increase in potential energy, the clamped down areas witness potential energies lower than the rest of the universe.

This is equivalent to mass-bearing bodies pulling space-time together by the virtue of their inertia generated by the aforementioned Fundamental-Interaction.

Now, we shall note how the developments thus far have amazing implications.

The pulling together of the space-time fabric by mass-bearing bodies means that it cannot expand at its natural rate. Thus, the passage of universal time slows down and gives rise to time dilations in and around mass-bearing bodies.

Before we head on to the auxiliary implication of such noting, let us consider the biggest implication of all.

The clamping down of space-time by mass-bearing bodies causes not only slowing down of time but also drop in potential energy of that area of space-time (as expansion of the comoving coordinates of our universe is a measure of its potential energy). But a homogenous and isotropic universe should be preserving $H(t)$ at any given time. Therefore, to compensate for such drop in potential energy and conserve the Hamiltonian $H(t)$, every inertial (mass-bearing) body in the vicinity of such an event will experience increase in its kinetic energy and hence an acceleration.

This acceleration follows the Newtonian inverse-square law and is proportional to mass of the space-time contracting object.

This leads us to a pertinent question: where do the relativistic corrections figure in this picture? Sparing the mathematical details, and circling back to the aforementioned facts, our space-time has contracted and Fundamental-Interactions exerted by each quantized comoving coordinate for a given area have increased. So, the effective distance, which we shall call quantum-distance, has increased due to such contraction of space. Such contraction of quantum-distance causes not only relativistic corrections to gravity but also causes Lorentz contraction for relativistic motion (motions at ultra high velocity).

As an inertial object accelerates (and it's kinetic energy increases) even in (gravity) free space, the H(t) needs to be conserved and a lowering in potential energy of free space happens, leading to our space-time contraction, which in turn, causes Lorentz contractions (leading to length contraction of the moving object and slowing down of time, as also observed in case of gravity).

How do we measure such space-time contractions in real life you ask? These contractions are observable if one pays heed. One such very prominent experiment was conducted in the premises of Harvard University in 1959 at the Howard Tower, using Gamma rays and is called the Pound-Rebka experiment. The gamma ray (a high-energy light), as it travelled towards Earth from the top of the tower into denser gravity, underwent a blue-shift of its frequency. Meaning, its frequency increased and the wavelength shrunk or decreased. These contractions in wavelength are Bosonic or light-related version of Lorentz contraction.

Such blue-shift of light frequency while travelling into the gravitational well helps preserves H(t) by an increase in energy of light particles and can be measured. Such measurements (of change in frequency or wavelength of light) are a fair approximation of the contraction of space-time at any point in space.

To conclude, space-time contracts under the influence of mass-bearing objects and this leads to the lowering of its potential. Conservation of Fundamental-Interactions or Hamiltonian H(t) leads to a constant acceleration of all mass-bearing object in the presence of such contractions. This leads to observance of the Equivalence principle, where being in the presence of gravitational field (or the area of space-time of lowered potential energy) is akin to standing in an accelerated (or, non-inertial) frame, causing downward acceleration.

In conclusion, gravitational acceleration happens to balance the drop in the rate of expansion of the space-time fabric.